WESTERN WINTER
WEDDING BELLS

CHERYL ST. JOHN
JENNA KERNAN
CHARLENE SANDS

HARLEQUIN®

TORONTO • NEW YORK • LONDON
AMSTERDAM • PARIS • SYDNEY • HAMBURG
STOCKHOLM • ATHENS • TOKYO • MILAN • MADRID
PRAGUE • WARSAW • BUDAPEST • AUCKLAND

ISBN-13: 978-0-373-29611-8

WESTERN WINTER WEDDING BELLS
Copyright © 2010 by Harlequin Books S.A.

The publisher acknowledges the copyright holders of the individual works as follows:

CHRISTMAS IN RED WILLOW
Copyright © 2010 by Cheryl Ludwigs

THE SHERIFF'S HOUSEKEEPER BRIDE
Copyright © 2010 by Jeannette H. Monaco

WEARING THE RANCHER'S RING
Copyright © 2010 by Charlene Swink

Recycling programs for this product may not exist in your area.

www.eHarlequin.com

Printed in U.S.A.

CONTENTS

CHRISTMAS IN RED WILLOW

Cheryl St.John

Dear Reader,

I'm often asked where I get my ideas. Writers get ideas just like anyone else. Most of my best ones come to me in the shower or in that moment right before falling asleep, when the right side of my brain is unfettered. When a good idea arises, I write it all down longhand and place it in a thick binder filled with other story thoughts. When I need a story, I open that binder and find one that appeals to me. Sometimes I wonder what I was thinking when I jotted it down. Other times the idea sparks an interest all over again.

That's what happened when I needed a Christmas story. I opened my binder and flipped to a page titled simply Christmas Story. My notes were about a heroine who was alone at Christmas and stayed busy with activities to cover up her loneliness. I liked the idea, so I created Chloe first, giving her a past and a goal. Then I needed a man to come into her life—an unlikely man—and there's where Owen came along. He's from a big family, works with his hands and is a quiet, analytical fellow.

And I always ask myself—what's the worst thing that could happen to this person? I have written myself into some jams that way, but the question sure keeps the stories interesting.

I especially love Christmas stories, because they are filled with optimism and good will. I hope Chloe and Owen's story brings you joy this holiday, and I trust the spirit of the season will live on in your heart throughout the coming year.

Christmas blessings,

Cheryl

This story is dedicated to the members of my critique group, who at any given moment will drop what they are doing and read pages when I need help in a crunch.
They are brilliant, funny, generous and incredible women, and I am honored to be in their company.

Bernadette Duquette, Debra Hines,
Barb Hunt, Donna Knoell,
*Cheri LaClaire, Eve Savage, *lizzie starr*

Chapter One

Red Willow, Colorado, 1880

"That old building is an eyesore," Richard Reardon declared, standing before the town council in his brown-and-gray-plaid cassimere suit, his brown hair parted in sleek precision.

Chloe Hanley felt sick to her stomach at the thought of the beautiful old structure where her grandfather had been chaplain for most of his life being destroyed.

It was the week before Thanksgiving, and the council had gathered to discuss the Independence Day celebration the town would be hosting for the entire county in eight months. Much had to be done if the storefronts were going to be refurbished and the overgrown park brought back to life in time for that event.

"What's more," Richard continued, "it's a safety risk, now that the windows are broken out and animals and even drifters can get inside. We need to tear the whole thing down so work can begin on constructing a hotel. The property is right in the middle of Main Street, and anything less than a pristine new structure will reflect poorly on Red Willow and our citizens."

Chloe leaned forward on her chair. "But the church is a historical landmark. The stone foundation and the brickwork are unique in this part of the country."

"They're *old,* Miss Hanley," Richard pointed out. "Red Willow's most important street should be modernized."

"Edmund Rosemont designed that church," she argued. "He was one of the greatest architects ever to build this far west," she reminded him. "And what would you do with the cemetery if you tore down the church? Our founding fathers are buried there."

"We can move the graves to the newer cemetery out on Long View Road," he replied.

At that thought, Chloe wanted to cry, but she tamped down her emotions to be able to defend her position against his cool materialistic plans. Thinking that she'd once fancied herself in love with the man, humiliation warmed her cheeks.

Apparently, he thought he had bested her because he offered her a cool smile. She wanted to climb across the table and slap that smug expression from his face, but she folded her hands demurely. "I've already paid the taxes that were in arrears. The women's league fundraising provided enough."

His smile dissolved.

Frank Garrison, the council chairman, leafed through the papers in front of him and shuffled one to the top. "She's right. The taxes have been paid."

"The town owns the property the church sits on," Richard reminded the group.

"After the church was vandalized, my grandfather couldn't hold services there and people stopped coming and giving. That's the only reason the property reverted to the town." After ten years of struggling, the few remaining members still gathered at the school. "The town could have helped repair the damages at the time."

"A church that can't afford to support itself must not be needed," Richard said.

His derisive dismissal came as a personal insult to Chloe. Her grandfather had dedicated his life to serving the people of this community. "The church was here before the businesses and the school," she told him heatedly. "The town sprang up around it, for goodness' sake. Even though we don't have a building to meet in, we still serve Red Willow all through the year. We just delivered food baskets to seven families who wouldn't have had a Thanksgiving meal without our help."

"I agree the church is important to the community," the bank owner, Charlie Salburg, finally offered, to her immense satisfaction. He didn't attend, but his wife June did and had helped Chloe with the food baskets. "I've thought for a long time that it's a shame not to salvage the existing building. It was quite something in its day."

"There is a lot to be said for the historic value," Guy Allen agreed. "What if we set a deadline for the church to be restored? If it's not improved by then, we tear it down. At any rate, we can't have a dilapidated building in the center of town next summer."

Chloe experienced profound relief. Yes! Support for her cause at last. "How about the first of March?" she suggested, thinking four months would give her enough time to raise money and make repairs.

"Building a hotel in its place will require more time than what's left after that," Richard argued. "If the church is still an eyesore by Christmas, it comes down. That gives us six months to hire architects, contractors and have the work done by the Fourth of July."

"Christmas is only a month away," Chloe objected. "And it's winter."

"I think giving you a month is all we can afford," Frank said apologetically. "We do need to get things moving."

Chloe sat in silence as the council members agreed and voted. When all was said and done she had one month to find help to repair years of neglect and decay, do the actual work and have the place looking presentable. And she had no idea how or if the church board could pay for the work.

Trudging along the hallway of the municipal building on her way out, she noted each framed photograph lining the walls, settling on her grandfather's photograph. A similar likeness hung in the study of the house she'd inherited from him, and every time she looked at him in his flowing black robe with a white satin vestment, she missed him anew.

"Well, this is a fine how-do-you-do, isn't it?" He never answered when she spoke to his photograph, of course, but she imagined the corner of his mouth, defined by his neat white beard and mustache, curled upward. He'd always believed in her.

Owen Reardon used a brush made of short horsehair to clean the intricate carvings on the interior door lying atop sawhorses in his wood shop. The door was one of twelve, which were all sanded to a smooth finish and ready for stain. They were nearly ready to hang in the home he'd been working on for a wealthy local rancher with an eye for detail and craftsmanship.

Though it was a cold day in late November, his shop was warm from the lumber scraps and aged chunk of maple burning in the stove. The sense of accomplishment he felt looking over his handiwork gave him bone-deep satisfaction. Every piece of wood had a character of its own and what he loved best was bringing each piece to life.

He ran his fingers over the smooth design. The wood had been carved and prepared, but there was as much skill involved with the final steps of stain and varnish as with the original design. The image he'd seen in his mind's eye was a darker stain in the grooves, enhancing the design to its fullest.

Owen washed traces of dust from his hands, opened a tin of stain and stirred it with a clean stick.

Someone cranked the bell on the door at the front of the store, interrupting his concentration. It was late in the day, and he hadn't been expecting anyone. Of course sometimes a customer dropped by with an order. He walked from the back room through the dim store and pushed back the bolt.

A young woman in a cranberry-colored wool coat with beaver fur at the collar and wrists stood outside. She wore a scarf over her hair, and it took him a minute to place her.

"Miss Hanley? Come in."

"Are you closed for the day?"

"I keep the door locked because I work in back. What can I do for you?"

"Do you have a few minutes? I'd like to speak with you."

Chloe Hanley lived beside his mother and younger sister in an Italianate-style house she'd inherited from her grandfather. While her neighbors had progressed to the popular white and off-white tones, she'd preserved the original tricolor palette of her home. He admired her efforts each time he visited next door.

"It's gets chilly in here once the sun sets," he said. "It's warm in my work area, though, if you want to come back."

"Thank you." She removed her scarf. A lock of her fair hair trailed against the dark fur collar. The combined scents of outdoors and her fragrant hair drifted to where he stood, and it took him a moment to move.

She had been childhood friends with his sister Pamela, and in those days had often attended his family dinners. He'd once thought his brother might marry her, but while at law school in the east, Richard had married someone else.

"I don't get much company." He led her through the store into the back room, where he found a stool and wiped it with a clean rag. "Have a seat."

She perched on the stool, and her gaze flitted from the shelves of tools and brushes to the doors waiting for stain. "I'm in a bit of a quandary."

He wanted to pick up his brush and see what the color looked like on the wood, but instead he rested the lid on the can of stain and snagged another stool, this one multicolored by drips of various stains and varnishes, and sat, one boot heel on the floor, the other hooked on a rung.

She lifted her luminous blue gaze to him, and if he didn't know better he'd have thought his stool tilted off balance. "The town council is bent on having Main Street sleek and clean before July."

Of course. The Independence Day celebration had been in the planning stages for a good long time already.

"They've given me until Christmas to fix up the old church."

At the mention of Red Willow First Church, weighted memories flooded Owen. The household in which he'd grown up had been filled with the drama created by his older brother, Richard, and the constant chaos his three sisters kicked up. In their father's eyes, Owen had never measured up to Richard, and of course he'd never tried or wanted to.

As an escape, he'd discovered a way into the church through a loose window and had spent many a late night in its darkened interior. Lighting a few candles had illuminated the rich wood carvings and thrown the beams and altar into sharp relief. Owen had never been particularly religious, but he'd found peace in the silence and immeasurable beauty of the sanctuary.

"If it isn't restored by then, the building will be torn down."

Jolted out of his reverie, Owen stared at the woman across from him. "But that place is a landmark. It's a work of art."

"Well, I'm afraid your brother considers it an eyesore," she told him.

He might've known Richard was behind the blasphemous idea.

"The congregation raised enough to pay the taxes," she said. "There's a little left over, not enough for all the supplies or labor. I asked Hackett's and Jerome Gleason, but neither could take on the project until spring. And they wanted to be paid up front," she added with a shrug. She'd mentioned the two biggest builders in a three-county area.

Now he knew why she'd come to him. "You want me to take on the job of restoring the church."

"Everyone says you're the best. I saw the Bentleys' mantelpiece and the beams in their great room. You made them look as though they were original to their house. If anyone can do the work on the church, it's you." She paused and glanced down at the white wool mittens she still wore, as if just noticing they were there. She plucked off one and then the other and stuffed them into her coat pocket.

The sight of a woman, especially one as young and pretty as Chloe, seated beside the workbenches and storage bins in his solitary space contrasted like a graceful butterfly resting upon an anvil.

"You're my last hope," she said. "I've come to beg you to help me. I can't let the church my grandfather loved be hauled away in a pile of stone and brick rubble and replaced with a modern hotel."

He understood her attachment to the building. He had a special fondness for the architecture and workmanship himself. All those secluded hours within its walls had planted and nurtured his appreciation for beautiful craftsmanship. If not for that place, his future may have been shaped in an entirely different manner.

"Richard is used to getting what he wants," he said, thinking aloud. If Owen helped her, his participation would cause friction between the brothers—and maybe even within his family. He'd stopped rocking the boat a long time ago to keep peace.

She nodded, her expression grim. "I know. And his opinion holds a lot of sway with the council."

"Not so much his opinions as his money," Owen remarked.

"At any rate, they listen to him."

Owen was a thinker. He'd never made a rapid decision in his life that he could recall. His quiet contemplation was something that drove Richard crazy. He mulled the options and different scenarios around in his head. He considered his current list of scheduled work, pondering the idea of how to fit in an undertaking this big in a short length of time.

"I asked about the graves and Richard suggested the—" she paused and took a breath "—the remains could be moved out to Long View. I've had two days—and nights—to think about it. I know the people buried there wouldn't know the difference. They're long dead, but moving them seems…well, just *wrong*. Some of those sandstone markers are pretty weathered, and I don't know how they'd make the trip. I'm sure Richard would just as soon see them replaced with fresh new headstones, but those are the markers their families set in place to honor their loved ones."

If Owen remembered correctly, one of his uncles was buried there, as well as a brother and sister his mother had lost only weeks after their births.

"Some of the epitaphs are too worn to read," she went on. "But most still have their inscriptions and designs intact. Do you remember all the lambs and trees and flowers carved into the stones? One of my favorites is a tall marker that reads Until the Day Break. Below it are the graves of a brother and sister who died days apart. In early summer, pink-and-white phlox weaves around between those old headstones." She'd been gazing absently beyond his shoulder, but her attention focused on his face. "How can something like that be moved without destroying its sanctity and integrity?"

"It can't." In the end it was Chloe's passion that swayed his decision. Richard's need to accumulate yet another property and put a feather in his cap paled in comparison to Chloe Hanley's fervor regarding history, beauty and reverence.

Her eyes widened in expectation, but she didn't rush him. He liked that about her. She was patient.

"I haven't been inside for a long time," he said. "I expect the first thing we'll need to do is make a list of supplies and get them ordered. We can take a look around tomorrow and see how much can be salvaged and what needs replacing."

Chloe hopped down from her seat. "You'll do it? You'll help get the church ready by Christmas?"

Chapter Two

"I'm guessing if Richard thinks it can't be done, he's got good reason," he said. "I don't want to promise until I've looked at it and assessed the work. Five weeks isn't very long. Without hiring a crew, it could be slow going."

"There's a little money left over from fundraising," she told him. "And I've got some savings I can use."

He nodded. "Let's keep our decisions for tomorrow morning. I'll meet you at the church, and we'll make a plan then."

Her eyes filled with grateful tears. "Thank you, Owen. This means so much to me." She covered her lips with her fingertips for a moment while she gathered her emotions. "My grandfather would be so happy if he knew what we were doing. All along I've thought how heartbroken he'd have been to see the state the church is in. Now it's going to look like its old self again."

"Like I said, we'll have a better idea tomorrow." He didn't want her to get her hopes up if what she was planning would be impossible.

"We can hold Christmas Eve services there," she suggested with a bright smile. "It'll be just like when we were kids."

He tilted his head to the side noncommittally. For some unexplainable reason, he didn't want to disappoint her. She'd always seemed as frail as a delicate flower.

"Thank you so much," she said.

He raised a hand to silence her. "Thank me later."

He stood, intending to lead her from his workshop, but without warning she launched herself toward him, wrapping her arms in her bulky coat around his middle and hugging him soundly. The embrace placed her head right under his chin, her silky hair grazing his neck. Her feminine scent paralyzed him for a moment too long. This wasn't one of his sisters hugging him for all she was worth. He gathered his wits and peeled her arms away.

"What time in the morning?" she asked.

"Eight?" he answered.

"Eight it is." She took her fluffy white mittens from her pocket and pulled them on as he guided her toward the front door. She looked up at him again. "This means everything to me, Owen."

Her earnest gaze created as much havoc with his senses as her hug. He didn't have a reply, so he opened the door. The sun had nearly set and shadows lurked in the doorways of the storefronts across the street. "Wait until I get my jacket. I'll walk you home."

He grabbed his wool jacket and his hat and locked the door before joining her on the boardwalk. As they left the wooden walkway, dried leaves crunched underfoot.

"I love this time of year, right before the first snow," she said, tugging her collar up around her chin. "Like a promise, the air is saying, 'Winter's coming.'"

They reached her street and walked in silence. Owen spotted the home where his mother had lived for the past two years since his father had died and Richard had handled selling the ranch. Owen had helped his mother find this place, where two lots separated Lillith Reardon's house from Chloe's. In spring, the scent of the lilacs that formed a border along Chloe's yard wafted all the way to his mother's dining room. Now they stood in bleak formation, neatly clipped back in preparation for cold weather.

As they passed, he noted lights on in his mother's parlor. He considered stopping to see if there was enough supper for him to join them, but he needed to get back to the shop and finish staining the doors, especially if he was going to lose work time tomorrow morning.

They reached the two-and-a-half-story home where Chloe lived, and he stood at the bottom of the stairs while she hurried up onto the porch. The wicker furniture had been put away, and the porch looked large and empty.

A light shone from the window overlooking the porch, and muted organ music reached them.

"That would be Miss Sarah," Chloe said. "My boarder. She's probably just finishing up her evening recital."

He nodded. His mother had mentioned a renter.

"Well, good night, Owen."

He touched the brim of his hat. "'Night, miss."

She opened the front door and knelt to prevent a furry calico cat from escaping before turning and disappearing inside.

A bitter wind kicked up a dry batch of leaves and swirled them on the porch floor outside the door she'd just closed. Owen turned back the way they'd come, glancing absently again at his mother's house.

How long would it take for news of his agreement to work on Chloe Hanley's church project to reach his family? He should probably tell his mother himself. He might be in time for dessert. Leaping the three railroad tie steps that led up to the walk, he swung open the wrought-iron gate, noting it needed oiling again. He took in the rosebushes he'd covered for winter and the fresh coat of paint on her storm door. He'd done the chores while the weather was still warm, intending to cut enough wood to last them the winter, but now he'd probably have to have a load delivered. As if he didn't have enough to do...

What had he gotten himself into?

Chloe hung her coat on the tree inside the vestibule. She'd better get out her boots and have them at the ready before snow fell.

Antoinette sat in the center of the doorway to the study, her great long tail flicking back and forth in the air behind her. She meowed and gave Chloe an accusatory green-eyed stare.

"What is it? Have I missed your suppertime? I haven't eaten, either." She knelt to scoop up the heavy cat and stroke her head and neck as she carried her into the room warmed by a snapping fire.

Miss Sarah Wisdom had finished playing and was just settling into her rocker. She reached into the bag beside the chair and spread her knitting on her lap. She'd been working on a baby sweater since the previous summer. Chloe wondered if she deliberately tore out stitches so she had something to do the following night, but she wisely kept her silence. "Good evening, Miss Sarah."

"Good evening, Chloe. You're late this evening."

"I had business to attend to after the food baskets were delivered."

"Did you walk all that way?"

"No, Marcella hitched her buggy, and she and Jenetta accompanied me. We had heavy baskets, so walking would have been impossible." The two widowed women she spoke of were sisters who shared a small home nearby. Though what some might consider up in their years, the two were Chloe's most eager counterparts, sometimes even wearing Chloe to a frazzle with their energetic ideas.

Sarah had never been married. From stories she had shared over the past few years, Chloe guessed she was probably old enough to be her mother, though she didn't have a nurturing bone in her body. She obsessed over the smallest details of her appearance and her room, even being finicky about the kitchen and its contents. She rarely left the house, and when she did, she never asked if Chloe wanted to accompany her or needed anything while she was out.

Chloe had become accustomed to her persnickety ways, and they shared the living space amiably. Chloe needed an income for monthly expenses and taxes, and because Sarah didn't want her to take another boarder, she paid a goodly sum to live in this house.

Sarah didn't care for Antoinette, but the cat came along with the house and instinctively stayed clear of the woman.

Chloe carried the cat into the kitchen, where she set her down and washed her hands before slicing cheese and an apple and pouring milk into a glass for herself and a saucer for Antoinette.

After shaving a few scraps from the roast she had made the day before, she shared them. Antoinette ate, then dared to jump to the seat of the nearby chair and eyed the tabletop, but didn't attempt the leap.

Chloe was still basking in giddy delight over the fact that Owen Reardon had agreed to take on the church restoration. Well, all but agreed. He'd been hesitant to completely commit until he assessed things the following morning, but for some reason unknown to her, he seemed ready to take on the work.

She'd have done it herself if she'd had the know-how and skill, but what she lacked in handiness, she would make up for with determination and dedication.

She ate her meager meal with satisfaction, then put on water for a pot of tea and washed her plate and glass. Sarah had already washed and dried and put away the dishes she'd used, as she did each time she ate or drank.

Chloe glanced around the roomy kitchen, noting everything in its place, the table and workspaces bare. The pie safe held a pie she'd made earlier in the week, and over half of it still remained. She broke off a bite of crust and nibbled it while waiting for the water to boil.

Once it did, she poured it over tea leaves in her china pot and moved to glance out the window while the brew steeped.

Lights were on in the house next door. Ever since Lillith Reardon and her daughter JoDee had moved in beside her, her own quiet existence had been pointed out on more than one occasion—especially weekends. Sundays were the most difficult, drawing out into tedious boredom, with Chloe aware that families were gathering elsewhere.

On Sundays, Lillith Reardon made dinner for her growing brood, and they all came over to eat. During fair months, they played games in the yard. Children laughed and squealed, and parents sat on the shaded porch or joined them in croquet tournaments.

Owen was always at the center of the children's activities. At first she'd thought he must have married, but Lillith had told her all the children belonged to Richard and her oldest daughter, Millie.

On Saturdays, however, before their gathering on the Sabbath, Owen always cut the grass with a push mower. As though thinking of the man conjured him up, Owen Reardon exited the rear door of the neighboring house carrying a bin. He stopped at the fire pit and emptied trash into the charred indentation in the ground.

He lit the rubbish on fire and stood watching the flames. After a few minutes the fire died down. He banked the ashes and carried the bin back to the house. She remembered what it had been like when her grandfather had been alive and had needed her. Running his errands and preparing him meals had been satisfying. Owen obviously found the same reward in doing chores for his mother.

Chloe turned to pour her tea. She carried a cup to the table and sat in the dim silence. If he was going to be occupied with the church and his own business, she would offer to help his mother with chores. She tucked away the idea for morning.

It had been a long time since she'd had any hope regarding the building that held so many memories. In fact, it had been a long time since she'd had anything of consequence to look forward to. Things were definitely looking up.

Chapter Three

The following morning, Chloe handed the key she'd taken from its place in the top drawer of her grandfather's desk to Owen and watched him place it in the wrought-iron keyhole and turn it.

Even if she hadn't been able to find the key, they could have removed boards from a window and entered the church. Owen pushed open the right portal of the double entryway door with a loud creak.

The dark interior smelled like old wood and dust. "We won't be able to see anything unless I let some light in," he said. He strode back to the crowbar and leather bag he'd left outside the door and raised the flap, pulling out a hammer. Picking up the crowbar, he left the church, carrying both tools.

A minute later, Chloe turned at the crack and squeak of wood and nails being pried, and squinted at a spot in the darkness. After a lot more pounding and creaking, a sliver of light opened along one of the tall stained-glass windows. A kaleidoscope of color pointed across the dusty wooden floor, growing longer and wider.

With a final ripping sound, an entire square of light reflected on the ground. She raised her gaze to the intact window. "It's perfect!"

Unexpected tears welled in her eyes and she placed her palm over her racing heart.

She stood mesmerized as Owen uncovered three more windows, lighting the sanctuary in an ethereal glow. The exterior noise halted, leaving a calm silence.

She turned to the doorway just as he appeared, silhouetted

against the morning sun, tall and broad shouldered. He hadn't worn a hat, and his wavy brown hair glinted with golden fire in the sunlight. Unlike Richard's pomaded style, Owen's ruffled hair always looked as though he'd left it to dry without troubling himself with a comb.

His astute gaze moved from the windows to the colorful patterns on the floor and rose to the rafters and ceiling beams. Chloe followed his gaze upward.

Owen stopped, mesmerized by the sight of Chloe standing in the spill of color. Her breath created bursts of white in the crisp air and tears glistened in her eyes. Her passion for this place moved him, but her beauty distracted him from what he should be thinking about. He tilted his head back to focus his attention elsewhere.

The dovetail joints and fitted grooves sang of the perfection and precision the builder had poured into every beam and arch and cross support.

He immediately searched for the beam above the altar that had been carved with the faces and wings of angels and found it unchanged and breathtakingly beautiful after all this time.

A cursory glance revealed that the altar area had suffered the most damage. Someone had taken one of the shorter podiums and broken it apart, most likely using the pieces of ash to strike at and damage the altar, the ancient organ and pipes, and one window. From his initial inspection, it appeared the only one broken.

The interior windowsills were rotted and small animals had made nests under pews. At several places in the ceiling, boards hung down and underneath, flooring and pews were damaged from rain and snow.

One entire wall and the flooring at its base had been splashed with whitewash.

"What do you think?" Chloe's voice interrupted his mental assessment. "Can we fix it all in time?"

"The exterior windowsills are brick," he said. "That means we only have to tear the wood away from the interior to replace what's rotted. The roof will have to be changed.

"A lot of these floorboards will have to come up." He gestured to the wall. "We can probably clean all that off." He turned. "I can do most of this—or hire it done—but that window…"

Together they approached the broken window, still covered with boards from the outside.

"Even if we find someone to make a replacement, the new one will never match the others exactly." There were eight windows altogether, four on each side of the building, and the scenes in the glass depicted various Biblical events. "Do you remember what this one was?" he asked.

"Jesus holding a lamb in the crook of his arm and a staff in the other," she answered. She looked at the dusty pile of multicolored glass someone had long ago swept into a corner. "We could lay it out and put all the pieces together, then trace over them."

"But every artist's work and materials reflect a unique color and style," he said. "Even if we find someone to make it, the finished window might not look like the rest." He thought a moment. "We could have a mason brick up the opening."

Her expression made it obvious the idea didn't appeal to her. "Only as a last resort," she said. She brushed her mittens together and told him how much she had in the bank. "How much will the work and material cost?"

The roof alone would be ten times the remainder of her fund-raising money. After starting his business, he still had over half of the money from the sale of his father's ranch. He intended to send JoDee to university if she agreed and still have money left over. "That's almost enough," he hedged.

"I can add more of my own," she assured him.

"We'll see when we get there."

"But you're going to do it?"

Her hopeful expression melted his hesitation. That and his own connection to this place. "I told my mother last night, so she won't hear it elsewhere first. Richard will find out as soon as we make our first step. He won't be happy."

"I'm sure he won't." She touched the back of a pew and rubbed her palms together distractedly. "I know it was unfair for me to even ask you to take this on, but I had nowhere else to turn. Will it cause a problem in your family? I don't want it to, but I need your help."

"I don't care what Richard thinks," he assured her. "I'm doing this because it's the right thing to do."

She placed her mittened hand atop his bare one. "Can I thank you now?"

He glanced down at her white mitten against his skin and then back at her earnest face. Unexpected heat pooled in his belly. "Thank me later. After you've seen how it turns out."

"All right." She smiled and drew her hand away. "What's first?"

"I'll get a ladder and do some measurements on the roof." He glanced upward. "And then I'm going to wire a fellow over in Tommy Creek and ask him to take the roofing job. That will have to be finished before we get snow."

"He'll expect to be paid up front," she said.

"Let me worry about the cost and the hiring," he told her. "If there's a problem later, I'll let you know."

He could tell she didn't want to, but she said, "All right." She glanced around. "What can I do?"

"We'll start tomorrow. Round up as many volunteers as you can get to work on the grounds in this cold weather. Maybe take turns. The whole inside can be cleaned up, and then we'll get started on cleaning the whitewash off that wall. This afternoon, I'll make sure the heaters and the vents are safe and order a load of wood." He had to do the same for his mother anyway.

With her new assignment, Chloe's face brightened. "I'll have a crew here early in the morning."

The congregation who met in the schoolhouse wasn't large, but each person felt strongly about the work on their old church and those who were able showed up the following day.

Owen had both heaters glowing and radiating warmth, though every time someone opened the doors to carry out debris or clear the air, heat escaped and the air chilled before the burning wood could again do its job.

"I worried I'd never see the day that Red Willow First Church held services in this place again," Agnes Matthews said. She'd brought a big tray of warm cinnamon rolls and cleaned a spot on the communion table that had been pushed to a side wall before uncovering them.

"Mighta had a crew together sooner if they'd known you were bringing your rolls," Ernie Paulson said, taking off his glove to pick up a sweet.

Others gathered around and Chloe gestured for Owen to come get one. He knew almost everyone, except Willa and Annie White, a mother and daughter who'd moved to Red Willow from Kansas the summer past. Willa's son, Morris, had hired on as the town's newest doctor and brought his family with him.

"Morris stitched up my finger back a spell," he told Willa, and she admired the neat scar on his index finger.

Owen took charge and assigned three men the outdoor task of trimming shrubbery, raking leaves and supervising a burn pit to dispose of debris.

By midmorning there was so much dust raised, Chloe could barely see across the sanctuary, but eventually the air cleared and they began scrubbing.

Owen brought a tin of liquid that smelled awful and showed them how they'd be using it with steel wool to remove the white-wash the following day.

Nearly everyone showed up the next day, and two additional helpers even joined them.

Around noon, they took a break to eat their sack lunches.

Chloe was enjoying the sense of accomplishment and listening to Melvina Pierce's story of a raccoon on her laundry porch the previous morning when the door opened. A draft swirled around her ankles where she sat on a wooden folding chair with the others.

Richard Reardon stood in the opening, the collar of his tailored calf-length black coat pulled up around his neck.

"Hey, shut the door!" Ernie Paulson called out.

Richard ignored him and strode into the sanctuary.

Annie White got up and hurried over to close the door, then returned to her seat.

With his jaw set, Richard strolled along the east side of the room, surveying the work in progress where Owen had been removing rotted wood. Conversation had been cut short, and the workers cast the man uneasy glances.

A nervous feeling churned in Chloe's stomach.

He turned, his gaze narrowing on the opposite wall, where evidence of their progress could be seen on the whitewash removal.

Her gaze shot to Owen. He continued eating his sandwich, without obvious concern.

Richard stepped beside him. "So, little brother. You've joined forces with the people trying to impede Red Willow's progress." He turned his accusatory gaze from Owen to the workers gathered around the heater and back to his brother. "No reply?"

"What was the question?" Owen asked.

"What are you doing here?"

"I'm replacing the windowsills."

"I mean what are you doing helping that woman in what's going to be a useless effort? Surely you have something more productive you could be working on."

Chloe winced at being referred to as *that woman*.

"Since when did you take an interest in my work?"

Annie and her mother finished their sandwiches and tossed their paper wrappers into the heater. One by one, the others took their cue and moved away from the stove and returned to their tasks until only Chloe and Owen remained.

"I don't give a whit about your work," Richard said. "What I want to know is what the hell you are trying to do. You know this is where the town wants to put the new hotel."

"And by the town, do you mean everyone? Including these people in here? Because I don't think these townspeople want to see a hotel replace their church."

"I mean the council. We've been talking about it for months."

"Undoubtedly *you've* been talking about it for months," Owen replied, without raising his voice. "That doesn't mean it's the right thing to do. It's just what you want to do."

Richard's face reddened, and he pressed his lips into a straight line before replying. "You're never going to have this place ready by Christmas." He turned to include Chloe in his prediction. "What do church ladies know about replacing roofs and repairing structural damage?"

"There's actually very little structural damage," Owen answered without rising to his brother's bait. "Nothing a mason can't repair in a week's time. And so far the church ladies have been doing a great job."

Owen's calm response impressed Chloe as much as his skill as a carpenter and woodworker. The man was unflappable.

"The church can't afford everything that needs to be done," Richard reaffirmed and fixed Chloe with a stare. "You're wasting his time and everyone else's. You might as well bake cookies and sew costumes for the Sunday school pageant and leave city planning to the people who know what they're doing and can afford to carry out their strategies."

"We're carrying out our strategy just fine, thank you," she said, hating that her voice quivered when she got angry. "Now unless you want to pick up a brush and rags and help, I'd suggest you leave us to our work."

Richard leaned over her. "You, little missy, are going to be sorry."

Chapter Four

Chloe's chair slid backward, catching her by surprise and causing her to jerk to keep her balance. Stifling a yelp, she glanced at Owen, who had merely moved her seat away from Richard and now stood filling the space with his imposing form. "And *you* can deal with me if you have a complaint worth hearing."

"How typical of you to mix yourself up in this fanciful dream. You never had a lick of business sense in your foolhardy head."

"When I want your assessment of my character, I'll ask for it," Owen told him. "And I don't recall asking." Owen picked up his leather tool belt and hooked it around his waist, effectively dismissing Richard.

Chloe took her cue from him and went back to her task of cleaning the shards of glass and laying them out like a puzzle on a freshly scrubbed section of floor at the back of the room.

She carefully kept her focus on her task until the door opened. This time it closed again. She glanced up to find Richard gone.

Several feet away, Owen worked at prying a board out of the wall beneath a window as though nothing had ever happened. She'd expected Richard would be unhappy. She'd hoped Owen wouldn't be the target for his displeasure, but she'd been fooling herself. Part of her regretted placing Owen in the middle of this controversy, but the other part of her was overjoyed with his support and willingness to take a stand.

By midafternoon, Chloe had the pieces of colored glass arranged on the floor in their original places. She acquired a long piece of paper from the newspaper office and fastened it to the floor over her eight-foot puzzle. Once that was secure, she took a stick of charcoal and rubbed the design on, one section at a time. The lead separations in the glass divided colors, so she was able to trace the size each piece had been and label the drawing on the paper with the correct color.

She had no idea if her effort was going to be useful, but it was the only way she could think of to recreate the window to its exact proportions.

Owen took a break and paused to watch her laborious endeavor. After several minutes he said, "I think that's going to work."

She sat back on her heels and looked up at him. "Yes?"

He nodded. "We'll have a scale drawing along with a piece of each color of glass. Hopefully, the design will be clear enough for someone to create a new window."

"But who?" she asked. "How do we find someone?"

He hunkered down and touched his fingertips to the paper thoughtfully. "Gather newspapers, like the New York, Washington and Philadelphia papers—there's always a stack at the barber's—and read through all the advertisements. Make a list of the tradesmen who sound like what we might need or those you think might be able to lead you to the right person. Send them all telegrams." He glanced at her. "Tell Jim Gold to put it on my account."

His cinnamon-colored eyes were bright with an excitement that hadn't been there before. "This was a smart idea, Chloe."

His brother might think she was a useless meddling female, but Owen thought she was intelligent. His unexpected praise warmed her cheeks. "I'll go pick up newspapers before the barber closes and I'll read through them this evening."

"I'll be having supper at my mother's later," he said. "Why don't you join us, and we can look through the ads together?"

At the invitation, her heart leaped with pleasure, but she hesitated. "Lillith wouldn't be expecting me. I wouldn't want to impose."

"I'll send someone over to tell her now," he said. "She enjoys a crowd around the table and always makes too much."

"If you're sure…"

He nodded with finality, then glanced around for someone to deliver the message.

Chloe watched him go back to his task. She hadn't enjoyed

herself this much in a long time. Having a purpose made the days go so much more quickly, and the work was rewarding. She'd slept like a baby the night before and awakened eager to discover what the new day held.

She experienced an overwhelming gratefulness toward the workers who'd come to do what they could. She was indebted to Owen, not only for his time and skill, but for being her champion. There was something decidedly compelling about the man, and the more time she spent around him, the more she noticed things she liked about him. Of course on the surface his wide shoulders, strong hands and handsome face were all attractive features, and she'd have to be blind to miss them. But there was so much more she'd never had the opportunity to discover until now.

As much as she appreciated feeling useful, she liked the fact that Owen noticed her even more. She eagerly anticipated their meeting that evening.

Lillith Reardon welcomed her neighbor with a warm hug. "Hello, dear. I'm delighted Owen asked you to join us for dinner. You look lovely."

Chloe had bathed and donned a two-piece visiting dress, the long jacketlike top made of an oriental cashmere print and an underskirt of bronze satin with a pleated overskirt trimmed in the matching cashmere. The dress was a couple of years old, but she preferred a smaller bustle than was currently fashionable and didn't care for cumbersome trains.

"Thank you. Owen assured me I wouldn't be putting you out."

"Not at all. The more people at the table, the happier I am. It's probably ill-mannered for me to usher you straight from the door to the table, but the meal is ready." She took Chloe's hand and led her to the dining room.

Chloe had been in her house once or twice before, but never for a meal. Lillith's warm greeting set her at ease.

JoDee had already seated herself next to Owen and smiled when Lillith arrived with Chloe in tow. "Hello, Miss Hanley. It's so nice you were able to join us."

"Please call me Chloe."

Owen stood and came around the table to pull out a chair for her. "Good evening."

Unused to the gentlemanly conduct, she shyly averted her gaze to the table settings.

"Your church restoration was one of the topics of conversation after school this afternoon." Owen's younger sister was still in school, and probably at least sixteen years of age by now.

"What are the students saying?" Chloe asked, as Owen resumed his seat.

"Repeating their parents mostly. Mary Dunbar's father thinks Red Willow needs a new hotel, but her mother claims she'll be the first one through the doors for services when they begin."

"Goodness. It sounds as though your project is affecting more than one family," Lillith observed. She removed covers from the serving dishes.

"It wasn't my intent to cause any hard feelings," Chloe told the woman. "The church is important to our community. I couldn't bear to see it torn down."

"You don't have to explain anything to me," Lillith told her, passing a platter of roasted chicken. "I have two babies buried in that graveyard, bless their souls."

Chloe remembered the inscriptions on the matching flat stones that marked those particular tiny graves. "Yes, of course you do. I'm sorry for your losses."

"It was a long time ago, dear. Before JoDee was born. But your grandfather was a comfort to me during some of the worst months of my life, and I'll never forget him for that."

"He did have a way of putting a person's heart and mind at ease," Chloe said.

"At one time my husband remarked that he thought your father would follow in his footsteps," Lillith told her. "It seemed he would, but then his interests turned to surveying. It was a shame he met such an early death. How old were you?"

"Ten," Chloe replied. She'd been just a girl when her father had fallen from his horse and died from exposure. Her mother had remarried a few years later, but it wasn't long before she left the both of them, never to be heard from again. No one ever mentioned the subject, but Chloe suspected everyone wondered as much as she did what had prompted the woman's hasty departure. Chloe had gone to live with her grandfather and her stepfather had moved on.

"You were a blessing to your grandfather in his later years," Lillith told her.

"He took care of me," Chloe said. "It was the least I could do for him."

"Your dress is pretty, Chloe," JoDee told her. "It's very sophisticated."

"I don't much care for the ruffles and bustles that are all the rage," Chloe told her. "They only get in the way."

"I've been trying to convince Mother I need dresses befitting someone other than a schoolgirl," she said with a roll of her eyes.

"You are a schoolgirl," Owen said, speaking up for the first time. He'd taken large servings of the chicken and potatoes and was working his way through them.

"I'll be sixteen in three more months," she said indignantly. "That's hardly a child. I should have more fashionable dresses."

"She's my last one," Lillith said unapologetically. "And maybe I am trying to keep her young for a while longer." She turned to her daughter. "You have years ahead to wear all the fashionable dresses you can buy. For now, just enjoy being a girl and not having to bind and tuck and lace yourself until you can barely breathe. We're not in Philadelphia."

Chloe grinned at their disagreement. She understood JoDee's need to exert herself as a young lady and not a child. It was probably doubly hard being the last of several children, and the only one still living at home.

"Will you play your fiddle for us after supper?" Owen asked.

"It's a *violin*," his sister corrected in an exasperated tone that led Chloe to believe the error was one her brother made deliberately and most likely often. "And yes, it would be my pleasure."

The delicious meal was followed by a peach cobbler with cinnamon-flavored cream poured over the top and steaming cups of rich dark coffee.

Chloe hadn't enjoyed a dinner this much since she'd accompanied Lillith's older daughter, Pamela, to the ranch years ago and been seated at a table much like this one, where the siblings teased each other and their parents did their best to hold dinner conversation over the hubbub. Besides being served tasty food, the company had been thoroughly entertaining.

If she'd stayed home, Miss Sarah would have eaten already, so Chloe would have had the same sliced cheese and fruit and eaten alone in the silent kitchen.

"I always loved coming to the ranch with Pamela," Chloe told them. "I have good memories of those visits."

"You were friends with my sister?" JoDee asked in surprise.

Chloe nodded. "We attended school together."

"She was friends with Richard for a time, as well," Lillith remarked.

JoDee raised an eyebrow at that information. "*Why?*" she asked.

Embarrassment dipped in Chloe's chest and heat rose upward to her cheeks.

"Your brother has his charms," Lillith said. "He was always a handsome young man."

"Richard paid attention to several young ladies," Chloe quickly explained to JoDee. "We were never exclusive."

"Pamela said the girls were always fawning all over him," JoDee said. "Was Georgia one of those others?"

"No, dear. Richard met Georgia when he went to university," her mother replied.

Owen finished his coffee. "Chloe and I have work to do," he said, pushing his chair back and standing. "It was a good meal, Mother. Thank you."

"You're welcome. You know you could come to supper every night."

"I know." He stood behind Chloe, waiting for her to place her napkin beside her plate and rise.

"Thank you," she told his mother. "It's been a long time since I enjoyed a meal so much." She glanced over her shoulder at Owen. "I should help your mother clear the table and do the—"

"Nonsense," Lillith interrupted. "You two go do your business. JoDee will help me."

JoDee opened her mouth, but Lillith added, "If she wants to

prove she's mature enough for those new dresses she talks about incessantly."

The girl clamped her lips together and reached for Owen's empty plate. "You two go on. I have this."

"I'll bring you coffee later," Lillith told Owen.

He led Chloe out of the dining room and toward a parlor with a large rectangular pedestal table against one wall where he'd dropped the newspapers earlier. After turning up the wicks in the wall lamps, he lit them.

From a flat box, he took a sheaf of stationery, a pen and a bottle of ink, then he pulled two cushioned armchairs close and gestured for her to take one. Funny how his innocent gesture made her stomach flutter.

Chapter Five

Seeing how comfortable Owen was in his mother's home, Chloe realized at that moment there was a lot she didn't know about him. He'd been gone from Red Willow for quite a while, but he'd been back for at least two or three years. In that time she'd run into him at an occasional dance or in the mercantile, but they'd never gotten well acquainted.

"Where do you live?" she asked.

"Above my workshop. There are two good-sized rooms up there. Plenty of space for me."

"I smelled your workshop," she said. "How do you ever get a good night's sleep?"

He chuckled, surprising her. "I keep the windows open a lot, even in the winter. And it only smells like that when I've been using the finishes."

"No insult intended," she added belatedly.

He shrugged. "I'm used to those smells, but I'm aware of them."

"Did you finish those doors you were working on?"

"Stayed up late a couple of nights to get them done and then delivered and hung them."

"Who were they for?"

"Rancher this side of Windsor. He has a pretty spectacular log home with custom features."

"He must be one of your best customers."

"He is. I'd like to have a place like his someday."

Chloe glanced up from the page of advertisements she was reading. That was the first personal thing he'd ever said to her, the first glimpse into his usually private thoughts. "There's no reason you can't build your own place, is there?"

He shook his head. "I will one of these days."

"I'll bet it will be something to see when you do." She looked back at the newspaper page, refocused her thoughts and stifled a yawn.

"You're tired."

"I'm all right. This shouldn't take us too long."

He opened the bottle of ink and dipped the pen. "Here's a glassmaker in Indiana."

His handwriting was neat and legible. After half an hour, Lillith brought them coffee and JoDee entered, opening a case and removing a violin. After setting a music stand on the rug and adjusting sheets of music, she ran the bow across the strings in a warm-up. She then stood with perfect form, the instrument tucked under her chin, one foot with toes pointed forward, the heel of the other against that instep.

Owen capped the ink bottle and turned his chair and Chloe's so they could comfortably watch his sister.

The exquisite sounds JoDee coaxed from the violin were more beautiful than anything Chloe had ever heard. She watched the girl's fluid dexterity with growing appreciation. Lillith listened with her eyes closed, occasionally opening them to smile softly at her daughter.

Chloe stole a glance at Owen beside her. He listened with a relaxed and proud expression on his handsome face. At Chloe's look, he gave her an easy smile as if to ask, "What do you think?"

"She's amazing," Chloe said softly.

"I've been checking into a conservatory for next year."

Watching JoDee play, Chloe wondered what it was like to have attention and concern lavished upon her. Her family had obviously encouraged her from a young age. It was evident that the young woman was the apple of this family's eye, and deservingly so. She was sweet and smart and incredibly talented.

"Your daughter is a special young lady," Chloe said to Lillith.

"All of my children are special in their own way," Lillith replied.

Richard was her son, so of course she loved him, but Chloe had yet to recognize any of his redeeming qualities. She arrested her unkind thoughts.

Chloe lifted her gaze to Owen's and wondered if the half smile he wore meant he suspected what she was thinking. She gave him a sheepish grin.

After three stirring musical pieces, JoDee gave an impressively low curtsy, and they applauded her. "Excuse me now," she said politely. "I have a lesson to finish."

Once she'd left the room, Owen turned their chairs, seated himself and resumed making notes. Lillith glanced over at Chloe, where she sat. "What are your plans for Thanksgiving on Thursday?"

Chloe had been so busy she hadn't given the holiday much thought, which she considered a blessing. Hopefully, she'd be equally occupied during the weeks leading to Christmas, as well. "I suppose I'll fry a couple of slices of ham for the two of us," she replied. "We don't normally go out of our way much."

Lillith appeared mortified at the idea. "You will do no such thing," she said emphatically. "You will come eat dinner with us. I have a fat goose waiting for the occasion, and I've been preserving filling for the pies since midsummer. Tell her about my pies, Owen."

"She makes the best pies in three counties," he said. "Really. You should join us."

"I couldn't leave Miss Sarah," Chloe objected. "Besides, you have plenty of family to cook for, and I'm not—"

"Nonsense," Lillith argued. "Miss Sarah will join us, as well. I wouldn't enjoy my day if I knew the two of you were right next door eating alone."

"I'm quite used to occupying myself on holidays," Chloe told her. Besides not wanting to feel like an intruder, the other thing that skewed her thoughts about joining their lively and entertaining festivities was imagining the day spent with Richard.

"Well, not this one, you won't. You're joining us, and that's the last I will hear of your argument." Lillith stood and rearranged the pillows on the plush divan. "I'll leave the two of you to your endeavors now, but I will see you Thursday around midday, Chloe."

"Thank you," Chloe told her. "And thank you for a lovely supper. I had a good time."

The woman's kind hospitality moved her. Chloe had been invited to people's homes on many occasions, but she'd rarely felt as welcome as she had this evening. Lillith Reardon wasn't putting on airs or feeling sorry for her. Chloe didn't get the impression that Lillith had performed a charitable act and felt benevolent about taking in an orphan or a spinster for a meal.

Lillith simply enjoyed having people around her table and was an instinctively motherly woman.

"What can I bring to dinner?" Chloe asked as the woman headed toward the doorway. Lillith and Owen had already bragged about the woman's pies. Chloe could bake, but she doubted her pies would be needed.

Lillith paused and turned back. "How are you with dough? We can always use another basket of dinner rolls on the table."

"I'd love to bake rolls," she replied with a smile.

Lillith beamed with pleasure and left the room.

Glancing aside, Chloe caught Owen studying her. She wanted to ask him how his brother had grown into the man he'd become when his mother was such a kind and generous woman. Instead, she asked, "What did you do when you left Red Willow during those years?"

He leaned back in his chair. "I kicked around the country for a while. Mostly I stayed clear of cities and found places in the mountains where it seemed like no man had ever set foot before. I saw the Rockies in Wyoming, Montana, Idaho. Spent a winter in Saskatchewan. I hunted and trapped mostly. Sold furs and pelts and did a little mining."

She imagined him off on his own, wintering in the extreme climates and eating over a campfire. He was a quiet person, but setting out alone was a choice she had trouble understanding. "What about wild animals?"

"They mostly leave you alone if you leave them alone."

"Weren't you ever afraid?"

"Not really. When you're using your wits to survive day to day, life is pretty simple. Uncomplicated."

"But you came back."

He nodded. "My father got sick."

"Would you have come back if not for that?"

"I never intended to stay away indefinitely. My brother could've handled things, and my mother has the girls. I wanted to come home. I'd had a lot of time to think, and there were things I needed to do."

She wanted to ask what those things were, but she didn't have any right to pry into his privacy. "Well, I know your mother is thankful you're here."

He nodded. "Probably."

She deliberately moved her gaze to the list on the table. "I'm glad you're here."

He didn't say anything. Her heart rate increased. She stole a look at his face.

He was watching her with a soft expression, his eyes more like warm honey than cinnamon tonight. "Did you ever want to leave?" he asked.

She considered his question for a moment. As a very young girl she'd foolishly imagined going after her mother and finding her. She'd daydreamed scenarios where the woman was overjoyed to see her and accompanied her back to Red Willow. But all those imaginings had ended up with Chloe returning to her home.

This place was all she knew. She shook her head. "I wouldn't have had anywhere to go."

Owen had always dreamed about leaving Red Willow. The earliest plans he could recall involved enduring school so he could set out on his own. But even without a family tying her to this place, Chloe was content. There was much to be said about contentment, he decided.

"I think we've exhausted the ads in these papers," he said. "This list should do nicely."

"I'll send the telegrams first thing tomorrow," she assured him.

"Good. I have the man coming to start the roof. Can't be completed soon enough with the weather so uncertain."

"More snow would fall inside."

He rubbed at an ink stain at the joint of his index finger. "Yes, but the real problem would be ice and snow on the roof, making it too treacherous for the workers."

"Oh, yes, of course." She gathered up the newspapers. "Will you be returning these?"

He shook his head. "I'll put them in the kitchen. My mother has a hundred uses for newspaper."

"I really like your mother. She's lovely."

"She's a special lady," he agreed. He gestured to the doorway that led to the foyer. "Let's get our coats and I'll walk you home."

"It's right next door," she answered with mild surprise.

"You never know what could be lurking in the side yard."

She stood and walked ahead of him toward the front door. "I've never run across anything lurking in the side yard."

"How would you know? It's dark."

"Are you trying to frighten me?"

He took her cranberry wool coat from the tree and held it so she could slip her arms into the sleeves. Again he noticed her fair hair against the black-tipped brown fur. "Not at all. But those rabbits get pretty hungry this time of year."

She laughed, and he liked the musical sound. After pulling on his jacket, he led her outdoors. It was a cold, crisp night, every star in the heavens winking brightly.

"No sign of snow yet," he said. "The weather's in our favor."

They approached her house.

"You've painted your home its original colors," he said. "How did you know which colors to use?"

"I scraped away layers of paint in several places," she replied. "I was pretty convinced I was right about the colors, and then I thought to ask Mr. Gregory." She gestured to a dark house across the street.

The man who lived there had to be nearly a hundred. Occasionally Owen mowed his grass, and talking to him, he'd learned that the man had lived on the property nearly all his life. His house had belonged to his parents before him. Again Owen was impressed by her inventiveness and integrity regarding the preservation of old workmanship.

Chloe took a key from her pocket. The windows of her house were dark. "Looks like Miss Sarah has gone to bed," he said.

"She retires early."

"Want me to walk inside with you?"

Chapter Six

"**I**'ve entered my house in the dark plenty of times," Chloe assured Owen, and he supposed she was right about that. "Thank you for inviting me to dinner this evening. I don't know when I've had a better time."

They stood on the shadowed porch, the silence of the night cloaking them in intimacy. The evocative scent of her hair reached him. Completely inappropriate thoughts chipped away at his common sense. He wanted to pull her into his arms and kiss her to see if she tasted as good as she smelled. How was it Richard hadn't fallen hopelessly in love with her and wanted to marry her? "Good night, Chloe."

"Good night." She turned the key in the lock and within seconds had closed herself inside.

Owen retraced his steps, turning to study the dark, silent house. Finally, an upstairs window glowed from the lamp inside the curtains. He thought of this cheerful woman who loved people entering a silent house and spending her days and evenings with only an unfriendly boarder for company. But Chloe didn't seem unhappy. Far from it, in fact. She appeared quite content.

He walked out to the street and looked back up at the house and the backlit window.

Maybe Richard had been in love with her. Maybe in spite of his feelings for Chloe, he'd chosen to marry Georgia because of her family money. The choice sounded like one his brother would make without flinching. But Owen would likely never know.

Why hadn't Chloe married someone else? he wondered now. He couldn't imagine that Richard had broken her heart and spoiled her for anyone else. But then feelings were unpredictable and women more so. He had more pressing things to concern himself with.

Owen turned and headed for his shop.

The man Owen had hired brought an entire five-person crew, who assembled scaffolding and tore the roof down to bare wood and replaced all the damaged and rotted wood before spreading tar paper and laying shingles.

The sound of their hammers gave Chloe goose bumps as she stood in the yard beside the church and watched the activity with joy in her heart.

A buggy slowed to a stop on the street out front and Frank Garrison, chairman of the town council, climbed down. Chloe met him halfway.

"Looks as though things are well underway," he said.

Chloe stood beside him, and together they looked upward to see the men pounding nails into the shingles. "Owen hired these men, and they work as fast as lightning. I'm going to head home and prepare lunch for them."

"I thought I'd better come see the progress for myself," he told her.

"You might as well see the inside while you're here," she told him and gestured toward the double front doors.

Owen had finished replacing all the windowsills and had spent most of the week tearing out ruined floorboards and replacing them, then sanding and staining. All the pews had been moved to one end of the sanctuary and securely stacked to leave as much open space as possible. Owen glanced up from his task and got to his feet to greet Frank.

"I didn't think you'd have this much done," Frank told him.

"Chloe's a harsh taskmaster," Owen replied with a grin.

Frank's eyebrows rose at the joke and he gave Chloe a wide-eyed look.

"Truthfully, she bribes us with baked goods," Owen remarked. "And chicken salad sandwiches."

Chloe grinned. "Food does seem to keep them happy. I'm perfecting my dough recipe, so they've had rolls at least once a day this week."

Frank turned to the boarded-over window. "What about that window?"

"We're waiting to hear something on that," Owen replied. He explained how Chloe had salvaged all the pieces and created a pattern.

"You're quite the inventive young lady," Frank said. "Well, I wish you luck. Have a good Thanksgiving Day."

"Same to you," Chloe said and watched him leave. As soon as he was gone, she turned to Owen. "Do you think he was simply curious?"

Owen shrugged. "Sure. Why not?"

"I don't know. I'm going to prepare the noon meal now."

She headed home. She'd baked the chicken that morning. Sandwiches were easiest to transport and serve without dishes and silverware, so she prepared and wrapped the sandwiches, then packed a bag of apples and empty jars for drinks, filling two crates.

"Miss Sarah?" she called up the stairs.

Sarah appeared at the top of the landing. "Hello, Chloe."

"Would you consider helping me deliver lunch to the crew working at the church? I'm going to get the wagon I use for gardening from the shed and carry these crates in it. I really need someone to make sure they're steady while I pull it."

Miss Sarah didn't appear all too eager to join Chloe's team of volunteers, but she didn't say no right away. "How long will it take?"

"Perhaps an hour by the time we get there, pass out the food, they eat, and we clean up and bring the wagon home."

"Well." She glanced at the watch pinned to the front of her dress. "I suppose I have an hour."

Chloe reached for her coat and hung Sarah's on the banister knob. What else did the woman have to do? She halted her judgmental thoughts and thanked her.

The workers greeted the two women with appreciation. Miss Sarah looked all around at the inside of the church and her gaze touched on the workers. Chloe assigned her the task of doling out the paper-wrapped sandwiches, while she pumped a pail of fresh water from the well next door and dipped jars into it.

The workers had to share because there weren't enough to go around, but they didn't seem to mind.

"Agnes Matthews dropped off a basket while you were gone," Owen told her.

She located it and found it filled with fat sugar cookies. Chloe was delighted to let Miss Sarah pass them out.

A tall fellow the others called Zeb doffed his hat and accepted the cookie she handed him. He had a lean jaw, a good smile, and crow's feet from years of outdoor work. "Thank you, Miss Sarah. Can't tell you how pleasin' it is to have a pretty lady such as yourself bringing our lunch today."

Miss Sarah blushed to the roots of her hair, but she spared him a bashful smile.

"His name's Zebulon Tate," Owen said to Sarah when she carried the basket back to where he and Chloe were sitting. "He's a hard worker and a pleasant fellow."

Sarah handed Owen a cookie. "I'm sure it's of no consequence to me what the man's name is."

She set down the basket and moved away.

Owen chuckled.

"Were you matchmaking?" Chloe asked.

"Hardly." He gave her a frown, but there was no animosity behind it.

"You were. You were matchmaking."

"Don't be ridiculous."

"I liked it," she added. "It was sweet."

She turned, knowing Owen was following her gaze. Miss Sarah had busied herself opening the last few wrapped sandwiches and splitting the halves between those who wanted seconds, but every so often, she sneaked a glance at Zeb, seated on the floor.

A half hour passed rapidly, and soon it was time for everyone to go back to their tasks. Chloe and Miss Sarah gathered the papers and jars and packed the wagon. Miss Sarah didn't talk all the way home, and went directly to her room.

Chloe washed the jars and packed them for next time. Tomorrow was Thanksgiving, but the workers would be back on Friday.

She returned to run errands at the church for the rest of the day, and then came home and had a quiet supper.

She could hardly relax that night for thinking about the following day. But once she snuggled under her covers with Antoinette's warmth at her feet, she slept soundly and woke early, refreshed and energized.

After baking rolls, she bathed. She decided on one of the dresses she wore to church, since a day dress wasn't fancy enough and it wasn't an evening event. She chose one of her favorites, a jade-green silk polonaise dress. The neckline and cuffs were trimmed with ivory Brussels lace.

The long tunic-style bodice, which was hemmed with matching fringe, gathered around her hips to tie in the back, giving the appearance of a bustle, but with a lot less bulk and structure. The style would be convenient for sitting at the dinner table, and she liked how the color looked with her fair skin and hair.

Miss Sarah surprised Chloe in a plum-colored silk paisley visiting dress, with a ruffled hem on the bodice and the skirt, as well as a ruffle that ran up the front to the modest neckline under her chin. The back billowed out in a loose train. Chloe had never seen the dress before. But of course, it was a visiting dress and Miss Sarah never went visiting.

"You look so pretty," Chloe told her.

"Thank you. How long will we stay?"

Chloe had no idea. They'd been invited for midday dinner, and a dinner usually entailed conversation or games and a light meal in the evening. "I'm not sure. At least a few hours."

Miss Sarah plucked her coat from the tree. "All right then."

They traveled the short distance between houses, Chloe carrying the rolls, which had turned out perfectly. She reached to rap on the door, but it opened before her knuckles touched the wood.

"Welcome!" Lillith said, and gave them each a warm hug. Miss Sarah accepted the embrace with a stiff posture and immediately backed away.

Judd Valentine, Lillith's oldest daughter's husband, took their coats and whisked them away.

Pamela hurried into the foyer and paused with a broad smile. "Chloe! How wonderful to see you."

She embraced her, then turned to Miss Sarah. "How do you do? I'm Pamela Rhodes, an old friend of Chloe's."

"It's a pleasure to meet you," Sarah said with a tight smile.

Another young man showed up, and Pamela turned to beckon him forward. "This is my husband, Sully. Sully, meet Miss Chloe Hanley and…"

"Miss Sarah Wisdom," Chloe supplied.

Lillith had taken the basket of rolls from Chloe, and she peeled back the toweling and sniffed them. "These smell so good. Pamela, show our neighbors into the great room while I carry these to the dining table."

Pamela led them into a large room with plenty of seating.

"You remember my sister, Millie," Pamela said. "And her husband, Judd. These are their children, Rosalie and Elias."

Chloe had seen the youngsters playing on the lawn during fair weather. "You have a beautiful family," Chloe told Millie.

JoDee got up from where she'd been seated beside Rosalie at the piano and greeted them. "Miss Chloe. Miss Sarah."

Another youngster burst into the room and skidded to a halt, bunching up the fringed rug. "Where's Grandmother?"

"This is Mattias," Pamela said. "And Niles," she added when another boy joined them. "That means Richard and Georgia have arrived. Grandmother is setting out plates and silverware all by herself, so I'm going to help her."

A slender dark-haired woman entered the room, followed by Richard. JoDee introduced them to their guests.

"I understand you live right next door to Mother Reardon," Georgia said.

Chloe confirmed that indeed she did. Georgia had undoubtedly heard all about Chloe and the church from Richard, but if she had, she didn't let on that she shared any animosity.

Her sons immediately settled themselves at a small table with a checkerboard and decided who would go first.

Owen arrived next, his familiar visage a welcome sight. Chloe couldn't help a broad smile. Another man entered directly behind him, and Chloe looked twice, recognizing the older gentleman from the roofing crew. Zeb Tate had slicked back his dark hair and donned a suit.

Owen introduced Zeb to his family members.

Rosalie, who Chloe guessed to be about four, attached herself to Owen's leg and even stepped on his shoe to get higher. He reached down in an easy motion and swung her to sit on one shoulder. She squealed and dug one fist into his hair to hang on.

Owen made a face that indicated she had a tight hold. "Ease up a little, muffin," he called up. "You don't want to snatch your Uncle Owen bald, do you?"

She giggled and relaxed her grip on his hair.

Miss Sarah had inched closer to Chloe. When Chloe glanced aside, her face had turned pink, and she held her hands clasped together at her waist.

As accustomed as she was to being alone, it was possible the number of people at the gathering unnerved her. Or…Chloe followed Miss Sarah's shy gaze as it darted to Zeb and away more than once. Maybe it was the presence of one man in particular that set her on edge. How obvious of Owen to bring the man to dinner when he'd known Miss Sarah would be here. She'd kidded him about matchmaking, but now she was convinced there was some truth at the bottom of her suspicions.

Pamela appeared wearing a bright smile. "Dinner is ready!" she called. "Come to the table."

Family members and guests strolled down the hallway. The aromatic smells of meat and sage reached them long before they filed through the doorway into the dining room.

Chloe had questioned how so many would fit, but the table had been extended and extra wooden folding chairs tucked close together. White linens and sparkling silver set a festive tone, and yet when Lillith guided people to their places, the atmosphere felt informal and comfortable.

A golden-brown roasted duck had been placed in front of Richard at the head of the table. Bowls and platters were filled with potatoes and gravy, green beans, sliced carrots, a smoked ham and so many dishes Chloe wondered how they would eat it all. Her mouth watered at the scents. She'd never seen anything like this feast.

Chloe took the seat Sully held out for her, while Owen perched Rosalie on a chair padded with a thick dictionary beside her mother and Judd slid out a chair for Miss Sarah directly across from Chloe.

Once he'd finished settling his niece and helping Millie get Elias into a wooden high chair, Owen took his seat directly beside Chloe.

Chapter Seven

Chloe glanced from face to face, noting Lillith's extremely satisfied smile and Richard's tight expression. Perhaps Lillith had a bit of matchmaking on her mind, too.

Owen's tawny gaze met Chloe's and held. Above the hubbub of chatter and shifting of chairs, her heart beat faster.

"Richard?" Lillith said, folding her hands over her plate.

Everyone quieted in expectation, and even the children bowed their heads. Richard's brief, yet eloquent prayer of thanks for the food and their health and prosperity surprised Chloe. As the oldest son, he was no doubt expected to give a blessing for their meal, but he'd done a good job of it.

Richard sliced the fowl, placing a portion on the top plate in a towering stack. The plate passed and the task repeated until everyone had a serving. Lillith directed bowls and platters passed to the right, and before she knew it, Chloe's plate was heaped.

Owen held her own yeasty-smelling basket of rolls toward her.

"There's something I can pass on," she said with a smile.

"Something wrong with them?"

"No, but I made them and I had one earlier."

"Well, if you made them, I'll need to take another," he said and rested one on the edge of his plate.

"Chloe made the rolls," he announced, and passed the basket to JoDee on the other side of her.

Chloe tasted the flavorful rich duck and the sage-seasoned stuffing with appreciation.

Across from her, Zeb had been seated beside Miss Sarah, and

Sarah sat ramrod straight, her elbows tucked at her sides. She met Chloe's eyes and managed a stiff smile. Zeb spoke, and her face turned pink, but she answered.

Chloe took in the unfamiliar atmosphere, listening to Pamela and Millie as they spoke to their children and observing Lillith where she sat with one of Richard's sons on either side of her. The joy on her face was unmistakable. Chloe wondered if the woman's late husband was uppermost in her thoughts at that moment, because she caught the woman glancing around the table with tears shining in eyes the same color as Owen's.

The moment became overwhelmingly emotional and Chloe's own eyes stung. Her fork stilled because she couldn't eat and swallow past the welling feelings.

It had been many years since she'd visited the ranch house with Pamela and eaten with the boisterous Reardons. Back then their family hadn't been nearly this big, but she had always remembered the way they made her feel. Their big noisy family magnified her complete lack of connection to anyone in this world. While she'd loved every moment of those dinners, she'd also felt like an observer rather than a participant.

"Something wrong?" Owen asked.

She shook her head and blotted her lips with her napkin.

"You sure?"

"Yes. I'm fine. It's just—it's been a long time since I've eaten at a table with a family."

"They're a little overwhelming," he agreed.

She shook her head. "No, not at all. I'm enjoying it."

She dared a look into his eyes again.

"The rolls are good," he said.

She smiled. "Admit you're matchmaking."

"What? No. I don't know what you're talking about."

"You know what I'm talking about." She lowered her voice to a whisper. "You invited Zebulon Tate and asked your mother to seat him beside Miss Sarah."

"I did no such thing."

She skewered him with her gaze.

"I invited him, yes, but my mother planned the seating."

"And you knew where she'd place him because of the order of couples."

He paused a moment too long. "Maybe."

She wanted to laugh, but she didn't want to draw attention to their conversation, so she gave him a satisfied grin and returned to her meal.

"Only a few weeks until Christmas," Lillith said, and the words stood out from all the others to Chloe's ears.

The children took the news with excitement, but Chloe experienced a sinking feeling.

"Four short weeks," Richard agreed. "And it's getting colder. I expect we'll see snow fly soon." He lifted his dark gaze to Owen, who merely nodded and took another roll from the basket in front of him.

"How's the work on the church coming along?" Richard asked.

Conversation stilled and concerned gazes shot to Owen and Chloe.

"Maybe we don't need to discuss that today, Richard," Lillith said cautiously.

"It's all right," Owen said to his mother. "The work is coming along nicely. The roof is finished except for trimming the eaves. Now when the snow comes it won't be inside."

"How about that window?" Richard asked. "I'll bet that's proving to be a problem."

"I'm looking for someone who can create a new one to match the others," Chloe told him.

"If time runs out," Owen added, "we'll simply brick up the space over the winter and go back to it in the spring. One window won't prevent Christmas service from being held there."

"I was past the other day," Judd remarked. "The outside looks a lot different with all the shrubbery cleared away."

If the tight line of his mouth was any indication, Richard was none too pleased at the news. Georgia gave her husband a surreptitious glance.

"The volunteers have worked very hard," Chloe told him. "The community has been supportive."

Millie changed the subject, and Chloe experienced supreme

relief. The more she thought about it, especially now, being in the midst of their family, she was responsible for the friction between Richard and Owen regarding the church. No one seemed overly upset about the clash of purposes except Richard, however.

Desserts were served, and Lillith had indeed outdone herself with pies. Millie had contributed dainty layered white cakes with fluffy frosting and a spun sugar flower on each square.

Chloe managed to consume a sliver of each variety of pie and two of the little cakes. When Lillith brought out a pot of freshly brewed tea, she sighed with pleasure.

Most of the men drank coffee, but the ladies enjoyed the tea so much Lillith brewed second and third pots.

Eventually the men stood and moved to the great room, and the women picked up dishes and carried them to the kitchen. When Chloe asked for a job, Lillith put her to work washing plates and silverware.

Pamela handed Miss Sarah a towel, and the woman seemed pleased to participate in the cleanup. Lillith took the clean plates and silverware back to the dining room. "The sideboard is set for an easy supper this evening," she said.

"We'll eat the remainder of the food later," JoDee told her.

"I've never eaten so much in my life." Chloe pressed her hand to her full stomach. "Everything was so good, and I didn't want to miss anything."

"I know what you mean," Pamela said.

With so many of them working, the kitchen was tidy in no time, so they joined the others.

Lillith sat in a rocker, holding Elias until he fell asleep. Judd took him from her and carried him upstairs.

Richard's two sons had been playing checkers again, but when their grandmother beckoned them over, they sat close to her feet. "What shall we play?" he asked.

"Let's play charades," JoDee said.

Mattias had his own idea. "No, let's make limericks."

"I want to play knots," Rosalie disagreed.

"So many good ideas," Lillith said. "How will we ever choose?"

"Let Chloe select the first game and Miss Sarah the second," Pamela suggested.

"I know how to play charades, but the others are unfamiliar," Chloe told them. "How do you play knots?"

"Between five and eight people stand close together in a circle," JoDee explained. "On 'go' everybody scrambles and grabs two hands. Then you have to get untangled without letting go of hands."

"It requires much undignified climbing over, under and around to get untangled," Lillith said with a chuckle. "I don't join in, but I certainly enjoy a good laugh watching."

Chloe studied the other women in their dresses and skirts, imagining the scene. When she looked aside at Owen, he had a mischievous twinkle in his eye. "Okay," she said. "Knots it is."

The children squealed and all of them wanted to go first. "Remember one short person per group," Sully said. "Otherwise it's near impossible to accomplish anything."

Chloe was recruited for the first group. Sully called Owen to join them, and she soon stood in a tight circle that included Mattias. They stretched their hands forward and Sully shouted, "Go!"

Within a matter of seconds, Chloe was gripping a hand in each of hers. Her gaze traveled from the hand to the person. She held one of Mattias's and one of Millie's.

"All right, untie the knot," Sully said.

The process was slow going, with much thinking and discussion of strategy. The more they attempted to climb and dip under each other's arms, the more tangled they became. At one point she had to bend across Owen to unravel the knot, and just brushing against him, she became aware of his heat and hard muscles. She was glad she couldn't see his face, because she'd have blushed, but she glanced at Lillith to see the woman grinning.

At another point she became entangled with Millie, and Chloe laughed until her side hurt. Finally, the only remaining knot in the group was maneuvered, and they stood in a circle, holding hands.

"I'm the next short person!" Niles called.

This time Chloe sat beside Lillith and watched. Sully gave the command and hands grappled for a hold. Richard and Miss Sarah attempted to untwine their hands and arms, and when Miss Sarah's skirts got in the way, Lillith was tickled and laughed until tears streaked her face. After a flash of lacy petticoats, Sarah managed to stand upright and resume her dignity.

Chloe couldn't remember laughing so hard. Seeing Richard in this context, teasing his wife and being a good sport, gave her an entirely new perspective. Recently, she'd wondered why she'd ever been drawn to him, but seeing him with his family reminded her of his good qualities.

Limericks turned out to be less physically challenging, but just as funny. Everyone jotted down a few words on a piece of paper, and every other person drew a slip from a vase to see with which word their line of the limerick must end and to make the next person's rhyme.

Those who'd played before had deliberately listed nearly impossible to rhyme or funny-sounding words. Parents helped their children with this game, and Lillith participated.

The afternoon and evening passed so quickly that Chloe couldn't believe it when Lillith announced it was time to set out the rest of the food, prepare drinks and have a casual meal. "You're welcome to make a plate and bring it back here or sit in the dining room. Just be comfortable and enjoy yourself."

Chloe found Miss Sarah. When they got to the dining room, family members urged them to the front of the line. Still full from the last meal, Chloe prepared a plate with small servings and carried it back to the great room. Miss Sarah sat beside her. Zeb soon joined them, taking a chair to Miss Sarah's right. A few minutes later Owen found Chloe and seated himself on the ottoman nearby.

This had been a day unlike any Chloe had ever experienced. As others filtered in, she glanced from one family member to the next, thinking how fortunate the in-laws had been to marry Reardons and how wonderful it must have been to be born into this household.

She remembered well how taken she'd been with Lillith and the others all those years ago when she and Pamela had been friends and later when Richard had invited her to events.

When she'd learned that he'd married Georgia and brought her back to Red Willow, she hadn't been heartbroken over the fact that he hadn't asked *her* to marry him. She'd been disappointed that she would no longer be invited to their home.

Her uncomfortable realization was that she'd never been in love with Richard, but she'd been completely infatuated with his family.

Miss Sarah soon took her leave, and Zeb was quick to excuse himself, thank Lillith and walk her next door. Richard and Georgia gathered the boys and headed home. Lillith hugged everyone at the door.

"I can't thank you enough for the day," Chloe told her.

"Thank you for coming. It's been far too long since you've been here."

At her words, tears stung behind Chloe's eyes.

"You'll join us for Christmas, of course. Owen would miss your rolls if you didn't bring them." Lillith released her and motioned to Owen, standing several feet away. "Walk Miss Hanley home now."

"I'll come back and fill the wood box," he told her.

"I can do it tomorrow," she replied. "You go on home and rest." She raised her cheek, and he kissed it.

He held out Chloe's coat for her then grabbed his own.

"I'd forgotten what a warm person your mother is. She manages to do everything and be cheerful all the time."

Owen walked beside her. "She lives for her family."

"That's obvious." She stole a glance at him. "I don't want you to feel awkward or obligated in any way, so I don't think I'll accept her invitation for Christmas. You didn't sign up for having me intrude on your family time as well as work."

"Oh, malarkey. You saw today that a few more people barely make a dent."

"Will you play the same games?"

"Nope. By Christmas there will be ice and snow. We'll go skating and sledding."

"I haven't ice-skated since I was a girl."

"She should've mentioned that to you. I'm sure she will later, so you can dress warm. And the ladies wear shorter skirts to skate."

"Seriously?"

"Yes. Ask Pam or JoDee. Maybe one of them will loan you one."

They climbed her porch stairs. "And you're sure it won't be an imposition?"

"I want you there."

Surprised, she lifted her gaze. He looked entirely too serious. Butterflies fluttered in her stomach. "Maybe you'll be sick of me by then."

He grinned. "Maybe. If I am, I'll let you know."

"I'll go to the telegraph office in the morning and see if we've had any replies."

"I was serious," he told her. "If we have to brick up that window space, we will, in order to hold services four weeks from now."

"There's still a lot to be finished," she told him.

"Trust me." His amber eyes petitioned her to do just that. He reached for her hand. She hadn't bothered with mittens for such a short walk, and she liked the sensual warmth and strength of his fingers against hers.

She trusted him. It was herself she didn't trust in a situation like this, and her mistrust was validated when he leaned forward, and she eagerly raised her face. What was she thinking?

Chapter Eight

Owen moved his head lower until his warm lips covered hers in a soft, hesitant kiss. Chloe's head swam with the pleasure of it. A giddy happiness welled from inside.

Antoinette meowed from the other side of the door.

Owen moved only a few scant inches away, but the crisp air cooled her lips quickly.

"Thank you for inviting me," she said. "I had a wonderful day."

"I'm glad you came," he replied. He straightened then, and she swallowed the disappointment of the kiss ending too quickly.

I'm glad you kissed me. Of course she didn't say it, but she thought it. *I wish you'd do it again.*

"Good night," he said, then turned and jogged down the stairs and out to the street, where he pulled his collar up around his neck.

Chloe unlocked the door and greeted Antoinette.

The following week passed quickly. Owen had a job at his shop he needed to finish for a customer, so he only worked at the church in the late afternoons. Chloe became discouraged at the lack of replies to her telegrams, but finally on Friday a good message was delivered. She carried the folded paper to his shop and rang the bell.

"Come on in, Chloe."

"I'm sorry to bother you."

"You're not a bother."

"We got a telegram from a man in Ohio who is willing to make our window."

"How soon can he do it?"

"Two weeks," she answered. "I'll mail the glass and the pattern, and it should go out on the next train."

"And his fee?"

She shrugged. "It will take the last of the money we raised, but we haven't paid for a lot of the other materials yet."

"Those supplies are taken care of."

"How?"

"I worked out a few deals."

"You paid the roofers, didn't you?"

"I called in favors."

He hadn't mentioned money at all, and whenever she asked he brushed off the subject. She'd suspected for a while that some of the cost was coming out of his pocket. "Owen."

They were standing inside the front door of his shop. Dust motes drifted in beams of sunlight that pierced the front windows, and the room was pleasantly warm. He wiped his hands on a rag. He'd rolled his sleeves back, revealing strong, corded forearms. "What?"

"Have you spent your own money on material and labor for the church?" There was no way he could avoid the direct question now.

"Some."

"How much?"

He made an estimate, and she absorbed the figure. "Once we're holding services again, and people are giving, you'll get your money back."

"Don't worry about it." His eyes were a vivid caramel hue in the sunlight. "I mean it. I wouldn't have taken this on if I hadn't wanted to. And I didn't contribute the funds thinking I'd be getting it back."

"Why did you do it?"

"Because I wanted to."

"To foil Richard's plan?"

"Partly. But no matter who'd been trying to tear down the church, I'd have thought it was a bad idea."

"What's the rest of the reason?"

"It's personal."

He had personal reasons for taking on the job and spending his own money, but he wasn't being forthright about explaining what they were. "All right."

She let her gaze touch a few pieces of displayed furniture without really seeing them. But she couldn't let the subject go so easily. "Did you feel sorry for me when I came to you? Was that it?"

"No. Nothing like that."

"Good. Because I'm not a charity case."

"I never thought you were."

"Well." She folded the telegram. "I just wanted to share the news with you."

"It's good news," he said.

She took a step toward the door. Owen caught her arm, halting her and bringing her back to face him. "I liked your passion."

"What?" She widened her eyes and her heart pounded. Her gaze dropped to his lips.

"You're passionate about the church," he added. "About its preservation. I appreciate that."

"Oh. Well, I guess I am."

"Are you thinking about kissing me right now?"

His question jolted her out of her reverie. That's exactly what she'd been thinking about. "Were you thinking about kissing me?" she asked in return.

"Yes."

She met his eyes. He dropped the rag and his arms came around her, pulling her tightly against him until she felt every inch of his lean torso along her body. He was strong and warm, and being held this way made her light-headed.

He leaned to capture her mouth, and this time the kiss wasn't soft or tentative. He angled his lips over hers, and she'd had no idea that something as simple as a kiss could send shivers along her spine and take her breath away. Nothing had ever felt this right or this confusing.

She wanted to get closer to him, get inside his head—breathe the same air and lose herself in him. He made her feel things she'd never known about or expected. He made her feel wanted, and the knowledge that he wanted her was heady.

One arm cinched her close, and with his other hand he cupped the back of her head. As he held her securely, the kiss grew in intensity. When she thought she couldn't draw a full breath, he ended it and straightened.

Slowly, as though he regretted doing so, he loosened the embrace, but held her hand, and she clung to it to keep from spinning off the edge of the world.

Chloe collected her senses. Without another word, and before he could stop her, she opened the door and hurried out into the reviving wintry air.

It was Monday, and he hadn't seen her since the previous Friday. It was probably a good thing they'd had the weekend to cool off and think about what had happened between them. Owen hadn't started out with a plan to be taken by her. In fact, it hadn't even seemed like a good idea.

But if he was honest with himself, he would have to admit he'd been attracted that very first day she'd approached him about fixing up the church and the day he'd heard her speak with such passion about the project.

If the woman could fight so fiercely for a building, imagine what she would endure for someone she loved. If she was so passionate about the church, what kind of passion could she unleash for a man?

The question shamed him.

And excited him.

At a pounding at the back of his shop, Owen unlocked the single door.

Ivan Henry had already started back to his wide delivery wagon and now unlatched the rear gate. "Got a load for you. Invoice is in my pocket."

Fat white flakes swirled in the sky and covered the ground with the first glimmer of winter white. Cold snow dotted his face and landed on his shirt. "Is it from Ashton Mills?"

"Yup. Got a spot ready for it?"

"Let me go open the other door." He hurried back in and slid the wide door to the side. "Stack it back against this wall." He joined Ivan, carrying in the heavy lengths of wood.

Perfect timing. Now he could start on new pews that would match the remaining original ones. He hadn't dared mention the lumber he'd ordered from a mill in Oregon to Chloe, because the cost had been way beyond a practical amount.

"Looks like some nice pieces," Ivan commented, pausing for a breath.

"Pews," Owen replied.

The man squinted as the snowfall picked up. "Gonna have them done by Christmas?"

"That's my plan."

"Tell Miss Hanley me 'n' my family will be there for Christmas service."

"She'll be mighty pleased to hear that."

They finished piling the lumber and Owen signed the invoice. "I have some hinges coming, so you might see those in the next few days."

"I'll keep an eye out."

Owen pulled the door shut and ran his hand over a piece of wood, still cold from shipping. Timber like this always beckoned him. He flexed his fingers in anticipation of precise measuring and cutting.

He should go tell Chloe what he'd be doing this week, so she wouldn't be looking for him—or thinking he was avoiding her.

He grabbed a coat and his hat and headed for Red Willow First Church.

Chloe was avoiding Owen, so seeing him ride up on a sleek dark horse and tie the reins to the post at her front gate caught her by surprise. She'd been cleaning her windows and he couldn't have missed seeing her framed in the panes of glass. She might as well greet him.

She pulled open the door.

"I was surprised you weren't at the church." He leaped up the porch stairs two at a time.

"I've let my housecleaning get behind," she replied. "I needed to attend to a few tasks today."

"I stopped there to let you know I'd be working in my shop this week."

"Oh."

"So if you have things to do at the church, you can go about your business without seeing me."

What was he getting at?

"The wood arrived, so I'll be building pews."

"All right."

He started to turn away, but then swiveled back. "You were avoiding me today, weren't you? Staying home like this."

"I told you I have things to do," she denied, but heat rose in her face.

"It was that kiss, wasn't it?"

She glanced behind her, even though she knew good and well that Miss Sarah was upstairs in the sewing room and hadn't heard his question. "I don't know what you're talking about."

"Either you didn't like that kiss…or you *did,* and liking it scared you. Or I scared you."

"You didn't frighten me." But her heart beat erratically at just the mention of their kiss.

"If it was unwelcome and out of line, all you have to do is tell me, and it won't happen again."

She couldn't believe he was standing on her porch in broad daylight, talking to her about that kiss. She didn't know how to answer him. She didn't want to unfairly encourage his affections, but her rebellious nature didn't want to completely rule out the possibility of another kiss like that one. He was right; it had scared her, but not for the reasons he thought.

She owed it to him and to herself to acknowledge that she'd done this once before and was smart enough to learn from her mistakes. Certainly Owen was kind and good-looking, but it was surely his family she was most attracted to, and she wasn't going to use him to get to them.

"We're not obligated to each other in that way," she said.

He looked puzzled by that remark. "What do you mean by obligated?"

"You know what obligated means."

"Yes, I do, and I hope you're not saying what I think you're saying."

"What do you think I'm saying?"

"That maybe I expect my financial investment repaid in a more—" a muscle flexed in his jaw "—*intimate* manner. You're not obligated to me in any way, and I don't expect *anything* from you."

"That wasn't what I meant—"

"I'll be making pews." He turned and loped down the stairs.

"That wasn't what I meant!" she called after him. "It came out wrong."

Ignoring her, he untied the horse's reins from the gate, swung up onto the saddle, turned the animal's head away and rode off.

Disappointment sank in her chest. He'd completely misunderstood her concern, but maybe it was for the best this way. If he was mad at her, she wouldn't have to risk hurting him or being hurt when things didn't work out.

That mid-December week was one of the longest of her life.

Chapter Nine

By the following week, snow had settled several inches deep and still more fell from the sky. The wind kicked up, and drifts piled against homes and fences, and reports came of ranchers searching for stranded cattle. The nights were wrapped in the insulated silence of winter, and Chloe had trouble sleeping. Antoinette's purr was loud as the feline lay curled at the foot of Chloe's bed. The moon reflecting off the snow made her room brighter than normal, and one night Chloe got up to hang a blanket over the window nearest her bed.

The following day, she took down the curtains and replaced them with heavier drapes that pulled closed, and still she lay awake at night. Ernie Paulson dropped by midweek to tell her he and Owen would be delivering the new pews and fastening them down within the next few days. Owen wanted her input on alignment and had asked her to meet them the next morning.

After bundling in her warm coat and boots, she trudged the distance to the church.

At the sound of the door opening, Owen waited expectantly to see who would enter from the vestibule. Chloe's cheeks were reddened from the cold, and tresses of her hair tumbled loose when she removed her scarf. Seeing her brightened his day. His heart did a two-step in his chest, but he forced himself to tuck away those unwanted feelings.

"Good morning," he said. He'd made certain that Ernie was present when they came face-to-face this time.

"Mornin', Miss Hanley," Ernie called.

"Good morning, gentlemen." Entering, she surveyed the

wooden seating he'd labored over for the past nine days. After running her palm along the back and down the arm of one like a caress, she lifted her gaze. The sheen of tears in her blue eyes startled him.

"They're so beautiful, Owen." Emotion choked her voice, and she pressed a hand to her breast. "They look just like the others. In fact…" She took a moment to move from one bench to another all the way to the front of the sanctuary and back. "They all look the same."

"I refinished the old ones so the new would match. You can tell the difference if you get underneath or if you look hard and find the deep nicks I repaired."

"They're beautiful. They look just like I remember."

He remembered, too. That's why he'd worked so hard to achieve the original color and finish.

"I still have to affix holders to the backs of a few. For the hymnals."

"I have two boxes of hymnals in the coatroom that were in our attic. We only took a few to the school, and I stored the rest."

"The pews aren't fastened down yet," he told her. "I wanted to make sure I had the spacing right. I can tell by the marks on the old floor where most of them go, but I waited to see how you wanted to work in the old with the new."

"What if you use a new one in every other row?" she asked.

"That's sounds good to me."

She looked upward, where he'd used scaffolding to stand and replace the wood panels on the ceiling. "It's really coming together." Her tone revealed her awe and pleasure. Her gaze fell back to him. "This wouldn't have happened without you." She quickly turned to Ernie. "Without all of you."

"I wanted to do it," Owen replied. His hide was still chapped about her insinuation that he'd done the work with an ulterior motive.

He'd pretty much laid bare his feelings for her, and she'd let him know she felt no obligation to return them. That was fine with him. At least he knew where he stood.

"Four days until Christmas Eve," she said. "We've almost made it—except for the window." She glanced to where wood covered the opening to hold out the weather. "I got a telegram saying it had been put on a train, but Jim Gold says the trains are delayed because of drifting."

"I was thinking," he told her. "I can go cut down a couple of fairly good-sized conifers. If I set one right outside, it will block that boarded-up window from view. And if I put one in here, it'll be covered from this side, too. You can gather the ladies and decorate it before the first service."

"That's a good idea," she said. "I'd thought about hanging a tapestry over it. We might need to do both."

"That one window won't prevent us from holding Christmas Eve service," he told her.

"No," she agreed. "It's just that all along I had a vision of showing Richard he was wrong."

"He is wrong. The outside probably never even looked this good when the church was new."

"I had an idea, too," she said.

"What's that?"

"I thought about going up the mountainside a ways and gathering enough evergreen boughs to make wreaths and then placing them on the grave stones closest to the churchyard and the street."

He wanted to offer to help her, but held his tongue.

"Hello?" A woman's voice echoed in the empty room. "Oh, my!" Marcella Bell appeared in the doorway, wearing her coat and holding a fox muff. Her sister Jenetta Sparks was close on her heels.

"Just look at this!" Marcella said, her voice reflecting her surprise and appreciation. "My stars, Jenetta, will you take a look at this place!"

Her sister nodded her silver head while admiring the new interior.

"Chloe, dear," Marcella called, "we came looking for you,. because we have the food baskets ready to deliver. I hired a driver and a buggy, and we really wanted you to accompany us before the snow gets any worse."

"I'm finished here," Chloe replied. "I'll leave you to this," she said to Owen. "I don't want to be underfoot."

She joined the sisters and they left the church.

Owen gathered his tools and got to work.

On Thursday, Owen took a wagon up the wooded mountainside and cut down two trees. He made a stand for both and positioned one outside the boarded-over window, then stood back and watched flakes falling on its branches. By the next day, snow would fill his tracks and make the tree look like part of the landscape.

The other tree he carried in and set up directly in front of the missing window. The following day was Christmas Eve. The more he looked at those boards, the more it bothered him that Chloe wouldn't have her window in time for the following evening's service. A quick inspection showed hymnals on the back of each pew. He picked one up and flipped through the well-worn pages, then settled it back in place. Before leaving, he mopped up the snow he'd dragged in with the trees, then locked the door on his way out.

After taking the wagon back to the livery, he stopped by the telegraph office. Jim spotted him and waved a piece of paper. "Telegram came for you or Miss Hanley. I couldn't leave the place unattended and the boy never showed up today."

Owen scanned the message. "The window glass is in Bullhead City, and nobody's coming this way until the weather clears." He crumpled the paper in disgust. "Even the trains are waiting for the snow to stop drifting."

"Reckon that's to be expected this time of year," the other man said.

Owen thanked him and headed back out. It bothered him beyond reason that Chloe was going to be disappointed.

Chapter Ten

She'd slept better the night before, but Chloe woke early, thoughts of trimming the Christmas tree already swimming in her head.

The day before she'd asked Miss Sarah to give her a hand carrying boxes down from the attic. Chloe's German grandmother, whom she couldn't remember, had saved glass ornaments brought to this country from her homeland. Chloe had used them a few times while her grandfather had still been alive because they brought him pleasure, but the past few years she'd only placed a small feather tree on a table in the parlor.

The night before, the two women had wiped dust from the cartons and stacked them in the front hallway before bathing and washing their hair. This morning they were transporting the ornaments to church.

Surprisingly, Miss Sarah had started breakfast, soft-boiled eggs and cooked meal. Chloe brewed a pot of tea and they ate.

"Mr. Tate asked me to sit with him at the service this evening," Sarah said, her eyes downcast.

"That sounds nice," Chloe told her.

"I've been trying to decide what to wear." Slowly, she lifted her gaze.

"Would you like me to help you select something?"

Sarah nodded. "Thank you. I'd like that."

"We'll do it as soon as we finish the tree and get back," Chloe promised. "I haven't decided what I'm wearing yet, either."

"I think you should consider your jade skirt and jacket with the black velvet trim," the older woman said, surprising Chloe. Today was the first time they'd ever had a conversation like this one.

"It's a lovely festive shade and it complements your hair," Sarah added.

"That's a good suggestion. Thank you."

They finished, washed their dishes and prepared to leave the house. "I was thinking ahead," Chloe told her as she stepped onto the porch and pointed to a long sled. "I remembered this was in the carriage house, so I found it yesterday and set it here so we can load the crates on it."

Willa and Annie were waiting when they arrived at the church, and Chloe unlocked the doors. Agnes and Melvina joined them, both carrying bags. "I brought red ribbons for the ends of the pews," Agnes said.

"And I made strands of cranberries last night," Melvina told them.

The six of them made quick work of decorating the tree and the sanctuary, but before they had finished, the door opened and Zeb carried in fragrant boughs of evergreens he'd cut and trimmed and shaped into wreaths and swags. The fresh-cut boughs combined with the scent of the tree to fill the church with holiday smells.

Zeb helped Miss Sarah arrange a bough and watched her add a velvet bow. His unmistakable infatuation with Miss Sarah had become evident to everyone. The rest of the ladies left them alone with their task and stole sly glances, then looked at each other and grinned.

Seeing Miss Sarah's shy reactions and the way she looked at Zeb when he didn't know made Chloe's chest ache. His attention was completely uncommon for the introverted woman, but Chloe could tell she was growing more and more receptive. A romance was blooming right before her eyes, and Chloe was happy for both of them.

Chloe hadn't seen Owen yet that day, but his work there was done for now, and he did have his own jobs to do. Being unable to share these last accomplishments with him dimmed her satisfaction, but she had only herself to blame for his withdrawal. If she hadn't confused her feelings for his family with an attraction to him, things wouldn't have gotten so uncomfortable between them and they'd still be friends.

She'd let him think there was more to her feelings than just…

She stopped her thoughts, because she didn't know how their relationship had begun. They were partners in a job that both of them felt strongly about. The restoration had gone smoothly, even with his brother's animosity toward them, until those kisses.

Chloe blinked to clear her thoughts because she didn't want to think about kissing Owen anymore.

She draped the last greenery over the top of the piano Frank Garrison had donated. He'd said it had been his mother's and that he didn't need it. It was a shiny baby grand he'd even had tuned after it had been moved.

Miss Sarah approached Chloe. "Do you think I might play a few notes to see how the piano sounds?"

"Certainly," Chloe answered with a smile. "The committee didn't make any plans for accompaniment, because the organ was ruined and removed, and we had no instruments."

"Did you select songs?"

Chloe called to Melvina. "Mrs. Pierce, have you chosen the music for tonight's service?"

Melvina hurried to her handbag and took out a few papers. "I have lists for tonight and tomorrow morning right here. Willa and Agnes helped me."

Miss Sarah looked over the song list. "I'd be happy to play the piano. Of course I'm not a member of the First Church, so I don't know if I'd be allowed."

"Doesn't matter a whit," Melvina told her. "The Good Lord doesn't check a membership list at the door."

Miss Sarah carried the note over to the piano and positioned the bench, then flipped through a hymnal. She opened the wooden lid and played the opening measures of "Silent Night."

One at a time, the other women finished what they were doing until all of them stood around the piano. Annie White sang the words to the last verse, and the rest of them joined in.

When Miss Sarah played "O Little Town of Bethlehem," Chloe picked out harmony, and their voices blended in the resounding space. Goose bumps rose on Chloe's arms at the beautiful sounds they made. As the last notes faded away, she looked around, noting the emotion each woman showed at that moment.

"This is an exciting day." Agnes's voice quivered. "Having the church back is going to mean so much to the people of Red Willow. I've missed coming here. I've missed the sense of belonging and solidarity we used to know when we met inside these walls. It's a good thing you've done here, Chloe."

Chloe found her voice. "Owen did so much. Everyone worked hard, but he gave the most."

"It wouldn't have happened if you hadn't stood up to Richard Reardon and enlisted Owen and the rest of us." Willa reached for Chloe's hand. "Your grandfather would be so pleased and proud."

Chloe couldn't answer around the lump in her throat. She smiled and hugged each of the other ladies before they cleaned up their messes and headed their separate ways.

That afternoon, she helped Miss Sarah select a dress from her armoire for the evening. They decided on a gown of Oriental sapphire-blue lampas, with a velvet bodice and sea otter trim at the hem and collar. The graceful lines of the dress accentuated Miss Sarah's trim figure, and the soft and fully gathered front frill that spilled from the neck opening added femininity.

When Miss Sarah showed her a hat of blue plush felt that matched, Chloe stared. "Why haven't I seen any of these clothes before?"

"I haven't had anywhere to wear them," she replied. "I have dresses made, and then they just hang on the rod. It's a waste really."

"I dare say you'll have occasion to wear them this winter," Chloe told her.

"What do you think of Zebulon?" Sarah asked.

"I think he likes you a lot," Chloe answered.

The woman blushed.

"Owen says he's a good man who works hard," she added.

"Is it foolish of me to enter into something like this at my age?" Sarah asked.

Chloe used a soft brush to freshen the nap of the velvet bodice of Sarah's gown. She considered the woman's question. "Are we ever too old to want someone to love us?"

Miss Sarah's fingers stilled on the hat pin she'd been twirling. "It's *not* foolish, is it?"

"I don't think so."

After Sarah chose an underskirt and petticoat, Chloe left her and went downstairs to bake cookies. There were still a few hours remaining, and she wanted to add to the refreshments they'd be serving later. Once they'd baked and cooled, she layered them in a basket and headed to her room.

She wore the jade lampas skirt with a soft bustle and a quarter train Miss Sarah had suggested. The matching jacket had a pleated black satin belt and black trim in diamond shapes at the shoulders and cuffs.

The bell rang, and when Chloe went to the door, Zeb Tatc stood on the porch in a long brown coat and a Stetson. The sky behind him had turned dark. He touched the brim of his hat.

"Miss Chloe. I thought you two ladies might like to ride to church tonight." He gestured to the buggy and single horse at the curb.

"That's thoughtful of you," she told him. "You have saved us from wet feet and soggy skirt hems." She turned and called up the stairs. "Miss Sarah. We have transportation to the church."

Sarah appeared at the top of the stairs and made her way down. The closer she got, the wider Zeb opened his eyes. He doffed his hat. "You're the prettiest sight this sorry cowboy has seen in a month of Sundays, Miss Sarah."

He carried the basket of cookies for Chloe and escorted both women to the buggy and then to the meeting.

They were among the first to get there, and she thanked Zeb for thoughtfully coming early. Tables had been set up along the back wall for the cookies and coffee that would be served after the service. The whole place smelled like evergreen and tallow. Candles burned in the wall sconces and across the entire front of the sanctuary.

As townspeople arrived two and three at a time—some with entire families—each person's surprise showed on their face, and nearly everyone had something to say about the amazing transformation.

Chloe kept an eye out for Owen, and at last he arrived with his mother and JoDee. Millie and Judd had already taken seats, so

Owen showed the ladies to the pew beside them and returned to greet Chloe.

"That color suits you," he told her, then turned and studied the tree. "It's beautiful."

"Thank you." He was always handsome, but tonight he wore black trousers and a matching jacket with a white shirt. In her eyes he'd never looked so good.

"Well," he said. "This is it. Everything you worked for."

"Everything we worked for," she answered.

He glimpsed something or someone over her shoulder and his attention shifted. She turned and spotted Pamela and Sully.

"Are Richard and Georgia coming?" she asked.

"Don't know. I haven't heard."

Chloe was overjoyed at the number of people who arrived and took seats.

The church hadn't been assigned a chaplain in many years. Since they'd been meeting at the schoolhouse, the male members took turns planning the services and doing the readings. Occasionally a circuit preacher passed through, but they hadn't seen one for months.

Tonight, Dr. Morris White would be officiating. Willa had been beaming about her son's participation all week.

"Well, I guess it's about time to get started," Owen said.

She nodded and glanced around, wondering where she would sit. Perhaps in the front row beside Zeb. Sarah was already seated at the piano.

"Would you like to join me with my family?" Owen asked.

Chloe's gaze shot to the Reardons taking up most of two pews. His question riddled her with disappointment. There was nothing she'd like more in all the world, but she wasn't one of them and wanting to be was wishful thinking. She wanted to say yes, but sitting with the Reardons tonight didn't seem right. She'd already made the decision not to use Owen just so she could be part of his family.

"You know," he added, "I have a better idea. May I join you in the front, beside Zeb up there?"

"What about sitting with your family?"

"I see them all the time. There's no rule that says I can't change where I sit from time to time."

"All right then," she agreed.

They seated themselves in the front pew just as Dr. White stepped up to the pulpit.

"Well, this is an exciting evening, isn't it? Not only are we celebrating the birth of Jesus, but we're celebrating the rebirth of this beautiful church that was once and will again be an important part of our community."

After a few more opening words, he nodded to Miss Sarah, who played the opening chords of "O Little Town of Bethlehem." Men's and women's voices blended and swelled behind Chloe and around her, and the moment transported her back to her childhood, the church filled with worshippers and her grandfather presiding over the service. She could almost hear his deep baritone raised in song—and the sound became so pronounced that she stopped singing to listen. The resonating voice belonged to Zeb on the other side of Owen.

She and Owen exchanged a grin.

After a few songs, the children were invited to come up and sit on the floor at the front. They filed into place and Dr. White helped them get situated.

Zeb stood then, and Chloe realized he'd been holding a Bible with his finger marking a page. Morris had pulled over one of the heavy chairs, and Zeb now took a seat in front of the children, and facing the congregation. He opened his Bible.

"'And it came to pass in those days that there went out a decree from Caesar Augustus that all the world should be taxed.'"

In his deep vibrant voice, Zeb read the familiar story of the first Christmas. The children leaned forward eagerly. The entire room hushed in expectation and reverence. Chloe listened to the verses, remembering her grandfather reading them, thinking how no Christmas since had been as complete or as meaningful.

"'And she brought forth her firstborn and wrapped Him in swaddling clothes and laid Him in a manger, because there was no room for them in the inn.'"

When he got to the part and read, "'Peace and goodwill toward men,'" a shiver ran up Chloe's spine.

Owen reached over and took her hand at that moment, and she looked up. His eyes were filled with appreciation and something else…hope maybe.

Some dear soul—most likely Agnes—had coached the children ahead of time and now she came forward and urged them to stand and form two rows.

Miss Sarah played a couple of measures and the children sang "Silent Night." On the last verse, the rest of the congregation joined in. Chloe got tears in her eyes and had to dab them with a handkerchief.

Zeb resumed his seat on the pew, and Dr. White stood while the children found their way back to their parents. "That just about winds up our Christmas Eve service," he said. "Except we have one more thing to do." He glanced toward where Chloe and Owen sat. "And Owen Reardon is going to present something."

To Chloe's surprise, Owen released her hand and stood. Was he going to sing? Say a prayer? She couldn't have been more curious.

But instead of going to the pulpit, Owen walked forward and then turned and looked at Chloe. "Miss Hanley, I'd like you to come over here for a minute, please."

Chapter Eleven

Startled, she glanced at Zeb and the woman behind him before looking back at Owen. Slowly, she got to her feet.

He asked the people sitting on the opposite side of the room if they'd mind trading spots, and Chloe ended up on the left, near the Christmas tree.

"As most of you are aware, Miss Hanley is responsible for everything you see here. She took on the project of restoring the church and saw to it that every last detail was handled—with excellence, I might add."

Applause broke out, and Chloe's cheeks warmed. In embarrassment she shook her head.

"Well, there was one thing she had her heart set on that didn't quite happen because of the snow."

She tilted her head in question. The fact that they hadn't been able to get the window in place was a small blemish on an otherwise perfect occasion. He hadn't needed to bring it up—in fact, they'd gone to a lot of work to disguise the fact that the window was boarded up.

Owen nodded at Zeb, who got up and came to help him. Both men knelt and reached into the tree, where they extricated lengths of rope and, as if on cue, stood and stretched the rope until the tree slid toward them.

Completely taken off guard and expecting the whole thing to topple, Chloe covered her face with her hands and peeked between her fingers.

The entire tree slid as though it had been… She stared in wonder. The tree had been set on some sort of wooden sled and moved easily when they tugged. The two men pulled it completely away from the tapestry that hung over the boarded-up window.

Owen grabbed a stool and climbed upward until he could reach the cords that held the tapestry. He then paused and turned to Chloe. "This is for you."

He tugged, untying the cords, and the fabric fell in a heap.

Chloe didn't look at where it landed, because her attention was fixed on the stained-glass window he'd revealed.

There it was, in all its previous splendor—and while she watched, flames lit the colored glass from behind as though some-one had lit lanterns on the outside of the building.

Standing, she approached the window and stared up. Jesus, in a flowing robe against a green background, held a white lamb in the crook of His arm and a shepherd's staff in the other.

Men and women exclaimed in approval, and after a moment of hushed appreciation, soft applause broke out.

Chloe couldn't contain the overwhelming sense of well-being and joy that flowed up from inside. She smiled and laughed and even cried a little.

Dr. White closed the service to cheers and joyous laughter and conversation. Chloe couldn't seem to move away from where she stood.

"How did you— When did this—?" She stared at Owen. "Owen, however did you do this?"

"I made a trip to Bullhead yesterday and didn't get back until today. After you and the ladies left the church this afternoon, Zeb and Ernie helped me put it in." He gestured to the sill. "Paint's still wet."

"But travel was dangerous, wasn't it? That's why no one else was willing to bring the delivery."

"There *was* a lot of snow," he conceded.

She finally moved, stepping closer to where he stood. "But *why?*"

"Because I couldn't bear for you to be disappointed."

Confused and guilty about him risking his safety, she absorbed his words and tried to grasp what he'd done. Her mind wouldn't even wrap around the magnitude of this gift.

"You'd already done so much," she said.

"You wanted the window in time for tomorrow. To prove Richard was wrong. We *did* this thing, Chloe. You did it. The church is ready for Christmas Sunday. And Richard was wrong."

People milled about, eating cookies and drinking coffee. Chloe mingled, listening to words of praise and admiration for the workmanship. Nearly everyone mentioned how good it was to hold a service in this place once again. And she couldn't agree more.

Eventually everyone cleared out, and Miss Sarah told her she'd be leaving with Zeb. Chloe swept up crumbs and snuffed the wall candles, leaving those on the altar flickering.

Owen remained behind with her. They sat on a step that led up to the platform where a choir would soon be seated and studied their surroundings.

"Thank you for the window," she said.

"You're welcome."

"If anything had happened to you, your family would have held me responsible."

"No, they'd have held me responsible. I'm a big boy."

"Well, I'd have felt responsible."

"Nothing happened to me."

"Thank God."

He studied her.

She looked away. Considered the new window, no longer lit from outside. "I can't wait to see it tomorrow, with the sun streaming through."

"You did all the work to make replacing it possible."

"I'm just thankful the pieces were there." She reflected for a few minutes. "When I was a girl, this was my favorite place in the world. This was where my grandfather prayed and preached. I used to sit and listen right in that front pew where we sat tonight. He was everything to me."

Owen studied her profile in the candlelight. He understood the feeling of peace she experienced here. "I used to come here at night sometimes," he said, and his stomach dipped at the confession. No one else had ever known.

"At night?" she asked. "You mean to evening service?"

"No, I mean night." He gestured with a thumb. "There's a small window back there in that little room that will jimmy open with a thin file or an ice pick. I used to climb through that window and sit in here. There were always candles on the walls or the front tables, and I'd light a couple."

"How old were you?" she asked.

"Twelve, fourteen, fifteen."

"Which?"

"All." He looked at her. "I come from a big boisterous family. That meant crying sisters and a father who yelled and a brother who made things…more difficult." He looked away. "I never felt like I belonged there. And Richard worked to make certain I didn't. My father had definite ideas about what he wanted us to do and become. He was a good father. He only wanted the best for us.

"Richard did as was expected and did well in school. But me? I couldn't wait for school to be over. I'd watch the clock and stare out the window, seeing the trees on the mountains in the distance. I wanted to be hunting or fishing, not adding figures and studying."

Chloe just listened. He'd always liked that about her. A gust of wind whistled through the stovepipe.

"One time," he told her, "I pulled my father's prize bull out of the mud after a rain. Animals can die of exposure if you don't find 'em and get 'em out. It wasn't easy. He was one stubborn animal, and big. Anyway, after getting him out, I led him closer to home and then went to the house and bathed. I was covered with mud from head to toe.

"One of the hands saw me coming in, but didn't recognize my horse and told my father he'd seen someone leading the bull back. That night at supper, my father asked who'd saved his bull. Richard spoke up and said it had been him."

Chloe blinked. "Did you correct him?"

"Nope. While my father thanked him and clapped him on the back, I just thought that if the man couldn't recognize an obvious lie—if he believed him, knowing that Richard never went anywhere near the cattle, then he didn't know Richard and he sure didn't know me."

"What happened with Richard?"

"I was angrier with my father than I was with Richard. The

behavior was typical of Richard, but my father…should have known better. This place was my escape from things like that.

"I spent time alone here, enjoying the peace and quiet, admiring the architecture." He looked overhead at the carved beam that had always given him inspiration. "I had as much reason to want to see this place fixed up as you did. You wanted to preserve your grandfather's memory and his legacy. I wanted to honor the place that inspired me to learn a trade.

"As soon as I was out of school, I headed out. I traveled for a while. Did all the hunting and trapping I'd wanted to do. Finally I ended up being mentored by a master carpenter. The man took me on, and for three years I worked beside him and learned everything he had to teach me. I didn't come back until my mother wrote me about my father's health, and then I came home to help her."

Chloe studied him. "Did you make peace with your father?"

"More or less. I'd long gotten over the offense. If Richard hadn't been so obnoxious, I'd probably have never come here. And if I hadn't come here, I wouldn't have discovered the connection to woodworking as a craft and an art. And if my father had been any other way, I may not have left and found out what I wanted to do with my life."

"You never mentioned any of this before."

"I've never told anyone."

"Why did you tell me?"

He studied her ivory skin and fair hair in the candlelight. He liked the way she looked at him, waiting for a reply. "It's easy to jump to conclusions about people," he said. "And I just wanted you to understand that I took on this project as much for myself as I did for you. Granted, you were persuasive, and I didn't want to let you down, but you didn't twist my arm…and I never expected anything in return."

She turned her upper body so she was facing him and raised her hand to lay her palm along his jaw. His skin tingled with warmth where she touched him, and he wanted to close his eyes and fall into her caress, but he didn't want to miss her expression.

"I'm sorry," she said in a whisper that sent an arousing message to his heart and his body.

He fingered a silken tress of her hair that had lain against her neck, and then trailed his fingertips over the velvet-soft skin of her jaw and her ear.

Her lips parted.

She had turned toward him in an invitation, and he wasn't about to refuse it. She didn't shy away at his touch, so he wrapped his arm around her and pulled her close.

She immediately raised her head, and it was natural to capture her lips with his. She grasped the front of his shirt and clung to him. He kissed her the way he'd thought about kissing her for days, tasting her, nipping at her lower lip and finally probing the seam of her lips with his tongue until she understood and hesitantly returned the deeper contact.

Owen framed her face with both hands and held her fast for the duration of the kiss until he couldn't breathe for his blood pounding erratically, and he covered her cheek and jaw with a series of pecks and nips before holding her away and looking into her eyes.

"Tell me now that you didn't like that."

She reached up to cover the backs of his hands with hers, then drew them away from her face and released him to stand.

He remained seated and watched her.

She was quiet for a few minutes before saying, "I offended you that day when I said we weren't obligated to each other. But I didn't mean it the way you thought I did. You had me all flustered talking about…talking about…"

"Kissing?"

She nodded, but didn't meet his eyes.

"Is it kissing in general you object to—or kissing me that puts you off? Because it sure feels like you're kissing me back."

She sat back down, but turned away, so he saw only the curve of her cheek and the downward flutter of her lashes. She hadn't seemed to mind any of their kisses, which was why the woman had him so confounded.

At her lack of reply, he figured he'd pushed too far. He pushed to his feet in one movement. "I suppose we'd better go. Morning will be here before we know it, and I didn't get much sleep last night."

She didn't stand, but she stretched a hand toward him. "Thank you for the window, Owen. That's the nicest thing anyone's ever done for me."

The tight expression she wore seemed in contrast to her words of appreciation. "I wanted to do it," he answered. "I'll get our coats."

Before he'd turned completely away, she spoke again. "It's not that I don't like kissing you," she blurted.

Slowly, he turned back. And waited.

"I do, in fact, like kissing you."

He absorbed her confession, only a measure reassured. "What's the problem then?"

"The problem," she explained, "is your family."

Ah. Of course. They drove him crazy, too, and he was used to them. Kissing meant courting, and courting was a prelude to marriage, and who'd want to marry into his family and be related to Richard? "You don't have to explain. I understand."

"You do?"

"Perfectly." He headed back to the cloakroom, finding her cranberry coat and his black one the only remaining wraps, and carried them out. He held open her coat.

She walked toward him slowly. "You understand perfectly?"

"I do. And because I do, it won't be to any avail for me to confess love for you or cling to hope for a future together. Believe me, if they weren't already my family, I wouldn't voluntarily marry into them, either."

A look of distress drained color from her cheeks. "What?"

He lowered the coat. "I don't expect you to tie yourself to my stifling family. I *understand.*"

"You think the problem is that I don't like them?"

"Isn't that what you said?"

"Not at all."

"What did you say then?"

"Well, I didn't exactly get to explain."

He tossed both coats over the back of a pew. "Go ahead."

"I *do* like your family, Owen. I like them too much. And *that's* the problem. I imagined once that I felt something for Richard, too, but when he married Georgia, the only disappointment I experienced was in losing the family I had anticipated."

"As far as I'm concerned you dodged the bullet when Richard married Georgia," he told her.

"That's beside the point. The point is I didn't care."

"Of course you didn't care. He's a donkey."

She blinked. "But I was devastated that I wouldn't be part of your family. I wanted to marry your family."

He thought about her reasoning for about thirty seconds. "What about me?"

"What do you mean?"

"How would you feel if I walked out of here tonight and asked…" He paused to think. "And asked Annie White to marry me?"

Chloe heard those words fall from his lips and straightened in indignation. "Annie White? She's only eighteen or nineteen."

"Nothing wrong with that."

"She's…well, she's not suitable for you."

"Why not? She's sweet, isn't she? Pretty enough. Most likely she can cook." He gestured with a palm in the air. "We'd likely have a baby the first year."

Chloe almost choked at that thought. "Why are you talking about marrying Annie White when you've just been kissing me? And what was that you said about confessing love or hoping for a future? You went from those words to talking about marrying her?"

"I'm not actually talking about marrying her. I asked you how you'd feel if I did."

Angry now, she walked past him to pick up her coat. "Put out those last candles so the place doesn't burn down before morning."

She shoved her arms into her coat, pulled on her mittens and went into the cloakroom to find her boots and pull them on over her silk slippers.

"Why are you so mad?" Owen called as she headed for the door.

She pushed opened the door to breathe in cold air and nearly ran smack-dab into Richard.

Chapter Twelve

She drew herself up. Richard looked as surprised as she did.

Fast on her heels, Owen nearly ran into both of them. "What are you doing here?" he asked his brother.

"I didn't know anyone was still here," Richard replied.

Owen cocked his head.

"I just came back to have a look at the place."

"In the cold and dark?" Owen asked.

Richard produced a key and held it up. "Council had a key."

"What were you planning?" Owen asked. "Going to vandalize the inside—or set a fire? Anything to stop tomorrow's service and cause you to lose your hotel."

Owen's accusations shocked Chloe. "He wouldn't!" She turned to Richard. "You wouldn't, would you?"

"I might be a ruthless businessman, but I'm not a criminal. Or a madman."

"Let's go inside," Owen said. He hadn't pulled on his coat when he'd chased Chloe out of doors. He looked at her. "You, too."

She let him lead her back inside.

"The two of you stayed late," Richard said.

"Owen was telling me all about his plans to marry Annie White," she said.

Richard raised an eyebrow and stared at his younger brother.

Owen shook his head in exasperation. "You're jealous. What does that tell you?"

"I'm not jealous," she denied.

"Could've fooled me."

"Did I interrupt something?" Richard asked.

"Yes, I was just leaving," she replied.

"What were you coming to see the church for?" Owen asked.

Richard walked forward along the center aisle. After a minute he said, "I guess I wanted to see what it was about this place that fascinated you so much all those years ago."

Owen shot Chloe a look, then glanced back at his brother. "What are you talking about?"

"I followed you a couple of times. Saw you come here and sneak in that window. You always left me to deal with our father while you hid yourself here."

"You're the one he wanted to deal with."

Richard shrugged. "Water under the bridge."

Chloe felt as if she was the one intruding now. "I should go."

"Stay," both men said at once.

Richard looked around. "You did a good job. Both of you."

Chloe wasn't sure she'd heard right. Was this a trick of some sort?

Richard shrugged. "Tomorrow the council members will attend. They'll see you're finished and that the church is no longer an eyesore. You'll have their stamp of approval."

"And you won't have your hotel," Owen added. "Aren't you mad about that?"

"I'll put the hotel on a different lot. It wasn't my first choice to do so, but…it will have to do."

Chloe exchanged a look with Owen.

"I have to answer to my wife and our mother," he said to Owen. "I think you know what that's like. I concede this one."

After a long look up at the rafters, he headed back toward the door. "Snuff the candles. You don't want a fire."

Owen used a brass snuffer to extinguish the remaining candles.

Tired and confused, Chloe turned and left, removing her mittens to button her coat, and then tugging them on again. It was only a few moments before she heard Owen catching up to her. He walked alongside her with his collar around his ears, his hands stuffed in his pockets.

They didn't speak until nearing her house. "What do you make of that?" she asked finally.

He'd known she was referring to Richard. He'd probably been mulling it over the entire walk, too. "Richard's not evil," he told her. "He's my brother, and I love him. He's always been extremely competitive, though, to the point of thinking the end justifies the means. Maybe Georgia is influencing him for the better."

She stopped at her gate. "I can see myself the rest of the way. Good night."

"Good night, Chloe. Just so you know, I've never even thought about Annie White like that. I was just pointing out that you didn't care whether or not Richard married someone else, but you would care if I did. Think about why that is."

She went up the walk and stairs to unlock her door and let herself in. When she peeked out between her curtains, he was still standing in the moonlight, a dark figure against the white-crested night.

Even after undressing and donning her nightgown, she was still wide-awake. She pulled on her flannel robe and slippers. Maybe a cup of cocoa would help her sleep. She padded silently to the kitchen, warmed milk and added cocoa and sugar. Once she'd poured herself a cup, she carried it to the study and lit two lamps. Holding the steaming mug with both hands, she perused the shelves of books, the items on the desk and strolled over to her grandfather's photograph on the wall.

His solemn expression belied his true self. He'd always been smiling and joyful. She studied his neat white beard and his eyes. They'd been blue, like hers. She imagined him breaking into a smile and looking directly at her. "I wish you were here," she said. "I fear a good, kind, generous man has fallen in love with me. Unfortunately, he has a wonderful family—a family I already dreamed of being a part of years ago. It wouldn't be fair to him if I let myself think I felt more for him than I do for his family."

The photograph remained unchanged. No one spoke in the stillness of the room. But in her mind, she heard Owen's voice: *How would you feel if I walked out of here tonight and asked Annie White to marry me?*

Annie White? Chloe had been angry at his suggestion. She'd been… Heartbroken?

You're jealous. What does that tell you?

She thought over the words he'd spoken as they'd sat together in the church that night. Owen had always been guarded with his thoughts and kept things to himself. He was a private person, more private than she'd even guessed. But he'd shared his personal thoughts and feelings with her tonight. He'd told her things he'd never shared with anyone else. He'd let down his guard. And he'd hinted at love and marriage.

Pride got in the way of a lot of things. Chloe wanted to be loved and needed, but she hadn't wanted anyone feeling sorry for her or showing her kindness for the wrong reasons.

Owen had made it clear that he'd had his own reasons for restoring the church. He hadn't done the work because he felt sorry for her. He'd done it because he loved the workmanship, and the church had played a part in the man he'd become. And he'd committed to the job partly because he wanted to see her have something she wanted so desperately.

Because he cared about her.

She hadn't wanted to think about that, hadn't wanted to consider his feelings for her, because then she would be forced to analyze her feelings and motives and was afraid to fall short of the person she wanted to be.

It wasn't easy to disconnect Owen from his family, but she concentrated on him alone. If he loved her. If she loved him. And if they married and moved thousands of miles away, would she be content?

The answer took only seconds: Yes.

She was in love with Owen. His family completed the package, but it was the man who'd captured her heart and given her a new perspective on each day. Each time she anticipated seeing him again, her heart beat faster and joy flooded her being. She didn't get those feelings about his family. She loved *him*.

A calming, reassuring peace settled over her. She considered dressing and running down Main Street to his shop, but she decided tomorrow morning would be a better time to settle this. She looked forward to Christmas day in the place that meant so much to both of them. Chloe couldn't wait.

Owen had slept fitfully the night before, and he'd awakened early, dressed and arrived at church to get the heaters burning so the interior was warm by the time everyone arrived.

The entire sanctuary smelled like a forested mountainside until people entered carrying in the scents of perfume and damp wool. Richard and Georgia joined his family this morning, and Mattias and Niles took seats on either side of their grandmother. His entire family showed up to celebrate this special day and attend the special service.

As the room filled and there was still no sign of Chloe, the thought came to him that perhaps she wouldn't come. Miss Sarah was already here, and they usually came together.

Owen walked to the front pew where Zeb sat. "Chloe didn't ride with you?"

"No. I asked Miss Sarah to tell her she was welcome to join us, but apparently she declined the offer."

He would go to her house and confront her. If she wasn't coming because he was here and she'd doubled her efforts to avoid him, then—

At that moment, Chloe appeared framed in the doorway to the foyer. She had already removed her coat, and she wore a sapphire-blue two-piece dress. Even from this distance he knew the color intensified her eyes. He commanded his feet to move and hurried to the back of the church, where she met him in the aisle between the last few pews. "I thought you weren't coming."

"I changed clothing three times."

Her dress did indeed make her blue eyes vivid. "You're beautiful."

"I have something to tell you."

He raised his eyebrows. "All right."

She slid the strap of her reticule onto her forearm so she could reach for both of his hands. Hers were chilled, and he pressed them together, warming them between his. "Your hands are cold. Did you wear your mittens?"

"I love you."

The declaration caught him off guard. He blinked, letting the words become a reality in his head. "You said...?"

"I love you," she repeated. "If you asked Annie White to marry you, I'd simply die of a broken heart."

"I'm not going to ask—"

"I know. And if you asked me to marry you and move to another state or another land where we'd never see your family, I'd say yes. Yes. Yes. Yes."

"What if I asked you to marry me and live right here in Red Willow and attend church in this place every Sunday for the rest of our lives?"

"I'd say yes."

Owen noticed that the congregation had grown silent, and he chanced a sideways look, hoping the service was starting and that was what had flagged their attention, rather than the scene between him and Chloe unfolding. But, no. Jim Rhodes and his wife, along with Mary Dunbar, Ivan Henry and more people than he could name—all of them were watching and listening.

Chloe's attention remained on Owen.

If he was going to do this publicly, he was going to do it right. Keeping hold of Chloe's hands, he lowered himself to one knee and locked his gaze with hers.

"Chloe Hanley," he began. "I admire everything about you. You're focused and honest. You're inventive and smart and humble."

She blushed prettily.

"I love that you're sentimental, and your enthusiasm is catching. You inspire people. You inspire me. I feel about you a way I never imagined to feel. I love you. I can't imagine living the rest of my life without you. I want to marry you and have children with you and bring them to church here on Sunday mornings and Christmas Eve. I want to tell them the story about how their mother saved this church and that you're the reason why the people of Red Willow have this important piece of their history."

Chloe released a little sob and fought for a calming breath, but she never took her eyes from his face.

"I love you," he declared. "Will you marry me?"

She blinked then, a furious batting of her lashes. One of the nearby women pressed a handkerchief into their interlocked fingers and Chloe withdrew one hand to raise the white hankie and blot at her eyes and nose. She tucked it into her cuff and placed her fingers back in his.

She pursed her lips and took a deep breath, and he recognized how she gathered her composure.

"I love how you're such a deep thinker," she said to him. "I love how you're private and analytical, but how after you've thought things through you share them with me." She swallowed nervously. "I feel safe with you. You're perceptive and respectful and you do things with a confidence I admire. You're quiet, but you're *fearless*." She said the last with a kind of awe in her voice. "I love that you know who you are, and you're true to yourself. If you feel strongly about someone or something, you can't be budged. And I'm so…" She paused. Not a sound could be heard in the room. "I'm so *proud* that you feel deeply about me."

She lowered her gaze to their hands, and he waited, not daring to take a breath, anticipating the words that would change his life.

Her blue gaze lifted. "I love you, Owen. Nothing would make me happier than to be your wife."

He got to his feet swiftly and pulled her against him, kissing her with all the joy she inspired. *She loved him.*

Owen could have spent the rest of the morning holding her, celebrating the moment, but around them the gentle interruption of applause swelled.

He straightened without releasing her. Her expression revealed the moment she became aware of the audience they'd had while that scene had played out, and she blushed, but laughed at the same time.

He joined her, and they laughed until she used the hankie to blot her eyes again, and this time it was because she was so overjoyed.

He hugged her soundly.

Chloe's heart was filled to overflowing. She loved Owen with all her being, and she was confident in his love for her.

"If you two are ready," Frank Garrison called to them, and the crowd quieted. "Judd Valentine is going to officiate the service this morning."

Miss Sarah played "Joy to the World" and the people lifted their voices in song while Owen led Chloe into one of the pews where his family sat. Lillith reached across her grandson to grasp Chloe's hand and give her a tearful smile. "I couldn't be happier to have you as one of my daughters."

Chloe teared up again.

Owen opened the hymnal to the correct page and held it where she could see it with him.

They had many reasons to celebrate this particular day, and together they would celebrate all their future Christmases right here in Red Willow.

Her heart sang that morning as sun streaked through the colorful windows, creating patterns of color and light on the congregation and the floor. She and Owen had produced something wonderful and enduring together. And it wouldn't be the last time.

* * * * *

THE SHERIFF'S
HOUSEKEEPER BRIDE

Jenna Kernan

Dear Reader,

This story combines three things that I love—history, decorating the Christmas tree and holiday baking. Some of you know that I am unreasonably proud of my tree. If you are interested in seeing a photo, I will have one at my Web site at www.jennakernan.com.

This is my first attempt at a heroine who is incognito and I eagerly anticipated the moment when the real housekeeper arrives and Eliza is unmasked. As for Eliza's mistakes in the kitchen, I didn't have to do much research, because I have made many of them myself. Though cooking was never my strong suit, my mother did teach me how to bake, just as she learned from the women in her family. And so the recipes come down through generations and into our most important celebrations.

I hope you enjoy this story and have a lovely holiday season full of the aroma of delicious family recipes.

Merry Christmas.

Jenna

This book is dedicated to my grandmother,
Ruth Cunningham, who would not let my mother wed
until she knew how to make a proper cherry pie, and to
my mother, Margaret, who rendered herself unconscious
in the process through a combination of a short ladder,
a cherry tree and a great fear of heights.

Chapter One

Butte, Montana, 1888

Eliza Flannery dodged the railroad conductor, but he captured her upper arm. His meaty hand clamped about her and closed with viselike intensity, making her wince.

"This is a mistake." Her face flamed in shame as the passengers craned their necks to get a better look at her.

"No ticket, no funds—no mistake." He hustled her down the metal steps and onto the platform. "I'm turning you over to the authorities."

Oh, no. She absolutely could not allow that to happen, because the ticket was only one of the reasons she had fled. If he detained her, they might find out about the other.

This morning she had been a decent woman with a respectable situation. Now she was without a position, stealing her passage from the Northern Pacific and running from the law. How had her life veered so badly off course?

"Please. You're hurting me."

"Common thief, that's what," he blustered. "Did you think I'd let you go because of those big blue eyes?"

Eliza clutched her carpetbag in her free hand as they reached the crowded platform. She glanced about and spotted three lanky cowboys, faces still rosy and hairless. She made eye contact with one.

"Help!" she cried.

All three straightened, turning toward them. A moment later they surrounded the conductor.

One placed a hand on his pistol. "Let her go, mister."

He raised one hand as if the cowboys were train robbers. "Boys, she doesn't have a ticket."

"That true?" asked her would-be rescuer.

She nodded.

He grinned, grabbed her captor's hand and twisted. Suddenly she was free.

"Well?" he asked. "What are you waiting for? Run!"

Eliza did, lifting her skirts and dashing as if her hem was on fire. The conductor's voice followed her.

"I'm calling the sheriff!"

She glanced back and saw that the conductor had made an attempt to follow her, but one of the cowboys held him by the collar.

Eliza darted between the passengers and slid around a pile of luggage, somehow managing to keep her feet on the icy surface. She slowed only when she was out of breath and out of sight of her pursuer. Thank goodness for those cowpokes.

Eliza placed one hand on her middle and perceived she had drawn the notice of several of her fellow travelers. She struggled to gather her composure, walking stiffly along.

Where was she going?

She had not a nickel to her name. Where would she sleep tonight? How would she survive?

A wet snow had begun to fall, adding to her misery. She clutched her bag before her as the red-hot flush of panic gave way by slow degrees to the icy cold of fear. She could not reboard the train and she could not stay where the conductor might find her. He said he would call the authorities. Had he already?

Eliza continued on, weaving between passengers as she glanced back the way she had come.

She was innocent. But wasn't that what the last woman had told them? It hadn't stopped them from believing her employer and arresting her predecessor. The cook, Flora, had recounted the tale of Miss Gram's arrest and subsequent incarceration, frightening Eliza near to death. It proved adequately that declarations of blamelessness were pointless, for what thief would not declare their innocence? She had never been one to stand and fight. So, with

Flora's help, Eliza had fled from Mrs. Holloway's residence before the police could be summoned, before she could be incarcerated for a crime she didn't commit.

Oh, why hadn't Flora told her about her predecessor before this conundrum had reared its ugly head? And all because of a cameo brooch set with a diamond that Eliza had not even seen, let alone purloined. Her eyes burned and her vision blurred. She wiped at her eyes, glancing back to check for a pursuer and ran smack into something solid and unyielding.

Eliza spun about to find she had collided with a man. He reflexively clasped her by the shoulders, steadying her as he gazed down with smoky-gray eyes.

"Are you all right?" he asked.

The deep male voice rumbled through her, causing a vibration in her chest that reminded her of the hum of the locomotive gliding over the rails.

He must have topped six and a half feet and wore a wooly buffalo coat that made him look as wide as its original owner. There was an inch of snow on his wide-brimmed hat that now tipped slightly as he glanced down at her. She feared the action might cause a minor avalanche, but the sticky wet snow clung tenaciously to the black felt.

His cheek showed a darkening of whisker growth making his lips seem especially full in contrast. His nose was straight as a blade, but it was those eyes that transfixed her. Staring up at him, she momentarily forgot how to speak. Thankfully, he released her and her mind cleared in the crisp December air.

"Ma'am? Are you all right?" he asked again.

No, she wanted to shout. She had never in her entire life been further from right. But she couldn't say such a thing, nor could she ask a total stranger for help. So instead she nodded woodenly. His hands slid from her shoulders, and he retrieved the bag she had not realized she had dropped.

"I guess I wasn't paying attention. Never saw you. Of course you're just a slip of a thing." He extended her bag and she accepted it, her gloved fingers brushing his.

His smile made her breath catch again. He wasn't handsome, exactly, but his intense eyes still seemed to befuddle her completely.

"I am waiting for someone," she said, then felt her cheeks heat at the lie. She was never one for untruths or hadn't been until this morning. How she longed to go back just one day and be the woman she had been, with a bed and a situation and a little money put by.

"Good place for it," he said. "I'm waiting, too. Though I don't know what she looks like, exactly."

She wished he'd go away, instead of hovering a little too close. He had a kind of predatory glint in his eyes that made her exceedingly nervous. A single glance told her that a fellow would think hard before crossing such a man and a woman could count herself lucky to be under his protection. Her eyes swept over him again, extremely lucky, she decided. For a moment she considered throwing herself against his wide chest and begging his help. Instead, she stood battling between her fear of the unknown and her need for assistance.

She forced a smile and glanced about, trying to appear as if she were searching for a family member, when in actuality she was again looking for her pursuers.

"I'd help you look," he said, offering assistance without her having asked. "But I'm not from Butte."

Her smile felt as brittle as her composure.

"Waiting on your sweetheart?" he asked, hazarding a guess.

For some inexplicable reason she did not want him to think her attached. Why, she could not fathom, for she had long ago given up such fancies as having a man of her own. But the impulse led her to the next lie.

"My no," she added, giving him no more explanation. She wished he'd go, while simultaneously hoping he'd stay. "I have never met the man I'm waiting for."

If only that were true.

He quirked a brow and his smile faltered.

"You haven't?"

"No." She held her breath as those gray eyes seemed to bore into her. Could he tell she was lying?

"Another coincidence," he said. He was definitely frowning now. "Did you board at Cincinnati?"

She nodded absently, glancing the way she had come. Would it be safer to go through the station or duck around it?

"You're not Mrs. Guntherson, are you?" he asked. "No, you couldn't be. Could you?"

Eliza glanced over his shoulder and saw the conductor, flanked by several very intimidating-looking railroad police, all heading straight for her. Eliza sidestepped so she was hidden from view by the man in the wooly coat.

"You aren't, are you?" he asked again.

What had he said? He was waiting for someone…someone he had never seen? Desperation made her voice quaver like a woodwind. "Yes, I am." She hunched lower. They'd be on her in a moment.

His jaw dropped. "But I thought…that is, I assumed from your letter that you'd be…a more…" He paused as if uncertain how to proceed. "Didn't you write you had been married fifteen years?"

Eliza's bag slipped from her numb fingers at this. Whatever had possessed her? She doubted she could make anyone believe she'd been married a day, let alone fifteen years, though at twenty-three, she was well on the shelf. She might better confess than continue to play him for the fool.

He retrieved her satchel once more and placed a hand on her elbow when he noted that she was swaying precariously. He now stared at her as if she were some dangerous and unpredictable creature.

She was a terrible liar and could never keep her face from flaming at any untruth, so she considered running again. But surely the police would see her then. She peeked over his shoulder. The men were searching the faces of the females on the platform. Cold terror washed over her. She would not be locked in a cell and was prepared to do anything to prevent that.

"Fifteen?" Her laughter bordered on hysterical. "Dear me, no. There must have been a stray mark. Five years, only."

"I see. Well, I'm Trent Foerster."

She stared blankly at him.

He lifted his eyebrows and leaned forward. "I'm the one you're waiting for."

She could hear the conductor's footfall now. She extended her gloved hand and tried valiantly to hold her smile as he clasped hers briefly. At the contact, her stomach gave an unexpected flutter.

"Shall we go?" she asked, taking a step in the opposite direction of the approaching menace. "I'm afraid this coat is insufficient for the cold here."

That set him in motion. "Oh, of course."

He moved to grasp her elbow, hesitated and instead relieved her of the small carpetbag that held everything she owned in the world. "I have a sleigh out front." He glanced about then faced her, his brow knit. "Your baggage?"

The conductor was now only ten feet away. Eliza felt positively dizzy with fright. She leaned against him for support. Trent Foerster, bless the man, set them into motion.

"A terrible mix-up. It's been misplaced. The railroad has promised to forward it to your address."

Mr. Foerster glanced over his shoulder, but continued with her, which was fortunate, because had he not, she would have been forced to leave her bag and run.

He guided her to the steps at the platform's end and assisted her down the icy stairs. He led her to a lovely sleigh complete with many buffalo robes, but the contrivance was, sadly, an open one.

He seated her on the bench that was so cold the leather made a crackling sound. Mr. Foerster draped her with a buffalo robe. Goodness, she had no idea that it would be so heavy. She did not think she could lift a leg if she tried. It was just as he took the reins that the conductor and his associates burst onto the street. Eliza ducked down in her seat, trying to lose herself in the rough bison blanket. They made eye contact and he shouted, waving his arms as he charged into the road, nearly colliding with a buckboard. Mr. Foerster seemed oblivious to the hullabaloo behind them.

They were leaving the city limits of Butte before she could properly catch her breath. Only then did she think to wonder what position he thought he had hired her to fill.

Gracious, what had he called her? She could not remember

the name he had uttered, her name now, if she was to continue with this charade.

A thought jumped into her mind, unbidden. *What if he were expecting a mail-order bride?*

Chapter Two

Trent cast a sidelong look at the beauty seated beside him. This was not what he had envisioned when he had hired an experienced woman to run his household. Mrs. Viola Guntherson, born to German immigrants, married fifteen years or five, he wasn't certain now. But either way she did not look old enough to have been married at all.

The horse trotted on as Trent resisted the impulse to turn the sleigh around and bring Viola back to the station. What would folks say, for heaven's sakes? He was unmarried. He couldn't have a woman who looked like this under his roof. He'd have to explain things to her, admit that there had been a mistake and compensate her. But she'd come all the way from Cleveland and he just couldn't muster the guts to fire her for no other reason than that she was young and pretty.

He wanted a mature woman, a widow, like his mother. For the hundredth time he wished his mother were still alive. She'd know what to do. Trent braced against the rush of grief. Three months already and still he could not believe that she was gone. It might have helped if his mother had been ill, but there had been nothing, no sign. One minute she was reading and the next she was slumped in her favorite chair. The grief was made all the more sharp by the fear that raising a young child had been too much for her. But what else could he do? He couldn't leave her with a mother who would not even look at her own child.

He glanced at Mrs. Guntherson again and she smiled. Lord help him, that smile could melt ice faster than July sunshine. He could hardly breathe around her.

His past had shown he had no sense where women were concerned. Apparently, his bad luck continued. Trent gripped the reins tighter.

"Nearly there," he said, more to himself than to her. "I'm anxious for you to meet Addy."

She nodded, but said nothing. He might as well be speaking to the horse. Why on earth would a woman with her looks take such a position? It made no sense. So there had to be something wrong with her. Maybe she wasn't a widow; maybe she got fired from her last job. Had she been caught fooling with someone's husband? Either way, he'd get to the bottom of it, starting with that letter. Fifteen years, she'd written; she'd been married fifteen years, a childless widow. No one could sleep next to a woman like this and fail to conceive a child, unless…was there something wrong with her husband or with her?

He looked her over, seeing nothing more than her head, peeking from the robes. But she seemed fit enough, made for having children, lots of them, enough to fill a big empty house. Trent had always thought to have a home just like that.

His frown grew deeper.

"My mom's passing struck Addy hard." So hard that she had vowed to hate Mrs. Guntherson on sight out of fury at his attempt to replace her nana. "I'm determined to keep everything as it was. She needs stability and she deserves to have a traditional Christmas, same as it's always been."

"I'll see to it, Mr. Foerster."

He knew his mother had made the house a home, but Lord help him, he never realized how strongly he depended on her advice until he could not seek it. "As I said in my letter, I have all my mother's recipes. Some are in German. But you wrote that you read German, ya?"

She didn't return his smile. Instead, she looked extremely pale. He fidgeted with the reins. Perhaps he was not what she expected, either.

"Shouldn't be hard for a woman with such experience preparing meals to make a few simple cookies, cakes and pies."

Viola Guntherson's pretty blue eyes widened to startling diameter as if she'd just sat on a pincushion. "A cook?"

His smile slipped again. He'd been very clear about the cooking responsibilities, hadn't he? Managing his household, that's what he had said, *all* aspects of his household. Did she think he was wealthy enough to have a cook *and* a housekeeper?

Well, what had he expected, that he could just hire a new grandmother for his little girl?

The fear came back, trickling in, like water through an earthen dam. What if Addy turned out like her mother? No. He was here to see that never happened.

"She's used to a kind of Old-World Christmas. You understand? A tree covered with candles, cookies and nuts. Do you know many carols?"

She nodded stiffly and her lip quivered again. It was what had first drawn him to her, that gesture that made him think she might cry.

They glided into town at midday, but already the sun's final cold rays of light were spilling over the roof of McVane's General Store. Days were short now. He judged he only had about an hour of daylight left. The traffic had stirred the snow into a muddy, frozen mess, which caused the sleigh to bump along. He steered the horse wide, avoiding the center of the thoroughfare.

"My home is just up on the right a little so you can walk to everything, such as it is. Not like Cincinnati, I expect. Early's a cattle town, but we have some miners, too, of course. We have a good grocery, butcher, even a bakery next to the hotel and several churches." He realized he was blathering on. Trent snapped his mouth shut.

Eliza nodded her understanding and only belatedly realized that Early was the name of the place. She didn't know if she should be relieved to learn she had been retained as a cook, since she had no experience whatsoever in that field, but it was a better choice than a bride-for-hire.

She still hadn't learned who Addy was. Likely it would not matter once Mr. Foerster learned she couldn't tell a whisk from a carving knife. She wondered if she should just tell him now, explain the entire thing. It would be better to do so before the real Mrs. Guntherson appeared or he found out on his own.

But where would she go? She shivered.

No, she must tell him. It was one thing to lead him on to escape imminent harm, but to continue with such a charade was quite another. She opened her mouth and then stared at the forbidding visage. He scowled, glaring at some point beyond the horse's bobbing head, lost somewhere deep in thought. She mustered her courage, fear jousting with her moral compass. How she hated confrontations.

"Mr. Foerster, I have a confession to make." Where to begin, she wondered? As she was gathering her thoughts someone called out.

"Sheriff!" The male voice came from just behind them.

Mr. Foerster pulled up on the reins drawing them to a stop. Eliza's stomach dropped as she looked at him again with rising panic. It would explain the air of danger and aloofness. She thought all Western law enforcement wore a star. She glanced at his oversize coat, realizing he could have a pistol, star and rifle under there and she'd never know.

A heavy man drew even with them, grasping the side of the sleigh closest to her. He was in his late forties or early fifties, with jowly cheeks and a face made ruddy from the cold. His eyes were dark, and his eyebrows stuck out in every direction like briar bushes.

"Sheriff," he said, addressing Mr. Foerster and confirming her worst fear. "We got a telegram from the sheriff in Butte. He says they're searching for a thief who jumped the train east of town."

Eliza sank lower into the buffalo robe and tucked her chin, trying to become invisible.

"Joey, I got no time for this today."

"He said she stole some valuable jewelry from her employer back in Bozeman."

"Did she kill anyone?"

"Well, no."

"Then put it on my desk. I'll deal with it tomorrow."

Eliza released her breath at the short stay of execution.

"Better yet—" Mr. Foerster scratched his chin as he considered the messenger "—*you* handle it."

"Me? But, I never…" His words trailed off as he seemed to notice her for the first time. His gaze flicked from the sheriff and back to her. Then he puffed up like a bird in the cold. "Oh, sure. I'll handle it." He tugged up his britches, sporting a confident smile that almost immediately dropped away. "But you'll help me, right?"

"Tomorrow," growled Sheriff Foerster, lifting the reins.

The older man tipped his hat. "Hello, ma'am. I'm Joey Backer, town deputy. I work with Trent, here."

"A pleasure." She shook his offered hand.

His grin faded as he seemed to recognize her. Eliza prepared to be hauled from the sleigh and arrested. How ever had she hoped to pull off such a ruse?

"Why, this ain't your new housekeeper, is it?" This he directed to the sheriff.

Housekeeper! Eliza's shoulders sagged in relief, then immediately stiffened. He'd expected an elderly matron to replace his mother. How terribly disappointed he must be. Now she understood his disbelief and his hesitation. He didn't think her up to the task. And he was right.

The deputy continued on, seemingly unaware of her growing panic.

"Why, she's younger than you, even. Ain't cha, ma'am? She can't stay with you."

"You think I don't know that?" Trent Foerster's voice was clipped and hard as he leaned toward his deputy. "So instead of flapping your gums, go get her a room at the hotel."

"Oh, that's not necessary," Eliza protested, trying not to show the joy and optimism filling her. If she could just think for a moment she might be able to come up with a way out of this mess. Who could she contact for help? Her parents were out of the country again, but even if they were not the thought of contacting them about this positively sickened her. Jail might be preferable. Perhaps she could slip away this evening or early in the morning after she had rested a little.

"Do it, Joey. Tell them to start me a tab, then come to my house after supper so you can walk her to the hotel."

Her optimism was crushed under a wave of guilt. He should not have to pay for her room.

"Mr. Foerster, please." Please what? Don't worry about her

reputation because it was already ruined? Or should she tell him that she should more rightly be sleeping in his jail as she was the fugitive they were searching for? In the end Eliza clamped her mouth closed.

Mr. Foerster stared at her, but when she said nothing further, he lifted the reins and clicked his tongue, setting the horse in motion. He drew down the thoroughfare, turning at the next cross street and then halted at the third house on the left.

"This is home," he said.

Home. The word had such a lovely ring. How long had it been since Eliza felt at home? Before her father's calling certainly. She pushed down thoughts of her parents as she turned to glance at the house.

Already the downstairs glowed cheerily against the approaching twilight. The two-story clapboard had a wide front porch that dripped with icicles. Trent rounded the back of the sled and lifted a hand to assist her down.

Eliza swallowed hard, and then stepped onto the road before the home of Trent Foerster, sheriff of Early, Montana.

"Let's go. I want to get the rig back before full dark."

He offered his elbow to guide her up the icy steps and across the porch, now half-covered by blowing snow. He threw open the door and waited for her to precede him.

Inside, the wave of warm air, heavy with the aroma of roasting potatoes and meat, wafted all about her. Instantly, her mouth began to water. A crash sounded from above and three boys tore down the steps. Eliza felt panic seize her. Would she be responsible for these little hellions?

Trent grabbed the first one, and the others collided into their leader. "Where's your ma?"

He was married? Why did that information make her stomach pitch? She'd been disappointed enough times in her life to recognize the emotion, but why she was disappointed flummoxed her completely.

She eyed the boys and inched toward the door. She had no experience as a nanny, either, and these youngsters seemed wild as wolves.

"Kelly?" shouted Foerster.

"Trent, that you?"

A moment later a woman emerged from the back of the house, trailed by a small, frail girl with golden hair and familiar gray eyes. Eliza glanced at Trent to confirm her speculation and found their eyes a perfect match, but not their hair color. He held his hat now and she could see his clipped hair was thick and medium brown.

"I fed my crew already. Didn't figure Mrs. Guntherson should have to cook on her first night, even if she is some expert in German food." The woman brushed her hand over her forehead and then sought out Eliza. Their eyes met and the woman's jaw dropped.

"This her?" she said, her voice holding disbelief.

Trent gave one curt nod.

Kelly laughed. "Well, well. Things are about to get real interesting." She stepped forward and shook Eliza's hand. "Welcome to Early, Mrs. Guntherson. I'm Kelly Milward. Live right next door." She released Eliza and turned to Trent. "Got to get going now. Bob will be home soon."

"Thank you for coming over," said Trent, and opened the door.

"Get your coats, boys." She helped the youngest navigate his sleeves and then ushered them all out.

Trent followed her, pausing to glance at the little girl, standing hunched, with hands clasped before her. "I'm just going to ask Mrs. Milward a question, Adeline. Be right on the porch."

The girl nodded and then glanced at Eliza as the door closed.

The silence between them was deafening.

Chapter Three

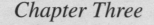

Eliza cleared her throat. "You're Addy?"

The girl nodded. Eliza felt disconcerted by the child's serious expression and constant stare. Well, she had good reason to look so dour. She'd lost her granny and now some stranger was trying to move into her place. Where was the girl's mother?

"I'm sorry about your grandmother."

This caused the girl to glance away. Eliza wondered if she might be about to cry. Why had she mentioned it? She should have said something benign, like complimenting her on her pretty face. She was a lovely girl, with smoke-gray eyes and dark, spiky lashes that matched her father's. But her hair was not thick and dark like his. Instead, Adeline's blond tresses curled in natural ringlets that looked as if they had not been combed.

The child took a step closer, pinning Eliza with her fixed stare once more.

"You're not old," she said, making her comment sound as if it were a condemnation.

"I am so."

"Not like Nana."

"No. That's true. No one is like her."

Addy's mouth twitched, and Eliza thought she might have seen the shadow of a smile. Then it dropped away.

"I don't have to listen to you."

"That's too bad, because I know a lot of fairy tales."

The child's brow lifted in speculation. "Ones with princesses?"

"Some, but also witches and giants and cats that wear boots."

"That's silly."

"Oh, no, Puss was a very serious fellow with a serious mission. He had to help his owner win the hand of his true love. Would you like to hear how he did it?"

Addy nodded. Eliza extended her hand and held her breath. Addy clasped hold, so Eliza led them to the third step and seated herself. Addy plopped beside her, staring up as Eliza recounted one of the many stories that had sustained her during her own difficult childhood. Fairy tales were not permitted in her home. Eliza's missionary parents did not approve of such whimsy, but Eliza was nothing if not resourceful. She had learned to read early and traded her hair ribbons for a battered copy of a book of fairy tales.

Addy listened intently as the world of Puss and his inept, but kindly owner poured from Eliza like water from a pitcher. She had not thought of these stories in years, yet she had stored them, unknowing, all this time.

When she finished, she waited for Addy to speak. At last she said, "Puss was very smart."

"Well, most cats are."

"Nana said she'd get me a kitten, but she died."

Eliza had her arm around Addy in a moment and pressed her close. She could think of nothing to say, so they sat, side by side. After a few moments, Addy's rigid frame relaxed and she leaned against Eliza.

The door opened and Trent stepped in. The heat of the room struck him first and then the sight before him. He stilled. There sat Addy, nestled against Mrs. Guntherson. His new employee encircled his daughter's narrow shoulders in an easy embrace. Was this the girl who had shouted and cried and promised to hate this housekeeper on sight? He understood her anger because it stemmed from loss. He did not blame her for missing her grandmother and resenting his attempt to replace her.

Addy's smile blossomed as she slipped from Mrs. Guntherson and bounded across the entrance. How long had it been since he had seen that lovely smile? Too long, he decided. Trent scooped her up in his arms and cradled her, closing his eyes for a moment against the sweetness of her smell. His eyes flicked open as he exhaled and found Mrs. Guntherson, standing now, with hands folded staring at the two of them. Vindication, relief and gratitude rumbled through his chest and then knotted in this throat.

"Do you know 'Puss in Boots,' Daddy?"

"Puss in…" He barely held his voice steady. It had been so hard to see Addy grieve, and her smile gave him a moment's hope.

"Boots," she chirped.

"No, button. I don't." He spoke to the girl but he kept his eyes on his new housekeeper, reassessing. Mrs. Guntherson had made his daughter happy and that was a point in her favor. He arched a brow. Perhaps, despite her youth, hiring her had not been a mistake.

She stood and he got his first good look at her without her shapeless woolen coat and he actually stopped breathing. She was slim and her bosom more than ample. The sight made his skin prickle. His breath came out in a rush that sounded like a cough as he lifted his attention to her pretty face.

She smiled at him and something flipped in his stomach. Instantly, he thought of the last woman who had made his stomach jump like that, and his admiration died in a sandstorm of determination not to repeat past mistakes.

He looked back at Addy as he covered the little hand that now pressed to his chest. "How was your day?"

"Good," she said as he carried her toward the back of the house. He paused in the doorway to glance back at his new employee.

"This way, Mrs. Guntherson."

His housekeeper trailed behind them. Trent seated his daughter at the large kitchen table. Eliza hovered, then carried the pot of stew from the back burner and set it on a trivet in the center of the table.

Trent held her chair, settling the matter. Eliza sat as he served them and then unceremoniously thumped a pitcher of water in the center of the table. Eliza placed her napkin, folded her hands and waited. Trent's eyes narrowed as he accepted the challenge, lifting his spoon in defiance. She cleared her throat.

"Would you like *me* to say grace?" she asked.

The sharp look she received gave her a serious pang of regret.

For goodness' sakes, she was safe for the moment—why was she rocking her very leaky boat?

Addy piped up. "Nana always said it. But we don't say it anymore."

Eliza felt a stab of regret that had nothing whatsoever to do with her situation and everything to do with Addy's.

She faced Mr. Foerster. "I'm sorry. I didn't mean to presume."

"You started it. Best see it through."

After throwing down that challenge, he folded his hands and inclined his head.

Eliza bowed her head and prayed for a way out of this mess.

Trent watched her above his folded hands. Something didn't fit. She looked every inch the lady, but he knew better than most that looks could be deceiving. It was why he had carefully checked all her references. He couldn't seem to concentrate as he watched her lips move as she spoke the blessing.

He endeavored to keep his eyes on his plate for the remainder of the meal and succeeded more or less. He had only needed to redirect himself a handful of times. After the meal, Mrs. Guntherson stood and cleared, without the least direction from him. He watched her hips sway as she washed the dishes and became mesmerized by the rhythmic spin of the cloth as she dried the plates. She lifted the stack of bowls and then turned, raising a brow. He pointed and she opened the cabinet he indicated, slipping the crockery into its proper place. He already looked forward to tomorrow night when he'd have a chance to sample her cooking. He hadn't had a decent meal since… Damn, it always came back to his mother's passing. Before he met Mrs. Guntherson, Trent thought her best attribute was that she could easily prepare the familiar meals. Now, however, he found her lovely face and form far more appealing than *schweinsbraten* and potato dumplings.

This was not good. All these years, he'd felt no urge to pursue a woman. He'd actually thought that he was done with that time in his life, chalking up his brain-numbing need as some passage endured by all young men. After all, he'd be thirty next year. But he recognized the building desire now as a danger sign, a warning that his mind was soon to be ruled by his body again.

"Coffee?" she asked.

He never drank coffee in the evenings.

"Absolutely." What the devil was wrong with him? He ground his teeth as he realized he'd agreed in order to keep her here a few minutes longer. Damn, he should drive her back to Butte right now.

"Daddy?"

He glanced to Addy, finding her staring at him with fork paused over the remains of her slice of blueberry cobbler. Her face held a slight frown.

"You look funny."

He let the smile grow wide as he hunched forward. Addy straightened, already anticipating the game. He lifted his arms like a bear and Addy shrieked, fleeing out of the kitchen. He growled and pursued her with the lumbering gait of a bear. The chase ended as it always did, with him swinging Addy up over his shoulder to carry her to her bedroom. They hadn't played this game in a very long time and he found he had missed it.

Funny, but today he did not have to pretend to laugh. His mirth was genuine. He didn't want to think what might have caused that. Relief, likely. Yes, the knowledge that he had secured someone who could help tend Addy and make the house more like the home it had once been.

He glanced about and found her drying her hands. The kitchen table was spotless.

"Can Mrs. Guntherson take me up?" asked Addy.

The smile was for his daughter, so why was his heart galloping like a wild mustang?

He cleared his throat. "I'll show you the way," he said to the woman.

Mrs. Guntherson nodded, hung the dish towel and trailed them as he mounted the stairs. He talked his way through their evening routine. She'd need that on the evenings that he was called away. He'd explain his mom's routine later, when Addy was asleep.

Once his daughter was scrubbed and changed into her nightie, he tucked her into her bed, smoothing the quilt that had covered her since she'd moved out of her crib.

He kissed her on the cheek and wished her good-night, lifting the lantern from her bedside table.

"Mrs. Guntherson, will you kiss me good-night?"

His jaw dropped before he could prevent it. Mrs. Guntherson did not hesitate, but swept across the room and perched beside Addy, bending low and sweeping her delicate hand across his daughter's forehead to push back the fine hair and then pressing a kiss to her smooth brow, exactly as her grandmother had done.

Trent held his breath. Addy smiled up at their new housekeeper. The relief Trent expected didn't come. Instead, the creeping unease continued to well within him as a new concern raised its head.

This stranger was an employee, hired to help raise his girl to be a proper lady. To her, Addy was just a job. She didn't love her. Hell, she didn't even know her, yet somehow, she'd already woven a dangerous spell over his daughter.

But what would he do if Addy fell in love with her and then she left them, too?

Chapter Four

Trent answered the door to find Joey, on time for once, but instead of handing Mrs. Guntherson over, as he had intended, he decided he had better see her to the hotel himself. After all, Joey wasn't known for his attention to detail.

His inner voice scoffed. He pushed back the alarm at the realization that he just wasn't ready to leave her yet. He slapped down a piece of Mrs. Milward's blueberry cobbler before his deputy and told him to sit tight until he came back. Joey might not be the most ambitious of employees, but he loved dessert and he loved Addy as dearly as any grandfather. So Trent had not one moment's concern over his daughter's safety.

"Could I check on Addy before we go?" asked his housekeeper.

Trent nodded and watched her leave, appreciating her graceful gait and the gentle sway of her hips. Joey gave a low whistle. Trent glanced at his deputy. The man's knowing grin nettled him.

Trent felt his face heat. "What?"

"That's a real thing of beauty to behold." Joey motioned toward the door with his head. "How's she doing?"

"Addy likes her."

"That girl of yours is smart—smarter than you. If Addy likes her, then she's all right by me. Say, how long you think she'll be willing to stay on as hired help?"

Trent reached for his coat, then paused with only one arm in a sleeve as the implication of Joey's words settled in.

"What's that supposed to mean?"

"She's pretty, shapely and she's a widow in a town full of single men. Seems to me you're going to be beating the men back with a stick. Tom O'Connor already asked me about her on my way over here."

Trent's eyes narrowed. "You tell that bean-counter to stay away from my house."

"Should I tell that to Evan Dauer, too?"

Now Trent's irritation blossomed into a simmering fury. *She was his.* "I hired her and I'm keeping her."

Joe laughed. "Only way I know to keep her permanent is to ask her to marry you before somebody else does."

The ridiculousness of that suggestion had Trent huffing like an angry bear. He'd only just met her today. And he'd damn well look before he leaped this time. He tugged on his coat and plopped his hat on his head, but shaking off the idea proved harder than he would have thought, for it clung to him like a burdock.

"You don't marry her, I will."

Trent ground his teeth together, resisting the urge to knock Joey to the floor for his audaciousness. The man had never been able to get his goat before. He exhaled sharply and felt no better.

"Be my guest," he said.

"Just saying, you could do worse," Joe called.

The creak of the floorboards above them alerted him that Mrs. Guntherson was returning. Trent waited as she descended the stairs, admitting to himself at least that she was a beautiful woman and realizing darkly that Joey was right. He'd have his hands full keeping other men from poking around after her like a bunch of damn tomcats. He chewed his lip as he considered this new dilemma.

"She's asleep," said Mrs. Guntherson, her smile fading as she glanced at Trent, now frowning as he stood already dressed and waiting to go. "Oh, I'll just be a moment."

Mrs. Guntherson snatched up her hat, tying the ribbons of her flimsy brown bonnet beneath her chin. Trent scowled, for the cap would do nothing to keep the snow from her head and did not even reach her ears. She might as well have slapped a tea cozy on top of her head for all the good it would do her. The dirty color of the wool was pale in comparison to the glossy dark luster of her hair.

This woman was not a snappy dresser, that was certain. Not like Helen Wagner. Trent allowed himself to compare Viola to Helen. They both had pointed chins and large eyes, but Helen's eyes were paler blue and she wore her blond hair twisted up in little corkscrew curls all around her face, instead of coiled into a practical knot. She had flashing eyes and expensive clothes. He'd spent a whole week's pay once on a crimson bonnet and was happy to do it. What a blind idiot he'd been.

His temper leaked out in his voice. "You ready yet?"

Viola jumped and scurried forward, her face flushing. "I'm so sorry. Yes, I'm ready."

But she wasn't. Her coat was still open and she held her gloves. Was it so warm in Cincinnati that women went about half-dressed?

He reached for the edges of her black wool coat and drew them together, fastening one button after another. His years dressing Addy must have addled him. That was his only defense, for when he reached her bosom she gasped and drew back.

His fingers stilled in midair and his mouth went dry.

"Then you do it. But fasten it up. Temperature's dropping."

She did and then drew on her gloves. Her figure was lovely, but she did nothing whatsoever to accentuate it. Her attire included no jewelry, ruffles or other gewgaws. She looked like a pretty little mouse, not at all like the brightly colored bird that had once attracted him. She was nothing like Helen—was she?

The insistent pulse he felt low in his groin was the same, the heat of blood and lust coursing through him, but now he also had a squeezing sensation in his chest. And that was completely new.

He held open the kitchen door and Mrs. Guntherson stepped out onto his porch. She stepped so crisply across the planking that he barely had a chance to close the door and catch her before she reached the icy steps.

She startled at his touch on her elbow.

"Oh," she said.

The woman seemed unused to assistance. Had no one ever pampered her? Helen insisted on it. And he'd borne it all, thrilled that she could love him.

Love—ha. She hadn't, not ever.

"I am especially sorry you feel it necessary to obtain a room for me."

He snapped his attention back to her, realizing that they were stopped in the street and she now stood before him, staring up with those large enchanting eyes.

Truth be told, he had little but the house his father had built. Paying her salary would be a strain, and the room was likely more than he could manage long-term. But he'd more pride than to say that, and he knew what came of sharing a room with a beautiful woman. Not that he regretted having Addy for she was the love of his life. But he had regrets—many regrets.

Viola stared up at him, her eyes wide with worry.

"Only proper," he said, and set them in motion again. "Not far, just halfway down the main street, so you can walk on down to the house. I rise early, but not as early as Addy. I swear she's up with the sun."

"What time would you like me there?"

"Round six should be all right. I'll get the stove started so it's hot when you get there. Maybe you could make us my mom's cinnamon crumb cake tomorrow with some eggs. Addy would like that."

Her footsteps faltered. "Oh, certainly."

"I'll lay out the recipe."

Viola said nothing to this, but her head hung now and her shoulders hunched as if bracing against the cold. Her breath streamed behind her like an arriving locomotive. The walkway before the hotel had been shoveled and so he steered them to that. She glanced up at the sign swinging slightly in the wind and slowed to a stop.

"Mr. Foerster?"

She had chosen to pause in a dark spot between the tobacco store and the hotel. He glanced down the alley, but saw nothing moving. Early could be rough at times, though he'd seen big changes in the past three years. More businesses and less bars. The miners were mostly company men and not the wild prospectors who had blown through with the silver boom.

"Yes, Mrs. Guntherson?"

A little line formed on her forehead between her eyes, and the corners of her mouth tipped down. He had a sudden premonition that she was going to quit him before even giving them a chance, and his stomach twisted.

"I know you are disappointed with me. I'm not what you expected. Perhaps it would be best—"

The unexpected wash of panic loosened his tongue. He didn't let her finish whatever she had meant to say.

"Mrs. Guntherson, I am not the type of man to make snap judgments. I'll admit you are younger than I expected and perhaps less..." He grappled for a word that wouldn't let her know that just standing by her made him long to pull her against him and kiss those pink lips. "Less matronly than I'd anticipated. But you are well recommended with exactly the sort of experience we need. And Addy is already taken with you. I hadn't expected that, either."

Her eyes darted this way and that, as if searching for some escape. Fingers of dread choked off his air. What would he tell his girl if she left them?

"If it's about the hotel, you must understand, I'm only trying to preserve your reputation. Or is it the position?"

Oh, dear Lord, had she expected Addy was older? He'd told her she was nearly five, hadn't he? Now he couldn't recall. She had been a wife and a housekeeper and a cook, but not a nanny. The children of her last employer were young adults, nearly out of the primary school. They'd need less attention than a child.

"No, it's not that at all. I just think *you* are disappointed."

"Where I come from you don't quit on something without giving it your best." His words mocked him as he recalled Helen and his attempts to make right his own mistake by marrying a woman who had no interest in being his wife.

"Give it a few days. Once you've settled in and gotten the feel of the place, then we'll talk again. Besides, Christmas is only ten days off. I wouldn't like to think of you alone and without a position at such a time."

She glanced up now and he stopped breathing. Two silver streams of tears flowed down her pink cheeks and crystallized on the collar of her coat.

"What's wrong?"

And then he was reaching for her. He grasped her shoulders, but somehow kept himself from drawing her in. But oh, he wanted to, wanted the feel of her pressed against him, wanted to mold those soft curves to his body so he could feel her warm breath on his neck. Instead, he reined in his longing. He was a sucker for a woman crying. Helen knew it and used it to her full advantage. But Viola made no demands.

Joey's words blasted him with the wind out of the alley. *Only way to keep her is to marry her.* Was that right? The very idea scared him more than any threat he'd ever faced. He could handle men, horses and Indians, but how could he handle a little girl who needed a mother and a woman he barely knew?

He leaned close, staring at her mouth, wondering what it would be like to kiss her. Suddenly he released her and stumbled back.

Her head dropped and she wiped her face.

"I'm sorry for misleading you," she whispered.

A wave of foreboding surged through him, making him feel sick. "Misleading?"

She nodded.

He regarded her, trying not to be taken in by her affectation of misery. Women were actresses, all of them, and he should know better than most what they were capable of. His tone turned harsher than he expected.

"If you've misled me, Mrs. Guntherson, you had best explain."

She shook her head. "You should not have to pay for a hotel room."

He released the breath he was holding. She was talking about her age then.

"I've got a reputation in this town, too. Don't see any other way."

She continued to stare at her woolen gloves.

"Now, we best get you inside before you freeze solid."

He touched her elbow, trying vainly to ignore the sniffle and surreptitious attempt to wipe her nose.

Trent hoped he had convinced her to stay, because his heart now ached as he fought against an unfamiliar optimism, one that he'd never again thought to allow himself. He'd only just met her, yet he knew he needed to figure out how to keep her without marrying her.

Mr. Foerster escorted Eliza into the lobby. She stopped a moment to stare. They had erected a ten-foot pine tree before the main window and strung it with garlands of silver beads. Large pinecones had also been dipped in silver paint and something that sparkled. On the top sat a blonde angel with a cherub face and white feather wings.

"She looks like Addy," she whispered.

Trent glanced in the direction of the tree and stared a moment, then headed to the registration desk, which was festooned with pine garlands trimmed with bows of red velvet ribbon. Even the chandelier in the center of the room had been decorated, holding a downturned bouquet of mistletoe.

Boxwood, pine and sugared fruit covered the mantel above a cheery fire. Eliza wanted to curl up in one of the wingback chairs before the blaze with a novel. She eyed the shelves of books flanking the hearth, wondering if they were strictly decorative. Trent met her there, handing over a key and then laying out her responsibilities; cooking, cleaning, laundry once a week and seeing to Addy's care through the year. She'd have one Sunday a month off and he would pay her monthly. After he had finished, he still lingered, staring at her in a quizzical way that made her heart beat painfully against her breastbone. Should she tell him the truth?

He's the sheriff, you ninny. Do you want to spend the night in a hotel or in his jail?

She noticed him staring at her mouth again.

"Is there anything else?" she asked.

He shook his head, as one does to rouse the mind, and then tipped his hat.

"Six," was all he said.

A chambermaid greeted Mr. Foerster by name, and she was not the first person; more like a dozen since he walked through the front door.

The younger woman lifted Eliza's small bag and preceded her up. Eliza climbed the stairs, feeling his eyes drilling into her back.

Sure enough, he stood in the lobby speaking to a tall man, but his eyes were on her as if he knew she planned to sneak down the back stairs and disappear the moment she was out of his sight.

She unlocked her room door and accepted her bag from the waiting maid, who seemed in a hurry to return to the lobby. Eliza knew why. What female wouldn't want a chance to talk to Sheriff Foerster? The moment she was alone, Eliza continued on along the corridor, down the servants' stairs and out the back door. She stood in the freezing yard beneath a cloudy sky, and already the icy cold bit through her wool gloves to nip at her fingers. Eliza stilled. Where exactly was she going?

Nothing had changed but her location. Somehow, Flora, who had thought to pack Eliza's things before the authorities arrived, had failed to gather her purse, which contained nineteen dollars and sixty cents. As a result she was penniless. The selection of garments could not be used to gain passage back to Butte. She considered begging a mule skinner to take pity on her, but did not like the idea of being alone on the road at night with an unknown man. Unseemly did not begin to cover it. The notion was downright dangerous. She could try to stow away, though it was exactly that idea which had landed her in the custody of the train conductor. And she might actually freeze to death on the way.

Eliza crept down the alley and onto the main street. There she stilled. The snow had changed to a stinging sleet. There were no wagons out now.

She glanced about, noticing things that had escaped her when she had walked with Trent. There were two saloons directly across the street. Rough-looking men strode from one to the other, the collars of their sheepskin coats lifted against the biting wind.

A chill that had nothing to do with the temperature crept down her spine. A large cowboy escorted a woman out of the Silver Strike. Eliza's eyes widened as she wondered if she was seeing what she suspected. Was this actually a soiled dove?

When the cowpoke threw the woman over his shoulder, peals of laughter filled the air. Eliza backed up and bumped into something.

"Ma'am? You looking for a little company?"

Chapter Five

Eliza stared into the face of a young man who weaved forward, tipping his hat. His coat flapped open and he staggered in front of her, seemingly impervious to the sleet. His exuberant smile and whiskey breath told her the reason he did not feel the cold.

He grabbed hold of her arm, dragging her from the shadows and onto the public thoroughfare. Good God, he mistook her for a common harlot.

She tore her arm from his grasp and slapped him across the cheek. Her woolen glove deadened the blow, which had the same effect as being batted by a kitten that had lost its claws. Still, it seemed to startle him.

He staggered back, hand raised to his face and eyes as round as twin saucers.

Light from the hotel now streamed out across their path, and he took a good long look at her.

"What the dickens you doing out here alone?"

First he insulted her and now he had the gall to raise his voice. She narrowed her eyes and aimed a finger at him.

"Does your mother know what you are up to?"

That sent him back several more steps. He turned and staggered across the street. Eliza lifted her skirts and dashed into the sanctuary of the hotel.

She reached the lobby, out of breath and puffing like a steam engine.

"Mrs. Guntherson?" The manager took in her coat and the satchel clasped in her hand. "Is there something wrong with the room?"

"Ah…" She could think of no reason she might be out walking at night with her bag.

"I just needed a breath of air."

He rounded the desk to come and stand before her, his face now worried.

"Oh, no, ma'am. Early can be a wild place after dark. Ladies do not venture out alone."

So she had just learned. Eliza realized that she was trapped here until the morning. Her heart squeezed and she felt the burning that preceded tears.

"I can see you have an escort if you need one. And there's no need to tote your gear. Our rooms are quite safe if you lock up when you leave," he said.

When she did not reply, but continued to glance about, he continued on.

"Of course should you have anything of high value, we do have a hotel safe."

Had he assumed she was afraid to leave her belongings unattended and thus had taken them with her? Her shoulders sank with relief that his conjecture had kept her from telling yet another lie. She hated lying, yet it seemed she had done nothing else the entire day.

She forced a smile. "That is a great relief to me." She needed to change the subject. Eliza glanced about, her gaze settling on the bookshelves flanking the hearth. "Would it be possible to borrow a book?"

He turned to follow the direction of her gaze. His smile broadened. "Oh, absolutely. Anything for a guest of Mr. Foerster." He ushered her toward the collection. "You know he has made this town safe for business. He's even, fair and no-nonsense. He was a Texas Ranger! Can you imagine? We are lucky to have a man like that here in Early. Why, I'd imagine he could have a position anywhere he wished, and now that his mother has passed, well, we're all crossing our fingers that he stays because his reputation is so good it keeps trouble away. I feel sorry for the criminals now."

Eliza's heart pounded so loudly she was certain the man could hear it. But he gave no sign. Trent Foerster had been a Ranger, the fiercest, most relentless of lawmen. She reached for a volume and found her hand shaking. Eliza drew back. How long would it take such a man to see through her?

"Perhaps *Bleak House?*" he offered.

The very last thing she needed was a book about debtors' prison. "I was rather looking for something to read to Addy."

"Oh well, we have *Kidnapped.*"

"No, not *Kidnapped. A Christmas Carol?*"

The manager slipped a slim volume from the shelf. "Take them both. As I said, any friend of Foerster's…"

She held a tight smile as she accepted the book, knowing without question that she would not be reading a story that was full of ghosts to Addy. But the volume had served its purpose. She said her good-nights.

A few moments later Eliza sat alone on the coverlet that draped the bed of the small room on the top floor. She stared bleakly at the orange glow of the fire just visible around the crack of the hinged door of the woodstove. At her feet lay her bag, untouched. She still clutched the book in her hand.

What should she do now? She thought to have the whole night to get out of town. She had not counted on contending with a rowdy, drunken man. She glanced wearily at the plump, white pillow with bleary eyes. If she could just rest for a few moments she might be able to think of a way out of this conundrum. Had she really let Mr. Foerster see her cry?

Perhaps she could pull this off for one month, take her wages and run. And what about the other Mrs. Guntherson? She had only to send a telegram explaining her delay and Eliza would be finished. Perhaps she was at Mr. Foerster's doorstep right now.

She sank to her side, staring out at the dark window, listening to the tiny shards of ice beat against the glass. Eliza shivered. She would rest a bit, let the storm blow itself out and then leave before dawn. She set the book on the bedside table. The maid could return it tomorrow, for she'd never have a chance to read it and despite what Mrs. Holloway thought, she was not a thief. Her heart gave an uncharacteristic twinge. She hadn't felt so sad since her first Christmas in the boarding school.

Enough of that now. You have to get out of this mess.

Surely she could find a freight wagon that would agree to take her back to Butte. From there she could disappear, become a server or scullery maid. Yes, that was the thing to do.

Don't think about Trent Foerster's handsome concerned face or the downy-soft hair on his daughter's head. Her chest ached as she wished she *was* the woman he was waiting for. She could think of nothing sweeter than looking after Trent's daughter and becoming a part of a real family. Her sigh was heavy and she did not recall closing her eyes, but the next thing she knew there was a loud knock at her door.

"It's five-thirty, Mrs. Guntherson. Mr. Foerster asked us to wake you. Mrs. Guntherson?"

Eliza sprang to her feet and started to run. She had the door open before she could recall where she was.

"Yes?"

"Oh, I see you are dressed already," said the young maid in the hall. "Coffee, biscuits and gravy are complimentary. Ham, steak or eggs is extra. Dining room opens at six."

Eliza blinked after her as she retreated.

"Say hello to Mr. Foerster for me." She giggled before disappearing down the stairs.

Who? Eliza shut the door, leaning back as her addled wits returned to some semblance of order. Her first coherent thought was to wonder how the chambermaid knew Trent. She pressed her lips together in irritation and then realized she was expected at his home in twenty minutes.

She glanced down at herself to see she still wore all her clothes from yesterday, including her coat. She flew to the washstand and poured the freezing water into the bowl, then scrubbed her face until it was pink. Her hair had suffered and she had time to set it straight and use the chamber pot. Would he notice she wore the same clothing? She hoped not. Her father never noticed such things. In fact, he never noticed anything about her. She had been born late to elderly parents, already nearly forty when she arrived. They had not taken to rearing a child. She'd always thought they were just set in their ways. It was preferable to thinking that they did not want her, but it amounted to the same thing.

Eliza paused before her bag. Small wonder she was uncomfortable about children. She had no siblings and spent most of her time with her nose in a book. She'd likely muddle Addy's life even further, having no experience with children. But the aching in her chest told her that she would miss the child. Eliza wondered how Addy had burrowed into her heart so quickly.

She lifted her bag. It wasn't fair to the girl to pop in and out of her life. It was reason enough to leave now. Eliza closed her eyes and prayed. *Dear God, what should I do—run or stay?*

There was a second knock on her door.

"Mrs. Guntherson?"

Her eyes popped open as she recognized the voice of Mr. Foerster.

"You up?"

She dropped her bag and opened the door.

"Ready?"

"What are you doing here?" she managed.

He glanced away and color rose in his face. "I had to see about some property damage. Brought me near the hotel, so I thought I'd walk you home."

"Who's with Addy?" The man wasn't fool enough to leave a small child alone, was he?

"Neighbor's girl is sitting with her. She comes at night when I'm called away."

Which she wouldn't need to do if his housekeeper had been the matron he had expected. She realized again what a sacrifice he was making for her, a woman too old to marry, but too young to be left alone beneath his roof. Her chin sank to her chest, and she felt miserable again that she was not the woman he needed.

"I'm sorry. I should be there to see to her at night."

She glanced up in time to see his smile fade.

"None of that now. I have it in hand."

"Perhaps you could come and get me when you are called away?"

His smile was back. "I'll think on it."

Trent's expression reminded her of a schoolboy who had once carried her books. Then it hit her, the look he had given her last night, as if he wanted to kiss her and then today, the thin excuse to appear at her door.

Was it possible that Mr. Foerster was attracted to her? Oh, no, that would not do. She was his employee, or she wished she were. But in any case, she had more self-respect than that and if he thought she'd allow him to take liberties he was much mistaken. She intended to tell him so if he tried to kiss her again.

"You packed up your bag again?" he asked, gazing past her into the room. His smile dropped away and he stared steadily at her. "*Or* you haven't unpacked." He frowned. "I thought you agreed to give it a few days?"

Ignoring his question, Eliza stepped into the hallway and tied her bonnet strings. "Shall we go?"

Chapter Six

Eliza clung to Trent's elbow. On more than one occasion she lost her footing. Her high-laced boots had lost any tread years earlier and the soles were now nearly as smooth as the ice beneath them. Despite her difficulties, he managed to get to his home before the church tower struck six.

The stove fires were already glowing. Trent showed her where the baking ingredients were stored and brought out his mother's darkly stained, wooden recipe box.

"I think Addy would like her granma's cinnamon crumb cake today with some eggs and bacon." He placed a small square card on the butcher block that dominated the center of the large kitchen.

Grease spattered the yellowing paper of the card. The recipe itself had been written in pencil in a tight, looping hand. She peered and could make out the numbers and absolutely nothing else. German, she realized. Trent hovered.

"Anything wrong?" he asked.

Other than the fact she felt sick to her stomach?

"Do you have all these ingredients?" she managed.

"Yup." He opened a cupboard and pointed. "Flour, soda, salt, cinnamon, brown sugar, white sugar and—" he closed the door "—eggs, butter and milk in the icebox. I'll give you a line of credit down at McVane's so you can pick up anything else you need."

If she had the first idea how to stock a larder that might be an appealing prospect; as it was, the notion filled her with dread. She forced a tight smile.

"I'll get out of your way." He picked up his coffee cup and headed through the door whistling "Jingle Bells."

Eliza snatched up the card and studied the squiggle scratched upon it and felt defeat press down upon her. There was definitely one and a half cups of something and a teaspoon of two other somethings, one of which might be cinnamon. Butter was clear enough. Was that the same in German? She did not know the order or which measurement went with which ingredient.

Eliza measured flour, salt, soda and cinnamon into a mixing bowl. Then she added three eggs for no particular reason followed by two cups of sugar. She stirred the ingredients until her arm ached and belatedly decided to add milk to make the mixture more doughlike. The resulting concoction went into a greased pan. She sprinkled cinnamon on the top and then slid the batter into the oven.

From somewhere upstairs, she heard whistling—"Jingle Bells" again. Eliza had the coffee on the stove when Addy appeared in the doorway, bleary-eyed, barefoot and crying.

Eliza scooped her off the cold floor and carried her back up the stairs.

"What's the matter, kitten?" she cooed.

Addy pressed her face into the juncture of Eliza's shoulder and neck. Eliza closed her eyes a moment, relishing the warm, sweet smell of the child. She'd never thought to have the opportunity to have a child of her own, but now, for just this moment she could make believe. Addy's sobbing began again.

"Penelope's arm came off!"

Eliza only then realized that the girl was clutching a rag doll in her hand. She paused halfway up the stairs and sat the child upon her lap.

"Let's see it then."

Penelope had blond hair, braided at each side of her squarish head, and her dress was prettily done in a nice green plaid wool, but her arm was indeed severed from her body.

"Oh, well, I can fix this right up."

Sewing, thankfully, was something that Eliza did very well, having made all her clothing since she was a girl. She fingered the frayed hem of the doll's stained apron. Perhaps they could make Penelope a new one today.

"Would you like to make your dolly a new apron?" asked Eliza.

Addy's face brightened. "Could we?"

"If you have some fabric scraps."

She dashed away her tears. "And fix the hole in her heel? I have to keep poking the rags back in."

Trent appeared at the top of the stairs, clutching the banister as he leaned over. His face was half-covered in lather and he held a straight razor pressed to the wood rail.

"What happened?"

"Penelope suffered an involuntary amputation."

His concerned frown vanished.

"Sewing kit?" she asked.

"Parlor, beside the rocker."

Her employer returned to his bedroom, and she led Addy to her room, dressed the girl and gave her hair the good brushing that it needed. She plaited her fine curls in one long braid down her back, securing it with a bit of green ribbon. Then she led Addy and Penelope down the stairs.

Addy stood beside the rocker, stoic as any mother as Eliza rapidly threaded a needle and reattached the limb. Then Eliza turned her attention to darning Penelope's heel and was just about to sever the thread when Mr. Foerster thundered down the stairs shouting, "Fire!"

Eliza glanced up to see black smoke billowing from the kitchen. She snatched up Addy and headed for the front door, carrying them both to the safety of the sidewalk.

A moment later Trent appeared, holding a dish towel about a familiar sort of cake pan that was fully engulfed in flames. He hurled the blazing meteor out over the porch rail where it disengaged from the pan and fell with a hiss into the bank of snow.

Eliza clutched Addy closer, sheltering her from the cold as she took in Mr. Foerster's glowering face. His expression was icy as the bricks beneath her feet. The condemnation was clear as well as the banked fury. She'd nearly burned down his house in the first hour of darkening his doorstep. There was no question that he'd fire her, but would he also discover her secret? If he fired her, she could leave. Why did that knowledge make her stomach ache?

Didn't she want to go? She held Addy tighter, grieved already at the notion of their parting.

Mrs. Milward poked her head out the door of her home, one down from Mr. Foerster's.

"Everything all right?"

Eliza flushed, knowing her humiliation would be public knowledge.

"Fine, fine. Kitchen fire," said Trent from the doorway.

She waved and retreated from the cold. Trent's smile dissolved as he turned his attention to his new employee. In that moment, Eliza knew what it was like to face a Texas Ranger.

She made the short walk and ascended the stairs, much like a condemned man awaiting his final punishment.

Addy reached for her father and he took her instantly, keeping his flinty gaze leveled on his housekeeper. He'd been looking forward to that cinnamon cake more than he cared to admit and was extremely put out that it would be biscuits and gravy at the jail. Surely Addy was no fonder of the bread and jam he'd been dishing up for her before dropping her at his neighbor's home.

"Daddy, look!" Addy held out her doll. "She fixed her!"

Addy's joyful expression melted some of his disgruntlement. His daughter was already scrubbed and dressed and her hair neatly fashioned. Trent felt a lump rise in his throat at the sight. Mrs. Guntherson stepped forward to break the thread, stowing the needle with a half stitch through her shirtsleeve.

"That was quick thinking, bringing her out here," he said to Viola.

Her mouth dropped open, but she quickly closed it, nodding her understanding. Her face was pale as paste, and he wondered, for the first time, just what she had expected him to say.

"I'm so sorry, Mr. Foerster. It's entirely my fault."

"Well, I'm disappointed. I do love that mixture of brown sugar, cinnamon and butter crumbled up on top of that cake." He glanced at the rectangular hole in the snow. "Don't expect it's worth saving."

"Butter and…" Viola's words trailed off.

Addy glanced from him, then to Viola and leaned away, clasping Viola's neck and drawing her close for a clumsy kiss.

"You fixed Penelope."

Trent stilled at the sudden nearness of the woman. Even in the crisp air, he could feel the heat of her. His heart took up a violent hammering and he stepped back, breaking the hold his daughter had on Mrs. Guntherson. Addy, however still studied her new caretaker's face, which now tipped down as if she took a sudden notion to stare at his boots.

"Don't worry," she cooed. "We have bread and jam."

His smile lasted only until Viola lifted her chin and he saw her eyes now brimmed with tears. He didn't think before he acted, looping one arm about her narrow shoulders and ushering her toward the door. She was trembling from the cold. Was it the cold?

"I'll just have to wait until dinner to sample your cooking, Mrs. Guntherson."

He thought his words would reassure, but instead she grimaced.

"What would you like?" she asked, her voice barely a whisper.

"What about a stroganoff with egg noodles and apple pie?"

He heard her gulp.

They reached the door and he was forced to release her as she slipped inside. It felt right somehow, having her beside him. *Now, don't get carried away again.* He'd been down that road, and no matter what jackass things his deputy said, he'd be damned if he'd ask another woman to marry him. And that meant he couldn't bed her, for he'd not make that mistake again. He glanced at Addy.

"Daddy?" Addy tugged at his neck. "I'm cold."

How long had he been standing half in and half out of his door?

He toted Addy to the kitchen, grabbed a cup of coffee and gulped it down black as Viola set out the mixing bowl. "No time now. Tomorrow's soon enough."

Trent set the tin cup into the sink and kissed Addy goodbye. Eliza stilled, waiting to see if Addy would feel any anxiety at being alone with her. But the little girl just hugged her father and went back to her bread and jam. Trent looked quizzically at his daughter then glanced at the woman.

"Since my mother…well…I usually have to peel her off me," he muttered. "I don't know how you do it, Mrs. Guntherson, but you're a marvel."

Mrs. Guntherson didn't suit her, somehow. He wondered what her maiden name had been.

Addy lowered her bread. "We're making an apron for Penelope today."

Mr. Foerster retrieved his hat from a peg near the stove. "Are you? Well, Granma's bag of rags is in the sewing basket. You know where."

Eliza stilled at the mention of Addy's grandmother and glanced toward the girl. Addy's bright smile faded and she pushed aside her plate. Mr. Foerster seemed to realize what he had said now.

His mouth turned grim, and he tugged his hat down low, wheeled about and headed out the door. "See you at supper," he called over his shoulder.

A moment later the door hinges squeaked.

Coward, thought Eliza, and then turned her attention to Addy, who seemed to have shrunk in on herself in the chair.

Chapter Seven

Damn, thought Trent. Why had he mentioned his mother's old bag of rags? He hated to see Addy grieve. It just ripped him up inside.

He paused on the front steps. He should go back.

He spun about, retracing his steps until he peeked into the kitchen, where he found Addy sitting on Viola's lap. At first he thought Addy might be crying, but then he realized she was listening to Mrs. Guntherson. Trent smiled. Was Viola telling Addy another story?

He paused to listen to the lyrical rhythm of her voice, enchanted with his daughter in the magic of the moment.

Astonishing. Viola had a way with Addy and a manner that gave him complete confidence that his daughter would be well taken care of. That was, if Viola didn't burn the house down making lunch.

Viola glanced up, noticing him. Her eyes widened, but she never faltered in her tale. He tipped his hat and retraced his steps, continuing out the door. He lost his smile somewhere before reaching the jail.

His deputy stretched as he entered and waited as Trent sorted the mail. Joey had learned from experience that Trent did not like to be ambushed with a lot of talk the minute he cleared the threshold.

"Anything happen overnight?" he asked.

Joey nodded. "I walked Mr. Jordan home, drunk again. His wife locked him out, so I had to do some talking."

His deputy could talk a possum out of a tree. It was why Trent hired him. He was not quick or accurate with his gun, but he was well liked, polite to all, and he showed up where he was told and when he was told, mostly. On more than one occasion Joey had soothed a situation that might have exploded into violence. Trent didn't always share his methods, but he approved of the results.

"How's that pretty gal?" he asked.

Trent glared. "Addy's fine."

Joey laughed. "Getting under your skin already, is she?"

She was, but he'd not tell that to a man who gossiped more than the old men down at the general store. "*She's* not. You are."

Joey drew on his coat and headed out.

"Well, you tell her I was asking after her, and if she needs someone who can carry on a conversation, she just has to ask me."

"What's that supposed to mean?"

"Women like you to talk to them. They don't read sign language, like the Apache."

He let that gibe pass and waved his employee out.

The day was busier than Trent had expected. First he had to ride through a heavy snow to Mr. Mathewson's spread to see about some horses that had gone missing. His own mount actually got turned toward town once, because he'd been wondering what Viola and Addy were doing, instead of watching where he was going.

Eliza's first order of business was to retrieve the cake pan from the yard. Then she cleaned up the breakfast dishes, after which she searched every cupboard and sideboard to familiarize herself with the kitchen. She glanced through the cards in the dreaded recipe box, all in German of course, but she also found a copy of *The Young Wife's Cook Book* by Hannah Mary Peterson.

Addy showed her the root cellar beneath the house, and they returned above stairs with six fine potatoes, a carrot and one onion.

The morning fled with chores. It seemed no one had bothered to dust or use the carpet sweeper in quite some time. She made Addy's bed and then wondered if she should also make Mr. Foerster's. Addy dragged her into her father's room.

Eliza stilled, feeling she had invaded some sanctuary. The bed was made with a lovely blue-and-white pinwheel quilt. Addy touched it reverently.

"Nana made this. I can thread a needle and sew. But I can't tie knots yet."

"Well I can teach you that after lunch."

Trent's room was spotless, dusted, with no soiled laundry in evidence. But neither did he have any personal items. The room looked as if it was ready to rent, and had she not known better she would have thought this had been intended for her.

Why did he live like a stranger in his own home?

Ah, but perhaps this was actually his mother's house and not his at all.

"How long have you lived here?" asked Eliza.

Addy leaned forward and smelled her father's pillow, then smiled. "Papa brought me home wrapped in a wolf hide all the way from Texas. It took him weeks and weeks because the goat kept getting tired, so he slung that goat over the back of his saddle and it rode behind us all the way here."

She giggled.

A goat? Eliza stilled. *For the milk,* she wondered.

She wanted to ask what had happened to Addy's mother, but thought a child who had only just lost her nana did not need to be reminded of another loss.

"I don't remember on account of I was a baby, but the wolf hide is in my room. Wanna see?"

"Certainly."

Addy led the way and Eliza admired the fine pelt.

"Shall we go downstairs and have some lunch?" she asked, extending her hand, which Addy immediately clasped.

"Don't you want to see your room?" She drew Eliza to the door at the top of the stairs, situated between Addy's and her father's. "This one."

Addy turned the squeaky knob and stepped inside. The room was cold from having been shut up.

"Nana's room, but we got new curtains and I got the quilt that used to be on Nana's bed 'cause it smells like her."

Eliza's heart ached at Addy's words.

"Daddy bought this new one for you so you could have flowers on a winter day. But you gotta stay at the hotel so as people don't talk."

Eliza peered at a narrow bed draped in a colorful flower basket–pattern quilt. Each of the many squares had been set on point and every one held a different color flower. Above the headboard a sampler showed fine promise and included the saying, Mother's Love Is Like a Fragrant Rose with Sweetness in Every Fold.

Eliza frowned, thinking of her mother's harsh criticism. No matter how she tried, she never could make her mother proud.

Addy pointed. "Nana did that when she was eight. She was going to teach me, but her hands were mostly sore."

Addy rubbed the knuckle of her index finger in a way that Eliza thought might be an imitation of her nana.

How hard must it have been for her grandmother to be faced with raising an infant while she had been in the autumn of her years? Had she known she wouldn't see Adeline grown?

Eliza ushered Addy out. "It's a lovely room."

"I wish you could stay here."

Together they descended the stairs. After lunch, Eliza headed straight for the bag of rags, but after seeing the girl's stitches, Elia decided they best begin with a few simple four-patch quilt squares. Addy worked diligently and did improve with practice, transforming the bits of fabric into a very pretty quilt for Penelope.

The afternoon was waning when Eliza turned toward the kitchen. She had not the first notion how to make homemade noodles and had never heard of stroganoff. But she did know what an apple pie looked like and had once made a crust, badly. So she set to work peeling apples. She gave Addy a butter knife and by the time she was through, they had mauled and massacred five helpless apples, added cinnamon and sugar and poured the mixture into a crust that looked more like another quilting project than a pie. She stood back with her floury hands on her hips, studying their creation.

Addy frowned. "It doesn't look like Nana's."

Eliza sighed as she wrapped her hand about the girl's shoulders. "But it will taste just as good." She hoped!

A knock at the front door made Eliza jump.

"I'll get it." Addy ran from the room, braid flying out behind her. "It's Mrs. Milward!" she called from the hallway.

Addy had the door open when Eliza entered.

"Oh," said the woman she had met yesterday and who had witnessed her breakfast humiliation this morning. "I've caught you in the middle of something."

Eliza only then noticed she was dusted with flour from elbow to knee.

"Yes." She tried for a smile but couldn't hold it.

"I just wanted to see how you are settling in and ask if there is anything I can do?"

Bake a stroganoff, she thought, but she said, "I have it all in hand." Then she bit her lip and considered asking for help. "Do you, by chance read German?"

Mrs. Milward smiled broadly. "Not a word, but I thought…"

Eliza stared at her folded hands. "Yes…well, I can't make out Mrs. Foerster's recipes."

"Oh, dear. Let's have a look." Mrs. Milward headed into the kitchen without invitation and with the confidence of someone who knew the way. She came to a rather abrupt halt when she noticed the misshapen pie. "Oh, my."

The two women regarded each other. Eliza wanted to slip through the floorboards.

Mrs. Milward lifted the recipe on the counter. "Hmm, I can't, but my husband can. Would you like me to have it translated?"

Eliza's shoulders sagged with relief. "Yes, please."

"I won't have it until tomorrow. Will that be all right?"

Eliza gave a stiff nod. "Yes, of course. I'd be very grateful."

"Oh, you were planning to make it tonight. Is that it? Well, just whip up a batch of chicken and dumplings or use the leftover lamb for potpie. That should do."

Eliza's smile felt brittle as spun sugar. "Yes, I'm sure."

The woman made no move to leave.

It was dark already and Eliza had no notion of when Trent might come home. She wanted to show Mrs. Milward the door, but did not wish to be rude. But the woman just stood there staring.

"Would you like a cup of coffee?" asked Eliza, reluctantly extending her hospitality.

"Love some."

Eliza pressed her lips together to stifle a groan.

* * *

Trent spoke to Mathewson, who had been quick to call it theft and blame his neighbor. The two former partners now hated each other. Trent promised to look into the incident, which he did, but, not surprisingly, found no stock with Mathewson's brand at Adkins's spread. Hell, he wasn't sure the creatures didn't just wander off, as stock did, before a big snowfall. The weather made it impossible to track them, so he headed back to town around sunset to discover that Joey had been called in during his absence to arrest a drifter who had intentionally broken a window to get locked up so he could have a hot meal and a warm bed. Amazing what desperate people would do.

Trent warmed his hands at the stove as Joey got the prisoner stowed.

"You got some telegrams waiting at the office," said his deputy.

"How do you know?"

"Well, Henry told me, is how."

"But he wouldn't give them to you?"

"Well," said Joey, scratching beneath his hat. "I reckon he would have, except I didn't ask him. You said I was to do it only when you was away, and you're here."

"For the love of…" He raked his hand through his hair and then pushed his hat down low over his eyes. Trent pointed at the prisoner. "Feed this one and then go pick up the telegrams. Open them. If they're important, bring them to me at home. Otherwise leave 'em on my desk."

Trent got half a dozen telegrams a week now from other law enforcement officers around the state. But today he'd never gotten over to the office to check.

Joey nodded. "Sure, sure. I'll get right on it. So, easy night. Only one prisoner."

Trent tugged on his Stetson. "Yeah, but it's early yet."

"You think about what I said yesterday?"

"No," he lied.

Joey's eyes danced as if he knew, but he didn't smile. Instead, he turned serious. "You promised your mom, boss. I was sitting right there beside her when she gave you her ring." Joey's expression was one Trent had never seen. He almost looked stern.

Trent narrowed his eyes. Most men would have shut up, but not Joey.

"She wanted your bride to have the ring your daddy gave her. I seen the ring. It's got red—"

"I know what the damn ring looks like. I told you, I don't want to get married."

Joey pursed his lips, and for a minute, Trent thought he'd hush up.

"But it ain't just about what you want, now, is it Trent? That little gal of yours needs a mother. Seems like Mrs. Guntherson might fit that bill."

Trent held his scowl, despite the fact that Joey had struck a nerve. He knew his deputy was right. Had he really thought he could just hire a mother for Addy? Somehow his plan had gone badly wrong. His housekeeper was lovely, kind and wonderful with his little girl, plus she made his skin tingle whenever he got within sight of her. Damn, he'd thought of Viola all day long!

Trent cast Joey one final glare, then headed out, slamming the door behind him.

Joey sighed. His boss was respected, tough, conscientious and fair to a fault. Every eligible woman in town, respectable and otherwise had let the sheriff know they were interested. They'd only grown more insistent since he'd buried his mom. But he'd stayed solitary as a grizzly bear, and Joey would bet his bottom dollar that the reason lay somewhere back in Texas.

The deputy had been in town when Trent had arrived carrying a newborn in his arms. Speculation about the girl's mother swirled, but neither Trent nor his ma had a word to say on the matter. Gossip continued, with some folks assuming that the gal's ma had died, but not Joey. He recognized a man who'd been hurt and hurt bad. Dying just didn't do that to a fella. He had a theory that the gal's ma was still alive.

He was eaten up with curiosity, but the only time he'd asked, Trent had near torn his head off.

The deputy grabbed his coat and buttoned up the front. The snow crunched beneath his feet as he crossed to the telegraph office. Benjamin had closed shop and he had to track him down at the Longhorn Saloon. He collected two messages and then he had to pick up the supper plate for his prisoner.

Once back in the jail, he fed his charge and then sat by the stove to read the telegrams. The first was a description of the female thief from Bozeman. Five two, dark hair, blue eyes, petite, name: Eliza Flannery. Well, Joey thought, he'd be on the lookout for her. If she passed through Early, he'd be waiting. After all, Sheriff Foerster had given this one to him, his first real case, and he intended to do his very best. He used his penknife to open the second message.

Unexpectedly delayed until next Sunday STOP
Apologies STOP
Mrs. V. Guntherson STOP

Joe stared at the date—December 14, 1888. Well that made no sense at all. She'd arrived yesterday just as expected. She must have gotten this off and then made the train after all. He crumbled the page and tossed it into the woodstove.

Eliza washed up, then poured two cups of coffee and a teacup of milk for Addy.

"My oldest is watching the boys. They should be fine, if they don't burn the house down…oh." Her smile faltered, and Eliza was certain she was thinking of what she had witnessed this morning. "I take mine black."

Eliza set the cup before her guest and then took her own seat. Thankfully Addy jabbered away and kept Mrs. Milward from learning every blasted detail of Eliza's past. Finally, after two cups, the woman left.

Eliza stifled a sigh of relief. Her moment of peace was fleeting as she realized she still had nothing to serve for dinner.

Having no other recourse, and with time running short, she made one of the few things she knew how to cook—a shepherd's pie. She ground the leftover lamb she found and made yet another piecrust. Then she layered crisp slices of potato with the meat and loaded the top with heaps of mashed potatoes.

The shepherd's pie was half-cooked when she lifted the dessert out of the oven, its golden crust showing each imperfection. She stood back, frowning at the offending dish when the front door opened and Mr. Foerster called from the hallway.

Addy charged from the room and a moment later the two appeared, Addy riding on her father's hip. His cheeks were pink from the cold and he wore a smile that made her insides tremble.

"How's my girl?" he asked her.

Eliza's heart gave an unexpected flutter, as if he had been directing the question to her. Wouldn't that be heaven, to have this man and this child for her very own?

Woolgathering, that's what her mother called it. Also stuff and nonsense.

He lowered Addy to the floor and inhaled deeply. "Something smells good."

Trent made a sound of pleasure that made Eliza's stomach jump. But his smile faded when he noticed the apple pie. It did have a nice domed shape, but bubbly apple mixture had seeped out of the numerous fissures in the surface.

"Mrs. Guntherson let me help!" chirped Addy.

His smile returned, and he glanced up at her with a knowing look as if it was all clear to him now. Of course no grown woman would have created such a monstrosity. She held a tight smile as her stomach roiled.

He searched the stove top. "No stroganoff?"

"Hmm, well, no. We had some trouble with that."

"Trouble?"

"Well, I didn't know, that is I wasn't certain about…"

"Oh, I see. We don't have any cream in the house, do we?" he finished.

Relief flooded her. "Not that I could find."

"I have a tab at McVane's. I forgot to tell you that. You can get what you need there." He looked around. "Well, I smell something cooking."

Eliza used the hook to open the oven and two dish towel retrieve the shepherd's pie. The mashed potato was golde gravy dribbled from the sides.

Mr. Foerster stood just behind her, leaning in, as she slid her handiwork onto the stovetop. He inhaled, then sighed. His chest brushed her shoulder as his warm breath fanned her. She let her eyes drift closed for just an instant to savor the contact. When she opened them, he was beside her, staring down at her. The mirth was gone from his gaze, replaced by a riveting heat that bored into her.

"Mrs. Guntherson?"

She turned toward him. He reached for her just as Addy pushed between them.

"I want to see." She stood on her toes. "Ooh!"

Eliza, rescued from her own folly by Addy's timely interruption, stepped back. What had he meant to do? she wondered. It almost seemed as though he intended to kiss her, right here in his kitchen.

She scooped up their dinner and placed it in the center of the trivet upon the table and then seated Addy and laid a napkin across the child's lap. Then she took her own place and bowed her head.

Trent removed his hat and coat and joined them, folding his hands.

"God, we thank You for bringing Mrs. Guntherson to us and for all of Your many blessings, Amen."

Eliza choked out, "Amen." But the grinding guilt ruined her pride in the meal and her joy at pleasing him. It was a lie, start to finish. She needed to tell him the truth.

She would do so, as soon as Addy was in bed.

She served him and Addy, but found her own appetite had fled. The apple pie crumbled in serving, but Trent told her it did not spoil the taste.

Addy was excused to retrieve the patches for the doll quilt, which her father studied carefully and praised lavishly, despite the awkward seams. How wonderful to have a father who was so easy with his approval. Addy positively glowed with joy.

Eliza cleared the table as Addy told her father all about the quilt and the apple slicing and how she sprinkled the sugar and added "pads" of butter.

When Eliza turned, still drying her hands, she found him

smiling at her again as Addy, perched before him, traced the lines of stitches that held the piecework together.

"Would you like to walk Mrs. Guntherson to the hotel with me, sweet pea?"

Eliza was quite ashamed at the relief she felt. She would not have to tell Trent, not with Addy there. Still, the real housekeeper was overdue, and that hung over Eliza's head like the Sword of Damocles.

Addy bounced with delight. "Yes, oh, yes!"

"Get your coat then."

Eliza made a weak attempt to dissuade him from bringing Addy out in the cold. "But it's dangerous out at night."

Trent's smile didn't waver. "I can take care of my own."

"But I thought it was my responsibility to see her put to bed."

"I'll manage tonight."

She retrieved her coat, feeling like an outcast, sent from the warm, cheery kitchen and into the cold.

"Your bag show up yet?"

Her cheeks heated. "Why, no. Not yet."

Eliza busied herself with her buttons so she wouldn't have to look at Mr. Foerster. When she finally dared to lift her gaze she found him holding a folded sheet out to her.

"I checked your letter. You *did* write you'd been widowed after fifteen years of marriage and you wrote it in script. There was no stray mark."

His cold eyes studied her as all the air seemed to leave her body.

"You lied to me, Mrs. Guntherson, and I'd like to know why."

She could not have answered if she had wanted to, not with him menacing her with his stony stare. Her notions of telling him the truth and confessing fled in a wave of panic. She barely recognized the loving father she had glimpsed a moment ago. This man—this stranger, frightened the wits from her.

"I thought…" She groped for some reasonable explanation and failed.

"Well?"

She shook her head.

"If you believed I would not have hired a woman of your age and obvious inexperience—" he glanced at the apple pie "—you were right. Your arrival is already causing gossip, and I absolutely will not have any shame brought down on my daughter's head because of this. Do you understand?"

Eliza jerked her head in a clumsy nod.

"Do you know why I am not firing you on the spot?"

She shook her head.

"Because my daughter adores you. She's happy for the first time, well, since my mom was here. I have you to thank for it. But this lie has put me to considerable trouble and expense. I've a mind to deduct the hotel costs from your wages."

Her head hung low as a puppy that had just wet the rug.

"If you have anything else you may have misrepresented, you had best tell me now, for I cannot abide a deceitful woman."

She swallowed past the lump. He wanted the truth, but if she told him, he would fire her—or worse. She squeezed her eyes shut and vowed that tonight she would flee.

"Daddy?" Addy's voice rang with concern. "Why is Mrs. Guntherson crying?"

"Put your scarf on, Adeline."

"Yes, sir."

He clasped Eliza's elbow and steered her out the front door. When they reached the main street he released her in order to scoop his daughter into his arms. Addy had been unusually quiet and now nestled close, her breath warming his neck. He knew his daughter well enough to know she was troubled by the palpable strain between him and Mrs. Guntherson.

He glanced at the woman beside him. Her head hung like a whipped dog. Perhaps he had been too hard on her. Had she discovered through experience that most families wanted an older woman? Such a pretty woman would be a distraction to any man, and Lord knew he was distracted to the point that he couldn't even sleep last night.

Damn it, why couldn't she have been an older woman as he expected? He wanted her out of his house and he wanted her in his bed.

Chapter Eight

Eliza waited upstairs for a time. She wanted to be sure she did not run into Mr. Foerster outside. When she judged enough time had passed, she retrieved her bag and fled down the back stairs again. She would have to find someone leaving town and beg for help. It would be humiliating, but she could not stay here. She reached the street and paused.

"Eliza!"

She turned at the call and only afterward realized her mistake. There stood Trent's deputy, not ten feet away, staring directly at her.

Her heart exploded into a wild thumping that made her light-headed. He knew her name! She swayed.

The deputy caught her elbow, steadying her.

"You are Eliza Flannery." It wasn't a question. He knew.

She tried to speak, but no words would come. The man took her bag.

"Come on now. Let's get you inside."

Jail. He was taking her to jail. Eliza stumbled along beside him and nearly through the hotel lobby before she realized she was not yet headed for a prison cell. He guided her into the restaurant on the ground floor. She glanced about dumbly, not understanding what was happening. Why had he brought her here?

He motioned to a seat and she sagged into it. He set her bag in the one beside her and then sat across the table from her.

"Joey Backer, ma'am. You remember me? Met you yester and looked after Addy last night while Trent walked you hotel." He removed his hat, hanging it on the back of the chair holding her bag.

She nodded.

He left her and returned with a glass of water. "Coffee's coming. Drink this. Ma'am, you're pale as snow. Now listen here, I'm not going to hurt you. You hear me? Drink this."

He pressed the glass into her hand and she took a swallow. Her hands shook, so she set the glass back on the table.

"You leaving town?"

She nodded.

The waitress brought their coffee and left the pot at Mr. Backer's request. His gentle smile disappeared when he turned his eyes back to her.

"From the beginning, now. Let's hear it."

She drew a breath and then told him about her predecessor and the arrest and how frightened she had been and how she had run. Eliza answered every question, and when he was done interrogating her, she sat numbly, waiting for what the deputy would do next.

"Why you running now? Why tonight?"

"Mr. Foerster knows I misrepresented my background. He said he'd fire me if I lied about anything else. How could I tell him?" She found no answers in Mr. Backer's steady stare. Eliza dropped her head and covered her face in her hands. "I never should have come here. I've interfered too much already. I don't want to hurt Addy or disappoint Mr. Foerster any further."

"Why not?"

She shook her head.

"Best spit it out, now."

Her hands slipped to her lap. "I—I love his daughter already, and I'm afraid I have feelings for Mr. Foerster, as well."

"That's fine."

Eliza glanced up in astonishment, to find Mr. Backer grinning at her over the rim of his coffee cup.

"He tell you about Addy's ma?" He waited until Eliza shook her head. "He never told me, either. I guess she hurt him bad. Won't have nothing to do with women now. Won't court them, won't even speak to them hardly. But you, well, you got under his skin faster than a chigger. Burrowed in good and tight, too. He walked right by the jail this morning. Never done that before. And, according to Trent, Addy's taken with you. Obvious to anyone that's seen you with the gal that you two belong together. First I thought he just made up the story about a housekeeper so he could sneak you in. Thought maybe you was the girl's real ma, but that was before I seen you in the light and your hair's too dark. Plus, why would he put you in a hotel? Didn't make sense. Then I got that telegram from the real Mrs. Guntherson."

"You what?" Eliza started to choke.

Deputy Backer pushed her untouched coffee cup at her and then continued as if she hadn't interrupted.

"Saying she'd be delayed. I figured that was a mistake, but after I seen you leave the hotel last night I changed my mind on that account and got suspicious." He laughed. "You sure told that Grogan boy what's what."

"You saw that?"

He nodded.

"Yet you didn't step in?"

"Wanted to see what you'd do. Thought you'd found another keeper but you sent him off. Question is, you staying now 'cause you want to or have to? You a common thief and an uncommon liar or are you telling the truth?"

"I assure you—"

"Don't. I don't believe you. Not yet anyway." He reached for her bag and unclipped the latch. "A thief, left alone all day in Trent's house might have helped herself to a few things to ease the journey. If you lied, there's hell to pay. But if it happened like you say, I'll back you with everything I got."

Eliza's eyes rounded. Her private things were in that satchel. "Mr. Backer, there must be another way."

"There is. I take you to Trent, then wire the sheriff in Bozeman."

Eliza sat back in her chair, gritting her teeth as Mr. Backer rummaged through her personal belongings in public. Satisfied at last, he sat back.

"Well, now, you sure do pack light." He closed the bag and placed it back on the chair. "Best tell him before he finds out."

Eliza nodded.

"If you try to leave town again, I'll track you like a Mississippi bloodhound." He stood and retrieved his hat, giving it a lighthearted spin. "'Night, Mrs. Guntherson."

Eliza arrived the next day knowing that flight was no longer an option. The deputy had seen to that. That left only one option, but she dreaded telling Trent more than she feared jail. She had such respect for him and wanted him to respect her, too. No, she wanted more than respect; she wanted to stay, and she knew in her heart that once he found out the truth her little dreams of keeping his house would burn to ash.

Upon reaching the Foerster's home, she discovered a note on the door instructing her to pick up Addy at Mrs. Milward's, which she did. Trent had been called away in the night to settle some matter with two ranchers and so she received another reprieve.

The morning flew by with shopping for the ingredients for beef stroganoff, with the help of the recipe that Mrs. Milward had handed her this morning. Eliza and Addy returned home before lunch and afterward they were back at the bag of rags selecting fabric for a new dress and apron for Penelope. Addy was a bright girl and her stitches were nearly straight. But she did repeatedly prick her finger.

Eliza went to her bag, retrieved her sewing kit and removed the only gift her mother had ever given her, a child's silver thimble.

"Here, Addy, you can borrow this."

"Ooh." Addy held up the small cap and ran her finger along the scrolling pattern of lilies of the valley. "Pretty."

Eliza sat beside the girl on the large window seat in the kitchen with the cold blue light of the winter afternoon streaming in behind them. "My mother gave me this for my fifth birthday."

"Nana said my mommy died. But Daddy won't say anything about her. If I ask him, he stops talking and looks away."

Something inside Eliza's belly flipped. Her troubles with her own parents suddenly seemed small. At least she knew them. Questions that were none of her business rolled through her mind.

Addy clamped her tongue between her teeth and squinted in her effort to coordinate the subtle movements of needle and thimble.

With a little practice she got the hang of it, and Eliza turned her attention to fashioning a prim white doll's apron. As the light began to fade, Eliza left Addy to finish the apron hem, as she lit the lanterns. Next she turned to browning the beef and making a batter for the egg noodles.

Mrs. Milward made noodles sound easy, but she found rolling the sticky concoction nearly impossible. The resulting misshapen blobs went into hot water to boil, bobbing on the top like ducklings on a pond. Eliza eyed them, wondering if egg noodles were supposed to look that slimy, but having never seen them, she was uncertain.

She left the meat on too long and it was very brown when she added the cream to the skillet. Eliza dumped in the quarter cup of flour. It turned instantly into a thick glutinous mass. Eliza tried to stir the flour, but it resisted, clinging and congealing like tallow, so she smashed it with a wooden spoon. Eventually the thick cream was flecked with clots of flour.

Addy's voice roused her focus from the skillet.

"That doesn't look right."

At that moment the pot of egg noodles boiled over.

Trent had run into Danny Strecker on the walk home. The man wanted to know if his housekeeper would be at church for Sunday services. Trent had been tempted to draw his gun and shoo him off. Damned if his deputy hadn't been right.

Men were already sniffing after Mrs. Guntherson like…well, he'd hired her. Let them go find their own housekeeper.

Trent stomped down the street, the snow muffling his steps. He knew he couldn't keep them back for long. There just weren't a lot of eligible women in Early and certainly none as lovely as Viola. What man wouldn't want to try sparking her? The idea of her seeing another man made him angry enough to grind nails between his teeth.

He didn't like being backed into a corner, but he saw only two choices. Let other men court her or claim her himself. Damn, but he didn't want to make a fool of himself again. Not after he'd finally finished wiping the egg off his face from the last time. How was it that he could read men at a glance and yet be so completely taken in by a woman? It burned his pride.

But then again, she was so good with Addy. His daughter had taken to her like a duck to water. Viola would make a good mother, of that he was sure. Perhaps that was reason enough to pursue her as a wife. For practical reasons alone, he should marry her. And he would have considered it, too, if not for the fact that his gut was in a knot just thinking of her with another man. He would not let another woman have that kind of power over him again. If he did marry, it would be to a nice, plain woman who was good to his daughter. Not someone he wanted so bad that he couldn't sleep at night from thinking what it would be like to love her.

He was wiser now. Wasn't he? He understood he was getting crazy over Viola, and that meant he wasn't thinking straight. But he couldn't send her off because she was good for Addy.

Trent stopped in the street as the truth he'd been fighting punched him in the gut. *Oh, no.* Addy's needs were only the excuse. He wanted her, needed her and knew he'd pursue her like a wolf after a wounded doe.

It was too late to send her away. Already the obsession controlled him and that meant *she* could control him if she found out. If she knew, she'd take advantage. All women did. Sweat broke out on his forehead.

She wasn't like Helen. So it could be different this time. Viola was quiet, demure and proper. Viola would never take advantage or use him as Helen had. But that didn't mean she wanted to marry him. He tried to imagine offering Viola the ring his mother had worn until well after his father died. What if she said no?

Damn, again.

He'd have to try. That was all.

Maybe he could keep her from knowing how much he wanted her, just tell her he needed a mother for Addy and…

His shoulders slumped. He was headed for another train wreck.

He stared up at the snow falling from the dark sky and then glanced about. Where the hell was he?

Trent realized he had walked clean past his house. He wheeled about and stormed down the street, reaching his home and stomping the snow off his feet before crossing the threshold inside.

His disquiet began to ebb the moment he inhaled. He paused to savor the warm air and the aroma of beef and…what? His brow furrowed.

"Daddy!"

Addy came dashing around the corner and leaped into his arms. He could feel the heat of her cheek against his cold skin. Her sweet smell calmed him and he found his smile came easily.

"Look!"

She held her doll too close for him to see what excited her so, but he accepted the toy and glanced down at her then back to Addy.

"Her dress, Daddy. It's new. I made it!"

"*You* did?"

"Well, most of it."

He glanced at the pretty pleating, trim sleeves and lopsided hem. Viola again, he thought, teaching his daughter the things that he never could, the skills she would need to be a good wife and mother someday. Gratitude welled, and he transferred Addy to his hip, carrying her into the kitchen.

There he found Mrs. Guntherson spooning a glutinous concoction that he very much feared was his supper into bowls. Had her duties with Addy so thoroughly distracted her that she had been unable to cook again?

Trent lowered his voice, "Did you help with dinner, too?"

Addy nodded and Trent's heart sank. The beef was chewy and the cream sauce lumpy. She seemed to have made dumplings instead of noodles and they were doughy and bland.

He needed to address this failing and be certain his housekeeper knew that this was unacceptable. This…glue could not be borne. She had written that she was a competent cook. Had she lied about this, as well? That thought brought him back to brooding. He could not abide a deceitful woman. He'd not have it. Not under his roof.

As he tentatively chewed his meal, he glanced at Addy, who seemed oblivious to the food's shortcomings. When he glanced at Viola, he discovered her head bowed and her lower lip quivering.

He knew enough about women to know this was a sign that forecasted imminent tears.

"Tasty," he lied.

Her shoulders shook and she lifted her napkin to her face.

Apparently, she could tell when he was lying. He wished to hell he could do the same with her.

Somehow he choked down his portion and then rejected seconds. Mrs. Guntherson removed the dishes and began washing as he sipped his coffee and listened to Addy explain the steps required to create Penelope's new wardrobe.

"I'll bet you could make yourself a dress, Addy, if Mrs. Guntherson would help you."

Addy was off her chair and at Viola's side a moment later, tugging at her skirts in excitement. The joyful laugh that escaped Viola was musical.

Trent paused, holding his coffee halfway to his mouth as he watched his housekeeper set aside her dishrag and kneel before Addy. The small act brought her eye to eye with his girl and showed a kind of respect not often afforded to a child. The warming of his insides had nothing to do with the coffee. He lowered his cup back to the saucer, watching the exchange.

His earlier notion roused again. The woman had a natural affinity to Addy. He had enough sense to recognize the rarity of the relationship the two had forged so effortlessly. And it could all vanish if she left them, or if some randy pup lured her away.

He thought of his deputy's words and found himself now clutching the saucer. He sure as hell didn't want another man to have her.

There was a pop and the china cup gave way, exploding into three jagged pieces.

"Oh, Mr. Foerster! What happened?"

He'd been picturing her with another man, was what, but he'd be whipped before he'd admit that.

"Just gave way," he lied.

She mopped up the coffee and quickly replaced the cup and saucer. A moment later she had the coffee poured and had rested a lovely flat cake before him. The top of the confection glittered with sugar and reminded him of snowflakes in the sun. The top had been scored to delineate eight pie-shaped wedges and each slice, while still connected to the whole, formed a flower pattern that might have been created with a fork or spoon. It seemed too pretty to eat.

"What's this?"

"Just a simple shortbread. You might like it with your coffee."

Bread? It sure hadn't risen any. He peered from the pan back to Viola to find her standing before him, hands folded, head still hanging. He wondered if this might be just as disappointing as his meal, but he was willing to eat sandpaper if it allowed Viola to lift her head up. So he cut a piece. The tip broke off and he worried over the pastry's lack of stability, but he shoveled it onto his plate, seeing it more resembled a cookie than a cake. He lifted the wedge and took a small, tentative bite.

The shortbread dissolved instantly and filled his mouth with a buttery sugary taste laced with vanilla and cinnamon. A smile spread across his face. He glanced at her and saw her sweet smile and twinkling eyes. Was that pride he saw shining in their blue depths? Suddenly he could not seem to swallow.

"Good!" he said.

She turned away and continued cleaning up. Addy polished off a piece of shortbread and then went to the window box near the stove to play with Penelope. He recalled his sisters playing together in that same spot. Addy, however, played her make-believe games alone. Trent pressed his lips together. Addy would make a wonderful big sister. A shame she'd never get the chance.

He glanced at Viola, noting her wide, flaring hips and narrow waist. She was young and healthy and looked in every way capable of being a wife and mother. Except for her cooking, he reminded himself.

She finished drying the dishes and then her hands, replaced the rag and went about returning the dried dishes to their places. There was a rightness to this moment that touched him on a bone-deep level. A tranquility and sense of peace on earth that had been long missing from his life. What a miracle that she should come so close to Christmas, an unexpected gift to his daughter and to himself.

It was something he'd never felt with Helen. She'd always kept him on tenterhooks, poised between ecstasy and despair. Her unpredictability and volatility had given him trouble like he would never have believed possible.

He felt none of that with Viola. Quite the opposite…in fact, she brought him calm, peace and a profound feeling of satisfaction with life. Except when he looked at how her hips swayed when she moved. Now that sight heated his blood.

Should he consider making her a permanent member of his family? Or was he poised on the brink of another colossal mistake? He'd only known her a few short days, but already the desire to hold her consumed him. Her skin looked so soft. Tendrils of hair kissed her neck.

Trent thumped his coffee down. He knew he'd be unable to defend that which was not his. Why would she want to cook and clean for him when she could be a wife, with a home of her own?

Viola closed the last cabinet, but did not return to him. Instead, she gripped the sink, head hung for a moment as if bracing for battle. He straightened in his seat, his senses now on alert.

She'd been uncharacteristically quiet during dinner, he realized, and had eaten little.

He'd been too harsh on her last night. That was it. Now she didn't feel comfortable or was she getting ready to quit on him? That thought flooded him with a cold panic.

She turned, revealing an anxious expression that set him on edge. "Mr. Foerster, I'd like a word."

"Would you join me?" he asked, and then stood to hold her chair.

She gave him a cautious look and then sat. He retrieved a cup and saucer and poured her some coffee. Before seating himself, he glanced at Addy, her eyes now drooping as she curled with Penelope in the window box by the stove. He turned back to Viola.

"I know what this is about." Trent took over the conversation. "And I'd like to apologize for my harsh words yesterday. I just… well, I've had some troubles and they make me hasty. So before you tell me this isn't working out, let me tell you that I've never seen my girl so happy, and as for me, well, truth is, after my ma's passing, I didn't want to come home. Now I do."

He met and held her gaze, watching her color rise. Was she embarrassed or did she feel some tenderness toward him, as well? He tried for a smile and then thought to take her hand. Reaching halfway across the table he wondered if he was being too forward and retreated, clutching his knees under the table.

She looked away first and his heart squeezed in worry. *Don't let her quit on me, too.*

"I'm sorry about dinner."

He wanted to ask her what had happened, but he resisted. Was that all she wanted to say? Relief made his smile genuine and he breathed a sigh of relief. "Forget that for now. Are you…well, that is, I'd like to know you a little better. Would you tell me something about yourself?" He'd almost asked her if she was happy, but fear had choked his words. What if she said no?

She looked startled. "Oh, well. What would you like to know?"

"What about your family? Do you have any?"

"Yes, my parents are still living."

"Siblings?"

Her face fell. "No, actually, I'm an only child. I was a late arrival, you see. My parents were unprepared for a baby at their stage of life. I think it quite embarrassed them." *A trial* were the words that her mother often used when referring to her.

Eliza felt sick thinking of her mother. She glanced up into Trent's frowning face. "Embarrassed?"

Was he angry at her for her choice of words or her parents? Eliza hurried on.

"They are missionaries in Venezuela, you see."

"What does that have to do with loving a baby?"

"Well, they needed to set a certain example. They were quite strict."

"There's no sin in the love between a husband and wife." His frown deepened. "Weren't they married?"

"Oh, of course!" She flushed. "For years and years before I came along. Perhaps they were just set in their ways. They'd already been to Tahiti and the Appalachian Mountains."

"*They* have been. What about you?"

"Well, it's hard, you see, to follow such a calling with a child in tow."

He frowned and Eliza shifted uncomfortably before her untouched coffee. She clasped her hands around the lip of the saucer as if protecting it from all sides.

"Didn't they raise you?"

She shook her head. "No. I attended a boarding school. But they visited when they were back in America. And of course I had their letters."

Filled with fire and brimstone and the threat of eternal damnation should she veer from the righteous path. The correspondence came less and less frequently over the years. Eliza could not recall how she had gotten in so deep and glanced about for some rescue from this topic.

Trent leaned forward, his hand now covering hers. The warmth and strength made her yearn for him in a way she had never experienced. "How old were you?"

She glanced at Addy and then back to him, in time to watch his face fall.

"Five?" he whispered.

"Four."

His gasp was audible. Why had she told him this? Why would she let him know that her own parents did not want her? Such a failing could only serve to draw attention to her many deficiencies. A child that was not wanted in her own home could not be wanted by others.

He leaned close. She closed her eyes so she would not have to witness the pity there.

"I'm so sorry."

Her eyes flew open. "Oh, no. They provided for my education and all my needs. They saw me raised up…" She was going to say *properly* until she realized how furious they would be to see what had become of her. They would not abide lies or the shadow of impropriety. If they discovered her circumstances, they would have nothing more to do with her. She had no doubt of that, for she knew they prided themselves on their sterling characters above all things. "You see, they had a calling."

Trent met her gaze with a steady stare.

"They abandoned you," he said.

Chapter Nine

Eliza glanced toward Addy now, seeing that she sat in the window box by the stove, cuddling Penelope against her as she curled on her side, half-asleep. It was easier to watch the child than face the pity in Trent's voice. But there was nothing she could do to block out his words.

"Your parents were right about one thing. A man should take a wife before he…"

She turned back in time to see him clamp his lips together. Then he lifted his coffee and took a long swallow, frowning deeply.

His words, of course, caused Eliza to begin wild conjecture as to the circumstances of Adeline's birth.

His voice turned low and intimate. "You're on track now, with what you're thinking. I tried to marry Addy's mother, but she'd have none of it or me." He lowered his voice again, so she had to strain to hear his words. "She left our child behind and took off after another man the minute he was released from prison. They were partners, gambling partners, which is another way of saying card cheats. But I couldn't see it, I couldn't see anything past my own…"

Trent stood, walked to the sink and dumped out the dregs. He kept his back to her as he gripped the counter and his head dropped.

She glanced back at Addy, who was sound asleep. Eliza found herself standing behind Trent, without recalling crossing the room. She already had a hand resting on his broad shoulder. He glanced around and turned. She drew back and found him staring at her. The sadness reflected in his eyes pressed down upon her.

"She left her own child?" whispered Eliza.

His eyes narrowed as he dipped his chin in slow affirmation. "Not a backward glance," he said.

Eliza could not prevent the sharp exhale of breath.

"So I brought her home to my mother. She was fifty-eight, thought she was through raising up babies, I imagine. But she took us in and never held her mother against Addy. She's the only one that knew…until now."

Eliza bit her lower lip, thinking she should move away, but the connection between them held her and she opened her heart, speaking when a wise woman would keep silent. "You haven't told anyone else?"

He shook his head.

"Good, for it cannot help but cause your daughter heartache."

"Don't know why I told you."

He sounded so dumbfounded she managed a slow smile.

"Well, I am no gossip. I think her mother made a grievous mistake." *For how could any woman leave such a man or her own baby girl?* She was rather glad she didn't say this aloud and took a moment to swallow back her first thought. "Addy is a wonderful child—a credit to you and to your mother." Eliza glanced back to see the little girl in question. "She'd make any woman proud."

"Not any. Helen was a coldhearted bitch."

Eliza drew a quick breath for she could not quite contain her shock at his harsh words. Trent pressed his lips together, but did not apologize or recant his severe condemnation.

He dropped his gaze. "It's not something a man gets over, being made a fool, but I *was* a fool for that woman, damn her lying heart. And I believed each word."

He glanced at her, his eyes beseeching, and Eliza knew she was about to do something foolish but could not seem to stop herself. She reached across the few inches that separated them and took his hand in hers. His skin was warm and his fingers callused. He clasped her so quickly it caused her to stiffen. But his troubled eyes held her and she forced herself to relax. He had been ill-used. That much was certain.

He placed his other hand at the small of her back and drew her closer. Her breath caught at the rightness of the intimate embrace that had her heart racing like storm clouds across the moon.

"I'm glad you've come, Viola."

Viola? Had she been on the verge of assuring him that not all women were callous or deceitful?

His utterance of the name he thought was hers brought her up short and she stiffened again. Now, she was the liar, taking advantage of him just as surely as Addy's mother once had. The fear returned, creeping over her like ice crystals on a windowpane. The intimacy they had shared was a lie and now she was the one making a fool of him. What would the town say when they found out the Texas Ranger had a fugitive living under his own roof?

She pulled back, breaking away and halting a step from him.

"I'm sorry," he said. "I shouldn't have taken liberties."

She lifted a hand, but did not touch him this time. "It isn't that."

His eyes narrowed on her. "Addy, then. I know what you are thinking. How does he know she's his? Well, I don't, not for certain. Helen was with me long enough. But for all I know…"

Didn't he have eyes? "Oh, Trent, she's yours. Certainly. You have only to look at her. She's like you in every way."

"Blonde," he said. "Like her. I hope to Christ that's all of her that my girl's got. She can't be like her mom. I won't allow it." He seemed to mentally shake himself, dragging his fingers through his thick hair. He sighed. "Shouldn't have told you."

"I'm glad you did."

"Why?"

"Because…"

She was about to say, "Because it shows you trust me," but she couldn't. She was not who he thought her to be. She blinked up at him, wanting to confess, but understanding now how very much it would hurt him if she did. Eliza felt her face heat as indecision turned her this way and that.

"Never mind." He pushed off the sink. "Best get you back." He retrieved his jacket, but paused, holding his hat. "Did you have anything else you wanted to tell me?"

She shook her head.

He waited a moment longer, but when she said nothing, he drew on his hat, gathered his sleeping child against his chest and folded his sheepskin jacket about her. Addy never roused as he buttoned the coat, cocooning her in the wooly hide and the warmth of his body.

The tenderness with which he treated his girl made Eliza's chest ache. She'd give anything in this world to have the protection of such a man. But she didn't deserve it, had earned it under false pretenses.

Eliza felt her throat burn and hurriedly slipped into her coat. In the darkness, her tears would not betray her. She followed him out into the frigid night. They walked in an uneasy silence to the hotel. The stars twinkled above them and oil lamps flickered in the windows. Her boots squeaked in the snow like the runners of a rocker.

He saw her to the door, tipped his hat, spun and retraced his steps. Eliza watched him go, wondering how a woman could ever leave such a man.

Trent marched home, holding Addy close to his chest. On returning to his house, he found Kelly Milward on her front porch loading firewood into her son's arms. She glanced at Trent then pushed her son toward the door.

"Go on inside, Tommy."

The last thing he needed was Kelly meddling in his affairs. The woman had tried on more than one occasion to get him to attend church socials and never failed to mention when a girl was of marrying age. He ducked his head and hurried up the steps. He was inches from his front door when she called out.

"Trent! You hold on a minute."

He froze and then turned. She motioned him over.

He pointed to his coat. "I got Addy."

"She'll keep." Kelly waited. He turned and descended the steps, crossed the little alley between their houses and stood like Romeo beneath her porch.

"How you getting on with Mrs. Guntherson?"

He made a face.

"Why? Ain't she good with your gal?"

Trent sighed. "Addy loves her. But she can't cook worth a damn."

"She'll learn."

"Yesterday, she set breakfast on fire. Dinner, I don't even know how to describe it."

"Why don't you fire her then?"

Trent felt as though someone had kicked him. Just thinking about her leaving made him grind his teeth.

"Ah, why don't you paint it like it is?"

He scowled up at her. "I don't know what you mean."

Kelly's smile needled him. "Don't you? You've avoided every pretty gal from here to Butte, but you can't avoid this one. You kissed her yet?"

"Almost."

Her smile broadened.

Damn, how did the woman do it? She always managed to wheedle information out of him. Lord, he ought to hire her as a deputy. Men round here wouldn't stand a chance under her questioning.

"How'd you know?" he asked

"You're a man, aren't cha?"

"She works for me. I can't go around kissing her."

"If you say so. But, if you don't, someone else will. And that girl needs kissing. And don't ask her first. Young women, proper ones like she is, they'll always say no if you ask. Pay no attention. Better to ask forgiveness than permission, I say."

"What if she doesn't want me to kiss her?"

"Oh, she'll let you know. Now get that child inside. Hear? And don't scowl so much. You'll frighten her to death."

Trent stood in dumbfounded silence as Kelly Milward sauntered into her home.

Chapter Ten

Eliza woke the next morning to the maid's familiar knock. Apparently, the real Mrs. Guntherson had still not arrived. Delayed, the deputy had said. How many days would it be until she was caught in her own web?

On the walk to the Foerster's, she weighed the deputy's advice against her new knowledge of how badly Trent had been hurt by the lies of Addy's mother. Finally, she decided it would be better to tell him, if only so he didn't find out some other way first. Her plan to speak with him privately upon arrival was foiled by Mr. Foerster himself, who did not even wait for her to take her coat off before heading out the door.

"You ever cut down a Christmas tree?" he asked from the porch.

She felt deeply inadequate and could only lower her chin.

"No, Mr. Foerster."

He pressed his lips tight. What was he thinking? "I guess you're not too old to learn. And call me Trent."

"Yes, Mr.…Trent."

His smile dazzled her. He turned and charged down the steps, calling back to her. "Have Addy fed and ready when I get home."

Addy's excitement was infectious. Truth be told, Eliza had never been on an outing for a Christmas tree and were she not still anchored by guilt, she would likely be bouncing up and down, as well. Instead, she fed Addy and bundled her into her bright green wool coat and red-and-green scarf. The mittens matched, but were too small to cover her wrists. Eliza wondered if her grandmother had knitted them for her.

Addy spent the next several minutes hopping up and down before the double-pane window, searching for some sign of her father.

The sound of sleigh bells reached them first. Addy rushed out, leaving Eliza to close the door behind them. From the steps she could see Trent, smiling brightly as he steered the fine bay trotter to a halt before them. The sticky snow clung to the bottom of the sleigh and the sun had already warmed the air so it did not bite at her nose and fingers.

"Daddy!"

Addy scrambled up and under the lap quilt beside her father, leaving Eliza to climb up next to her.

"There's my girls," he said as naturally as sunshine, and gave Eliza a wink that quite took her breath away.

The offhanded comment warmed her and gave her a secret thrill of delight. For just a moment, she could pretend that it was true, that they were a family and that she was really and truly his.

He tucked the quilt about them, his hand brushing her hip. He hesitated. Their eyes met, and his humor vanished as he waited for her to speak.

"I apologize for being forward last night."

He was apologizing to her? She should be apologizing. "Please don't."

"We'll start again?"

She nodded.

"'Cause I'd hate to do anything to run you off."

Really? He liked having her here? Her heart thudded and her face felt warm as a sunny day in May.

"Daddy, let's go!"

Trent straightened and smiled, his boyish charm startling her for it was a side of him she'd never seen.

"Yes, ma'am," he said and gave his daughter's chin a gentle tug.

Her giggle turned to a shriek of delight as Trent lifted the reins and set them in motion.

The sleigh sped along, gliding on the ice as the horse's hooves kicked up small saucer-sized discs of snow. It was like flying.

The silver bells on the sleigh jangled merrily with the fine high-stepping gait of the trotter.

Eliza gleefully gripped Addy's hand, glad for the moment they were all together. Christmas was a little over a week away. Would she be with them then? Oh, she hoped so, but first she must face her worst fears. She was surprised to realize that the worst now meant losing them. She feared that more than capture or even prison.

Tendrils of dread coiled within her.

Trent was honest, kind and tough. Was he also merciful and forgiving? He'd been ill-used and she knew she must prepare herself for failure.

The town receded behind them, opening into an expanse of frozen earth that ran along the valley. Beautiful, lush evergreens lined the road, but Trent never slowed.

"There's a good one, Daddy!"

Obviously, Addy had similar thoughts.

Trent chuckled. "But those are not on public land. It's not much farther."

After another half mile, he drew the horse to the side of the road, which now consisted of the twin marks from the runners and the well-worn path left by the horses that had passed before them.

Trent jumped down, carrying the reins along and looping them around the trunk of a sturdy pine, far too tall for their purposes. Addy scrambled after him and immediately found the snow reached up over her thighs. She did not stop, however, but waded in gamely, prepared to follow wherever he might lead.

Eliza knew exactly how she felt. How had she allowed herself to become so tangled up in their lives in so short a time? It seemed she had known them forever and that she had finally found a place where she belonged.

"Whoa, there, sweet pea. I'm afraid I'll lose you."

A moment later Trent had scooped his child up onto his shoulder. He returned to escort Eliza down. His gloved hand was sure and steady.

She caught him glancing at her ankle as she stepped onto the earth. He lifted his gaze and gave a boyish shrug and a smile that charmed and disarmed. Her heart was racing now and she had only taken the first step.

He released her to retrieve a fine, sharp ax he had tucked safely beneath the seat.

"Stay behind me so I can break a trail."

She did, wishing that they could keep on this way forever. She waded through the fine field of white that shone like polished silver. Eliza breathed in the crisp, clean air and smelled the scent of pine.

Addy turned back to grin at her from her perch upon her father's shoulder and then turned back to the path ahead. Trent broke the unmarred snow, cutting a direct path to the woods.

When he stopped, he caught her unaware and she ran right into his back. He didn't move an inch, but turned to grace her with another smile.

"Look here." He pointed. "Fox tracks."

And there they were. Eliza puzzled over the several deep holes in the snow.

"What made those?" she asked.

"The same fox. They listen for mice and voles under the snow and then dive right in and catch them."

"Really?"

He nodded.

She stared back in astonishment at the cleverness of the fox and the depth of knowledge of her companion.

"One of nature's miracles," she said.

They were off again, pausing to admire rabbit tracks and the delicate brushstroke of the wings of a grouse. The empty plain was not the tranquil scene it appeared, but alive with its inhabitants all revealed to her by Trent's narrative.

Once they reached the wooded area the snow was not so deep, and Addy dashed about searching for the perfect tree.

"Too big," said her father for the fourth time.

Addy dashed off again, remaining in sight, her bright green coat and colorful scarf flashing between the tree trunks.

Trent hooked his axe in the limb of a pine tree and stared at Eliza.

"You seem quiet."

She smiled. "Oh, I am just out of my element."

"Your first?" His smile faded. "But you've had a tree in your home before?"

She felt deeply inadequate and could only lower her chin.

"Not in my *parents'* home, and the school wouldn't allow it for safety reasons. My employer had a feather tree. They are quite the rage, you know."

"Never had a tree." He frowned now and Eliza realized she had made him feel sorry for her.

"But I'm sure I'll be able to decorate it. I've seen pictures and paintings of *tannenbaums*. Do you use candles?"

He nodded. A moment later he had clasped her hands and drew her forward.

"Eliza, I want this to be your Christmas, too. You're a part of the family now."

She felt her face heat. He was being polite, kind even. But she knew very well that an employee is not and never would be a true part of any family. She'd reconciled to that long ago. She, however, was not even a real employee. And she did not deserve to be included in this family until he knew it all.

"That is very generous of you to say," she began. "But—"

"I'm not just saying it. I mean it." He touched her chin, lifting it until her eyes met his. "I don't know how you did it, but Addy has never been so taken with anyone."

This was about his daughter then, not his feelings. How had it happened so quickly? How had she fallen in love with him in so short a course of days?

Tell him now. Tell him what you've done.

She looked into his eyes and saw everything she ever wanted shining back. His skin was rosy from the cold and his warm breath condensed into a vapor when he exhaled.

"Truth be told, it's not only Addy who's taken. I am, too."

Her breathing stopped. What was he saying?

"I only wanted someone to look after Addy. But now I want so much more."

Eliza lost her tongue completely and could only stare in mute astonishment. She'd already waited too long.

"I have something to tell you," she blurted.

"After I kiss you."

Chapter Eleven

Trent wanted this woman in every way a man wants a mate. He hadn't been looking; fact was he'd been licking his wounds for five years. But no longer. He was prepared to make her his, just as soon as she'd allow it. This time was different—had to be.

He held Viola's face firm in his two hands as his mouth slanted over hers. Her lips yielded and she gave a little gasp. Had he shocked her?

He hoped so.

Trent encircled her, cradling her head and holding her for his sensual assault. His tongue slid along the crease of her full lips and she opened her mouth. Her tongue emerged to duel with his, tentatively at first, and then with an abandon that thrilled and excited him.

Lord, she was sweet. How fortunate for him that Mr. Guntherson had departed this life and left Viola here—for him.

She drew back and he allowed it, but did not permit her to go far. He wasn't done kissing her yet, never would be done.

"Mr. Foerster, this isn't proper. People will talk."

"Let them." He realized with astonishment that it was true. He didn't care what the good people of Early thought. He'd have Viola if she'd have him.

"Mr. Foerster, please."

He felt the first inkling of worry. She had her arms braced on his chest now. "I have to tell you something."

"So do I. I want to court you, Viola."

Her brows lifted high. "But you hardly know me."

"And I'm looking forward to discovering every detail, each

secret and every habit. But for now, you're going to kiss me again."

He reeled her in, her resistance easily broken. She was sweet as a sugar cookie and fresh as a new day. He wasn't gentle this time, taking her mouth as he pressed her full against him.

Without any warning he could detect, she turned her head and leaned away, refusing him in the only way he'd left open to her.

The way she kissed him, that was not the kiss of a reluctant woman. But neither was it the kiss of an experienced one. Something didn't fit here.

"Viola? What is it?"

"I've been trying to tell you. I'm…I'm…not…"

Good God, Mr. Guntherson was dead, wasn't he? They weren't just separated. He let her go and she stumbled.

From somewhere to his left he heard Addy shriek. Viola's eyes widened and she ran in the direction of his daughter.

"Daddy!" came the panicked cry.

Trent grabbed the axe and followed, unbuttoning his coat as he went, so he could reach his gun. It took an instant to realize Viola was several feet in front of him, running like a deer, her skirts hitched up to her thigh and snow flying out behind her.

He saw a flash of green wool and then Addy came into sight. He stopped, relief flooding through him, blending with the fear. His heart still pounded, but he found himself chuckling.

"What happened?" he asked, trying very hard to keep from laughing.

Addy was not smiling, for she had somehow managed to catch the back of her coat on a broken tree branch and now hung like a rag doll on a clothes hook.

"Daddy! I'm stuck!" Her voice held irritation, because despite his efforts, Addy had caught him smiling.

Viola was doing her best to reach his girl, but Addy dangled above her grasp and her charming hopping had only managed to earn her one of Addy's boots.

He clasped Viola's arm and pulled her gently back, then set aside his axe and reached, disengaging his daughter from the clutches of the evil tree branch.

"Oh, Addy," said Viola. "You've sap all over the front of your coat." She fussed over the girl exactly as his own mother used to do, except there was a difference between an indulgent grandmother and a...*mother.*

He felt his stomach tighten as he realized that he wanted Viola to have his babies, that his dream, the desire he had long ago put upon the shelf, was now possible again. He might still fill that old house with children, *their children.*

The tenuous hope flickered within him, and he hardly dared breathe for fear he would extinguish it once more.

Once Addy had regained her footing, she took him to the tree she had selected. It was slightly too tall, but had a nice shape and a fine, straight trunk. He retrieved his axe, chopped through the wood and dragged the tree back to the sleigh with Addy riding the pine like a travois.

The tree fit nicely behind the seat, though the branches had to be tied to keep them from encroaching into the seating area. The horse was anxious to return to the shelter of the livery, where, no doubt, a nice bucket of oats awaited her, so her pace was brisk.

He and Addy sang "Jingle Bells" on the return trip, but Viola was unusually quiet. He wondered if her silence had something to do with whatever it was she had been trying to tell him or about his announcement that he planned to court her. He began to wonder about her first husband again. Why was it she had never mentioned him?

Perhaps that was what she meant to say, something about him. He'd be sure they had a moment's peace when they returned home, so she could speak plain.

The scent of pine filled the cold air about them as they jingled and jangled through town. He paused at his home to unload the tree before climbing back into his seat.

Viola did not go in, but stood beside the sleigh. "Mr. Foerster? We were interrupted in the forest."

"Yes, ma'am."

Addy came back down the steps to tug at Mrs. Guntherson's shirts. "I'm cold."

Viola looked from him to the girl and frowned.

"I'll be back in two shakes," he promised. "Soon as I get this sleigh stowed at the livery."

She pressed her lips together and nodded her consent. Her solemnity worried him. Whatever it was, it wasn't good.

He thought about the kiss. Had he been too forward? Damn Kelly Milward and her advice anyway. He'd gone too fast. But she was a widow; surely she was used to a man's appetites. He glanced back and found her following him with her worried eyes as he pulled into the street.

Trent returned the sleigh and was just leaving the livery stable when he spotted his deputy. The two fell into step together.

"I'm going home for lunch. Can you stay until I get back?" asked Trent.

Joey pushed his hat back on his head and grinned. "I reckon so."

"Sheriff!"

They turned toward the unfamiliar female voice and found a handsome woman, about Joey's age, striding purposefully toward them. She was out of breath when she reached them, her cheeks flushed and her blue eyes sparkling. Joey's mouth hung open as he gaped.

Trent released the brim of his Stetson. "Ma'am. What can I do for you?"

She pushed a strand of white hair back into the bun. He glanced at Joey to find he'd closed his mouth, but his face turned so red, Trent would have sworn he was choking to death.

"You're Sheriff Foerster?" she asked.

"Yes, ma'am, Trent Foerster and this is my deputy, Joey Backer."

Trent enjoyed watching Joey stammer out a hello. He'd never seen the man so befuddled.

"A pleasure." She turned back to Trent. "I do hope you received my telegram."

"I'm not sure. What's this about?" he asked.

"About my delay in arrival. I'm Viola Guntherson, your new housekeeper."

Eliza sagged into a kitchen chair. Now she must wait until he returned to tell him.

She'd reached a decision on the way back to town. She had

decided that if Trent did not arrest her on the spot, she would go back to Bozeman and clear her name because, for the first time in her life, she had something worth fighting for.

Under similar circumstances, Trent would never have run. She was certain of that. She wanted to be like him. And if she ever intended to regain control of her life she needed to stop hiding like some little rabbit and defend herself.

The sound of water rolling into a boil brought her to her feet. She poured it into the teapot and heated some milk to make hot cocoa for Addy.

What if he couldn't forgive her?

Eliza felt her heart wrench. What if this was all a lovely dream, a cruel taste of what she could never have?

She straightened her spine. If she was to deserve him, she must be the kind of woman that Trent Foerster and his beautiful daughter, Adeline, deserved.

One thing was certain, she would not return to the quiet, life-less situation she had held. She had not recognized how stagnant her existence had become until she stepped into this house, with its joyful laughter and energy. She wanted to be a part of it, to breathe in the excitement and dive back into the river of life. All families were not like hers. There was love and tenderness here. And she wanted to be a part of it all.

"Addy, your cocoa is ready," she called and heard the girl's footfalls on the stairs.

A moment later she appeared in the doorway, clutching her doll.

"Can Penelope have some, too?"

Eliza took another cup off the hook.

Chapter Twelve

"If this is the real Mrs. Guntherson, then who the hell is watching my daughter?"

"Now, Trent, don't do anything foolish," said Joey.

His panic turned to rage in just one single heartbeat. Now he understood his deputy's strange reaction on seeing the woman. It wasn't that he was taken by a fetching female—just the opposite, in fact. Trent grabbed his deputy by the throat.

"You knew about this."

Joey clutched at Trent's wrist and nodded. "Yes, but—"

Trent extended his arm and Joey fell hard to the sidewalk.

"You knew and you didn't tell me?" He whirled toward home, but Joey scrambled to his feet catching him by the arm.

"Listen, Trent."

He shook him off, worried he might shoot the man if he didn't get clear of him. But his deputy hung on, tenacious as a rattlesnake.

"You're fired, Joey. Clear up your stuff and be out of the office before I get back."

His deputy's face fell. "Fired?"

"Well, just what the hell did you think was going to happen?" With that, he took off toward home and his little girl.

A few moments later, Trent crashed through the front door, sending the wood panels ricocheting off the stopper and back at him. He catapulted through the now-closing door and registered a cry of alarm from the parlor. He changed directions, bolting into the room to find both his daughter and the imposter on their feet, staring wide-eyed in his direction. The imposter held a hand to her chest, a piece of chalk was wedged between her index and middle fingers.

Addy recovered first, jumping up and down, clutching a slate before her. She dashed across the room and into his waiting arms.

"Daddy! Look, I'm learning my letters!" From her perch upon his hip, she held up the slate for him to see, but he had eyes only for the woman.

He had carried his pounding heart in his throat all the way here, filled with a panic he had not known since Addy had the mumps. He held her tight and backed toward the door.

"What's happened?" asked the woman, as if she didn't know.

"Addy," he said, still not looking at his girl, but keeping his attention fixed on the possible threat. If she had harmed one hair on his daughter's head, he wouldn't be responsible. "Go to Mrs. Milward's house. Right now."

The woman set aside the chalk and her own slate.

"I'll get her coat."

He lifted a finger and aimed it at her. "Not you."

Her eyes rounded and the color drained from her flushed face. He'd been sheriff long enough to recognize the look of guilt that flashed in her features. She knew what was happening now. He would have liked to arrest her on the spot, but he didn't want to upset Addy. Damn her for using his little girl.

He backed toward the door. "I hope you run," he said through gritted teeth. "Because I sure would enjoy chasing you to ground."

She gasped.

"Daddy?" Addy's voice now rang with alarm. He knew tears were imminent. "What's happening?"

He had her out the door and down the steps and to his neighbor's threshold. He reached Kelly's door and pounded.

Kelly appeared a moment later, ushering them in. She gave him a once-over and her eyes flashed with alarm.

"What on earth?"

"My housekeeper just arrived. The real one. I have no idea who that woman over there is, but I'm going to find out."

Kelly Milward lifted Addy from her father's arms, sheltering her with her body.

"But she's…"

"Stay here." He wheeled and ran back the way he had come, hearing Addy crying his name. She was confused and frightened, but she was safe.

When he reached his home again he did not know what to expect, but certainly not to find the imposter sitting with her hands folded in her lap, in the very same chair where he had left her.

She stood as he stalked toward her, her body trembling.

Eliza stared up at Trent, knowing now without question what it must be like to be hunted by this man. No wonder the town hired him. His expression alone was so fierce it turned her knees to water.

The day she had feared had arrived. He knew of her lie, had somehow discovered it before she could explain. She knew that any confession now would ring hollow as a rotting log. She had been given opportunities aplenty and she had squandered each one.

All she could do now was lower her head to shield herself from the terrible rage that blazed in his eyes.

Hot tears scalded her cheeks.

"Don't you dare cry. Not after this."

She startled and stared. His eyes had narrowed to slits.

"Do you think I can't recognize crocodile tears? My God, I told you about Helen. And all the time you were lying to me. Was it all a lie then—everything?"

She could only shake her head.

He snorted. "As if I could believe anything you said. Damn it to hell! Why can't I tell when a woman is lying? Missionaries and a boarding school. Mercy, how you must have laughed at me. Made a fool of me—just like she did."

"They *are* missionaries," she whispered.

"Stop! No more." He loomed, sending her back a step. "You almost had me believing that things could be different."

He took three steps across the parlor, fury making him pace.

"You're the thief wanted in Butte, and I drove you out under their noses. I have your description on my desk." He glanced at her and resumed his pacing. "And here you are right under my own roof. That makes me the prize fool at the fair. Last place they'd look, isn't that right?"

She sat with her hands folded, head bowed, looking contrite and miserable. But she had all the acting skills of her gender. Born deceivers.

"How did you get Joey to help you?"

She lifted her tearstained cheeks, beautiful even in sorrow. But this time he did not allow her to see the twisting of his stomach or the squeezing pressure of his heart. He'd not let her know that she could affect him, even now.

"I wanted to tell you. I tried—"

"Not hard enough. You used me and you used Addy. I ought to handcuff you and drag you all the way back to Bozeman myself."

He stopped before her, the toe of his boot nearly touching the hem of her dress.

"Yes."

That stopped him. When faced with adversity, Helen always tried tears first. If that proved unsuccessful, she begged very prettily and when all else failed, she flew into a rage that would have made the Furies proud.

So why did this woman agree with him?

"What game is this?" he asked. Had he really thought of giving this woman the ring his father had bestowed on his mother? He must have been out of his mind.

She lifted her chin, facing him.

"No more games. Take me back. I want to go. It is what I tried to tell you this morning. I'm through running, done with hiding because of something I did not do."

His jaw dropped. If this was a trick it was a damn foolish one. Perhaps she expected him to drop his guard because she was a woman and because she appeared to be willing to go.

"I'm not buying it," he growled.

"Nor should you. You are justifiably wronged. But I am not a thief."

"That's not what the telegram says."

"Please listen."

"No. You're under arrest and will remain in your hotel room under guard until the sheriff from Bozeman can send someone for you, because I never want to see you again."

Chapter Thirteen

The dining-room table hadn't been used since Easter dinner. Trent's mother only used it for special occasions. All other family meals were served at the large kitchen table, which was closer to the stove. Now, on an ordinary Saturday night, the lace cloth draped the mahogany and the best china graced the table, except Addy's service. His daughter's plate was enamel and so was her cup.

Trent stood in the doorway, peering in. It seemed Mrs. Guntherson preferred to serve here. Trent had thought that last night she was just trying to make an impression, it being her first dinner and all. But now he feared this was to be a regular event, rather than an occasional ritual. He didn't like the dining room. It was cold, for one thing and the kitchen was more convenient to serve and…oh, damn it, he missed the other Mrs. Guntherson.

He might as well admit it.

Dinner was served the instant Trent finished washing up. He took his place, waiting while Mrs. Guntherson said grace in German. Then he poked at his stroganoff. The sauce was creamy and smooth, the noodles thick and yellow as the yoke of an egg. In fact, they were perfect in every way, and still he found himself wondering what disaster the other Mrs. Guntherson might have served him this evening.

He glanced at Addy's untouched meal. She stared at him, steely-eyed as any outlaw. He pointed his fork at her.

"Eat."

She lifted her own fork high, beside her ear and then threw it with all her might.

"Adeline Foerster!" he said, disguising none of his disapproval.

She sprang to her feet. "You made her go away! You 'rested her and made her go." His daughter pointed an accusing index finger at him. "You…you meanie!"

Addy fled in tears, charging up the stairs in a clumsy retreat.

Trent stood, laid his napkin beside his plate and faced the rosy-cheeked housekeeper, who was in every way what he had once believed he wanted. She was an experienced cook, an older woman familiar with raising children. Here was the replacement he had hired for that which could not be replaced. How could he have been so stupid?

You didn't get to choose who you loved, you didn't get to interview who you would let into your heart. Such decisions were not wise or practical or clean. They were messy.

Mrs. Guntherson began to clear the untouched meal.

Her German accent turned all *W*s into *V*s. "Perhaps you will have an appetite later on. It will keep, you know."

Trent nodded. "Thank you."

"Don't be silly. I'm just doing my job."

Trent blinked at her retreating back. Yes, her job. But Eliza Flannery had been doing much more than a job, hadn't she? Or was she just a consummate actress like Helen?

Why had she done it?

He didn't know, because he had not even given her time to explain. He'd been so angry and so full of self-righteous fury, he'd not allowed her to speak.

"You're a horse's ass," he muttered.

"What's that now?" asked his housekeeper, already banging and rattling around in the kitchen.

"Nothing."

He climbed the stairs, his feet leaden, and paused before his daughter's closed door. He knocked.

"Go away!"

He opened the door anyway, crossed the room and sat on the bed beside Addy, who had curled in a ball around Penelope. She didn't move away when he laid a hand on her shoulder.

"She wasn't really Mrs. Guntherson," he said, trying what he knew would not work on a child. Addy didn't want logic or reason. She wanted the woman she loved.

Addy rolled toward him and sat up. Her tears cut him like tiny flakes of glass.

"I don't care. I want her to stay and be my mother."

That shocked him speechless for a moment.

"But…but Addy, she told us lies."

"Only her name."

"No, she pretended to be someone she isn't."

"But why?"

He shook his head. "I don't know."

"Don't you love her, Daddy?"

His throat grew tight. He nodded and managed to growl, "Yes."

"Then don't let her go away. Bring her back, Daddy."

He didn't know why he allowed himself to say the next part, but he did.

"But Addy, what if she was just pretending to like us?"

His daughter clasped his hands and stared earnestly up at him. "She wasn't, Daddy. She loves us both. I know it in my heart."

His next words came out as a whisper. "How?"

"Penelope told me."

He managed a smile as he laid a hand on his daughter's head. "All right then. I'll try to bring her back." Or at least, try to learn the truth.

He tucked Addy into bed and read to her until she was sleeping. Then he told Mrs. Guntherson he was going out. He paused on the porch to stare at the Christmas tree that they had cut together. It lay on its side where it would wait until Christmas Eve, when Mrs. Guntherson would decorate it.

Trent dreaded Christmas already. It just wouldn't feel right without his mother and…

And it wouldn't feel right without Eliza.

He ran down the steps and into the snow.

Trent headed over to the hotel where Eliza Flannery, if that was her real name, was under guard by his new deputy.

Trent reached the second floor where his pace faltered as he took in the sight of Paul Landry sound asleep in his chair. He walked right by Landry, who sat propped against the wall beside Eliza Flannery's door. Joey would never have been so careless, but he'd fired him and in his place was a man who obviously liked his sleep more than his job.

He paused, trying to decide if he should kick the chair out and then it occurred to him that their prisoner might have fled.

Trent threw open the door. Eliza, dressed in a white cotton night rail, sprang to her feet, clutching a hairbrush in one hand. She held the other over her heart.

He'd never seen her hair down before. It flowed in dark ribbons over her shoulders, reaching all the way to her elbows.

Trent stepped into the room, mesmerized by the way the oil lamp on the bureau shone through the thin fabric, revealing her tempting shape.

Eliza snatched up her robe and slipped her arms through the sleeves.

"Is your deputy still asleep?" she asked.

That stopped him. "You knew?"

She nodded.

"How?"

Her smile did not reach the sorrow shimmering in her blue eyes.

"He has a sonorous snore. I went out to check on him and he didn't wake."

"Then why are you still here?"

The smile dropped away. "I told you. I want to go back and settle this."

Trent studied her features as she stared him straight in the eye, giving not the slightest indication that she lied. Even Helen looked away at such times. But not Eliza. Either she was a pro or she was innocent, and damned if he knew which.

"You want to go back and face justice?"

She lifted her chin and then nodded. She looked like a brave little soldier about to face battle for the first time. She trembled, but she did not run.

"Why didn't you do that right off?"

"I should have. But I didn't have a reason to fight then."

What did that mean? Was she talking about them? His heart ached in his chest. Just seeing her brought it all back, the hope and then the crushing disillusionment.

He took in her expression, the hope reflected in her eyes and the stiff uncertainty of her clenched jaw. She'd let him down, that was certain, but wasn't he now doing the same to her?

It occurred to him only then, that she had not one soul in the world that she could turn to for help and not one person in her corner, until now. He owed her that much, didn't he?

"Telegram says you're a thief."

"I'm not."

He nodded. "I believe you."

She gasped. "You…you what?"

He held out his hand.

"I believe you, Eliza. So why don't you tell me what really happened back there in Bozeman."

Although Eliza had told him all she knew, Trent sensed there was more to the story. He believed she withheld nothing, but all the pieces just didn't fit. His instincts had always served him well, so he didn't discount his hunch.

Eliza didn't do it. He knew that in his heart. So all he had to do now was prove who did.

Trent hugged his daughter and promised her he'd be home by Christmas Eve. Mrs. Guntherson, the real Mrs. Guntherson, took charge of Addy. Now that his girl didn't see the older woman as a threat to Eliza, she had warmed up to her nicely.

"I'll have the tree all decorated by the time you get back." Her heavy accent changed *the* into *zee*.

"I'll help!" cried Addy.

Mrs. Guntherson shook her head. "No. Children don't help. That's sure."

Trent smiled. It was exactly what his mother would have said. Addy would not see the tree until the grand moment when the doors to the parlor slid back to reveal the *tannenbaum* alive with a hundred white candles ablaze. Trent wondered, if next year, Eliza might perform the duty for them. His heart swelled with hope, but he pushed it back.

No woolgathering; he had work to do.

Addy hid her disappointment well as she kissed Eliza and clutched her dad about his neck, whispering in his ear.

"You'll find out who's telling big lies about Miss Flannery?" she asked.

"Yes, kitten. I sure will."

Trent had sent Joey to the telegraph office to send word to the sheriff of Bozeman to expect them. If all went well they'd be there by supper. The railroads certainly were a wonder.

He waved goodbye, lifted the reins and gave them a snap. They were off. The ride to Butte was smooth and clear. If it hadn't been for the threat looming over them, he might have enjoyed having Eliza snuggled up close to him beneath the blanket.

At the station, Trent paid for their tickets and a one-way passage from Bozeman to Butte then handed both to Eliza.

"Now if you see that same conductor, you show them the one you 'misplaced.'"

She leaned forward and kissed him on the cheek. His face heated. Trent offered his arm and led Eliza to the platform. The arriving train was something to see, with smoke streaming from the engine and steam from the wheel brakes blasting across the platform like a horizontal geyser.

Once aboard, Trent asked Eliza to tell him her story again. When she'd finished he asked his question.

"How did the cook know to pack your bag?"

"She was trying to be sure I wasn't arrested."

"And she was the one who told you about the last companion's arrest."

She nodded. "Yes. It frightened me half to death. They didn't believe a word of her denial. And how, may I ask you, is it possible to prove you *did not* do something?"

He nodded, gazing out the window. "How indeed?"

Trent assisted Eliza from the sled. He did not let her go as he escorted her into the city offices of Bozeman, and if he noted her trembling he did not mention it. Sheriff Jethro Carlson stood as they entered. At first he looked like a moving mountain with broad shoulders and a considerable paunch. However, when he came out from behind his desk, his spindly legs made him look like a large potato on stilts. He shook Trent's hand and then briefly clasped hers.

"I thank you both for coming in. I've got a murder trial, starts day after Christmas, so I'll say up front this case isn't my first concern." He motioned them to a pair of spindle-backed chairs beside his desk. "Mind the splinters. One of my prisoners gouged the seat with the shackles and I haven't had it sanded out yet."

Eliza froze a moment, then sank gingerly into the chair. She found it a struggle not to shift beneath his stare.

He focused his watery eyes on her. "So I'm wondering why you'd run instead of coming in right off?"

Eliza's chin sank to her chest and all the air left her lungs. When she had drawn another breath she spoke, but kept her eyes firmly pinned on her folded hands. "I was afraid of being thrown in jail."

"Innocent people don't think that way."

"Yet it happened to my predecessor, Miss Gram. Her innocence did not help her so why should I believe I would find justice here?"

"That was her choice. She could have disputed the charge. But leastwise, she didn't run."

"No, because you sent her to prison."

"Prison? What the Sam Hill do you mean? She scttled."

"Settle?" Eliza parroted. "Is that what you call being led away in shackles? Flora told me all about it."

Trent lifted a hand to stop her.

"Gram wasn't convicted?" asked Trent.

Eliza freed her skirt from the chair and leaned forward to hear the sheriff's reply.

Carlson lifted a pencil from his drawer and used the point to scratch behind his left ear. "Miss Gram said she didn't do it, but we found the money in her room so she agreed to make reparations."

"Hard to prove you didn't do something," said Trent, his gaze on Eliza.

"'Specially when you're holding the goods. Trouble is the thefts didn't stop."

"You catch the real culprit?"

"Not exactly. But I'm getting damned tired... Oh, excuse me, ma'am. I'm getting *real* tired of dragging my...self out to Mrs. Holloway's house every time she misplaces a hair comb."

"Anything go missing since Miss Flannery's flight?"

She wished heartily that Trent had said disappearance or absence. He made her seem more fugitive than ever.

"Yes. First she misplaced some fancy jewelry case. We found it *inside* the piano. The money she reported stolen was tucked inside a Bible, some of it anyways. As for the jewelry, it hasn't turned up yet. Neither have the silver grapefruit spoons. And who, in the name of our Lord, needs a special spoon just for grapefruits?"

"What's your opinion?" asked Trent.

He shrugged. "I called her son. The old girl is getting up there. Maybe forgetful is all. It happens."

Eliza stiffened. "She is not."

Both men turned to her, staring. She felt herself shrinking into her seat. Sliding back caused the fabric of her skirt to snag on the rough wood.

"Go on," coaxed Trent.

"Her memory is flawless. She's completely coherent and exceedingly bright. And she's far more organized than I am."

Mr. Carlson raised a bushy brow. "Then why would she need a companion?"

"For companionship, obviously. Also she can no longer perform some personal tasks because of her eyesight. But she is not, by any stretch of the imagination, losing her faculties."

Sheriff Carlson smiled. "Just agreeing would have had you off the hook."

"But it's not true."

The men exchanged a look.

Carlson spoke to Trent. "I see why you came in." Now he turned to Eliza. "How do you explain the recovered items?"

"I can't. But I know it was not Mrs. Holloway's doing."

"The son here yet?" asked Trent.

Carlson nodded. "For several days."

"Anything go missing?"

"All the butter knives, but he found them in his mother's knitting bag."

Trent nodded. "She was set up."

Carlson's mouth tipped down at the corners. "Beginning to think so myself. You got a suspect?"

"Yeah, I sure do," said Trent.

Eliza returned to the office with the sheriff's deputy to find Trent waiting.

"Well?" he asked.

Eliza opened her reticule. "Just as you suspected, the bills were removed from my purse and, when caught, Flora claimed the money was her life's savings."

"What did she say when they showed her that the bills were marked?"

"I don't know. I was shown out when she began to weep. I hate to see her so wretched," said Eliza.

"She tried to pin this all on you."

Eliza nodded. "Yes. The deputy who drove me back led me to believe she has a gambling problem. But I heard her say that she's building a fence with Mr. Jaffe, the owner of the Golden Spike."

Trent chuckled. "That he *was* her fence?"

"That might be it."

The deputy poked his head back inside, meeting Trent's eyes. "Sheriff said to get you two to the train. She's free to go. Sheriff Carlson said thanks."

Eliza breathed deep, the air somehow suddenly sweeter.

Trent escorted Eliza out and into the carriage that would take them to the train. Once underway, Eliza turned to him.

"How did you know?" she asked.

"She tried a little too hard to get you to run, even packed for you, everything but your money. And she lied about Miss Gram. Then there was the problem of things going missing and later turning up, but they never *all* turned up, only the things that were easy to trace or of no value."

Eliza smiled. "You're so clever. I could kiss you."

"What's stopping you?"

She glanced at the deputy who sat before them and lowered her voice.

"Absolutely nothing, Mr. Foerster."

And with that she slipped into his arms and kissed him on the lips.

Epilogue

Trent waited with Addy and Joey Backer in the hallway outside the closed parlor door. The air was heavy with the wonderful fragrance of roasting ham, potatoes, onions and the cinnamon that had recently been ground over the waiting eggnog resting in his mother's large punch bowl on the dining-room table.

Mrs. Guntherson was a wizard in the kitchen. With Eliza acting as assistant she had created a Christmas Eve feast that would long be remembered.

Since Trent had made amends with his old deputy, Joey had been a regular at his table, taking his dinner with them rather than at the hotel. What Trent couldn't figure was whether he was taken with his housekeeper's cooking or his housekeeper.

"You courting my cook?" he asked.

"That's a fact," said Joey. "Besides, the way you're sparking Miss Flannery, don't figure you'll be needing two women in your house for long." Joey glanced at Addy, who was so excited she jumped up and down before the closed door. "Though you might have need of a cook for a spell."

Trent thought of the cinnamon buns and winced. Eliza cooked little and badly. But she was a real fast study and picked up everything Mrs. Guntherson taught her. Once Mrs. Guntherson had learned that Eliza's own mother took little interest in her, she had taken her under her ample wing.

Eliza had mastered rolling a piecrust in one piece. It was a start.

Trent tried to give Joey a stern look. "You best treat her proper."

He'd never thought the old bachelor was much interested in women. But three days ago he had never seen Joey pull a chair out for a lady or wash a dish. Now he regularly did both.

"Trent, I swear, I'm taken. She's fetching, isn't she? Such pretty eyes and a perfect figure."

"You decide this before or after you tasted her apple strudel?"

"After, but it didn't sway me. She's got a warm heart. Woman like that, well, she deserves someone to look after her."

"Joey, you talking about…"

He nodded solemnly. "Yes, if she'll have me, I am. And if you're smart you'll get a ring round Eliza's finger right quick. All that spouting about you not being the marrying kind, it's hogwash. That little girl needs a mama and you sure couldn't do better than Miss Flannery. Why if I was a little younger—"

Trent raised his hands in submission. "All right, all right."

Joey stilled. "You asked her?"

"Not yet. But I can't think of a better night than tonight."

Joey rubbed his hands together in anticipation. "When? Can I watch ya?"

"Later, and no, you can't. In fact, I want you out of the parlor just as soon as Mrs. Guntherson calls us to the table."

"That I sure can do. Shall I bring Addy?"

"Yes." Trent knelt before Addy. "Remember to go when Mrs. Guntherson leaves."

Addy quieted and nodded solemnly. The doors slid open. Addy stilled.

"Oooh!" she whispered.

Beyond her, the room was dark except for the golden light pouring from their tree. Mrs. Guntherson stood by the open pocket doors, pressing her back to one to allow them to see beyond her to the evergreen.

Addy rushed past and stood still as stone, staring. Trent found Eliza, smiling proudly beside their first Christmas tree together. He prayed they would have many more. He pictured the room filled with their children all here before them.

Addy found her gift from him hanging on the tree, a doll with a china head, hands and feet from her father. She hugged it to her chest, while still gripping Penelope. Then she ran toward him. He squatted so she could throw her arms about his neck.

"Thank you, Daddy!"

"You be sure Penelope doesn't get jealous."

"Oh, no. Penelope loves her, too."

Addy found Mrs. Guntherson's addition to the tree—packets of sugared nuts, hung in paper cones, and she gave one to each adult. Joe had added a fat bundle of licorice and it hung awkwardly on a low branch. Addy gave him a kiss in exchange.

Eliza pointed out her gift, hanging from a red hair ribbon.

Addy bounced with joy. "Your thimble! The one your mother gave you."

"Not mine anymore because I want you to have it."

Addy hugged Eliza, and Trent had to blink to keep the image from going blurry on him.

Mrs. Guntherson waited for Addy to place her thimble on her finger and then bustled the child out. Eliza tried to follow them, but Trent caught her hand. Joey glanced at Trent. He must have just then recalled Trent's earlier directions, for he sprang to his feet, dashing out as if his britches were ablaze.

Eliza stared after him with a puzzled expression on her face. "Whatever is the matter with Mr. Backer?"

Trent ignored the question as he drew Eliza toward the tree. "You did a fine job."

Eliza's face glowed pale in the candlelight and he thought he'd never seen a more lovely sight.

Trent cleared his throat, his fine speech suddenly forgotten as she turned to face him. He clasped her other hand and swallowed hard. He knew she was the right one, knew he loved her and that his daughter loved her. What he didn't know was if she'd take him. After all, he'd had some harsh words for her and she'd seen him at his worst. She'd said she forgave him, but…

She glanced toward the hall. "Trent? I need to help serve the meal."

"I'd like you to stay."

"All right." She waited.

"I mean, I want you to stay here with me and with Addy."

Eliza brightened, but then her smile faded. "You needn't worry. Mrs. Holloway has offered me my old position back."

Trent felt suddenly ill.

"Do you want to go back there?"

"No, but you already have a housekeeper."

"That's true. But I don't have a wife."

She stilled, her voice now breathless. "What?"

He turned to the tree, locating the heart-shaped leather box hanging at eye level. He slipped his index finger through the red satin ribbon of this very special ornament and offered it to her.

"This one is for you." He flipped open the lid, revealing the red garnet encircled with small sparkling diamonds. He sank to his knee. "My father gave this ring to my mother. She asked me to give it to my bride."

When she didn't speak, he removed the ring from its nest and held it out to her.

"I love you, Eliza. Will you be my wife?"

A little line formed between her brows. "I can't. Not unless…"

He stood, his heart hammering so loudly he could barely hear her. "Unless?"

"Well, Mr. Foerster, I do have strong feelings for you, and I would like nothing better than to share my life with you and Adeline. But I'd want to be certain that Addy is agreeable."

Trent's smile returned, relief and happiness filled him. "I have already broached the subject. She's over the moon about the possibility."

Eliza drew a sharp breath. "Truly?"

He nodded.

"Then, Mr. Foerster, I will wed you and be your wife."

He slipped the ring upon her finger knowing that this was a promise she would keep and a vow he would honor. This woman was loyal and loving. He did not know what he ever did to deserve her, but he'd spend the rest of his life making certain she didn't regret her decision.

He caught movement from the door and glanced up to see Addy peeking around the edge.

"Did she take the ring, Daddy?"

Eliza held up her left hand to show his daughter. He could feel her holding her breath. He squeezed her other hand in reassurance as Addy's shriek split the air.

His daughter ran across the room and jumped. Somehow Eliza caught her, taking only one bracing step back. Addy captured Trent about the neck, as well, pulling him in until all three of their foreheads were touching.

"I got what I prayed for," said Addy. "I asked the baby Jesus to make us a family and he did!"

Trent's throat constricted. Life had truly blessed him with a lovely bride and wonderful daughter. What more could a man ask for?

Mrs. Guntherson spoke from the hallway. "Dinner is ready."

Trent lowered Addy to the floor, took Eliza's hand and followed his daughter, who had already cleared the hallway. Eliza hesitated and he paused to give her a quizzical stare. She glanced upward and he followed the direction of her gaze, finding them standing squarely beneath a sprig of mistletoe.

* * * * *

WEARING THE RANCHER'S RING

Charlene Sands

Dear Reader,

After I wrote *Bodine's Bounty,* two female characters' futures were left to our imagination and I wasn't entirely sure if there was a story for either of them. Never leave a character's fate to a blank page is my motto. So, Theresa Metcalf's journey popped into my head and shortly after, I wrote *Taming the Texan.*

That left widow Rachel Bodine, the heroine of this story, "Wearing the Rancher's Ring," without love in her life on her small ranch in Northern California. Certainly she and her adorable toddler son, Johnny, needed a happy ending, too. After all, this is the season of giving.

But happy endings are not in Cooper Garnett's future. Found shot in cold blood on Rachel's property, Cooper isn't about to reveal his secrets to his new lady boss. He's on a dangerous mission and not even the pretty young widow nursing him back to health can talk him out of it. He doesn't deserve her love or the warmth of her home during the Christmas holiday.

I hope you enjoy this heartfelt holiday story about redemption and second chances. What better time for both than the Christmas season?

May your holidays be merry!

Charlene

*This story is dedicated to Charles Griemsman,
my new fantastic editor at Harlequin Books.
Thank you for your insights, support and all that you do.
It's truly a pleasure working with you!*

Chapter One

Cedar Flat, California, 1883

Early December snowdrifts sent a powerful chill clear through Rachel Bodine's body, despite her heavy winter coat and fur-lined boots. After checking on her livestock and closing the barn door, she scooted across the Double J yard just as Jess, her cook, and Mikey Ray, her youngest ranch hand, came barreling up the road in the wagon.

"Miss Rachel! Miss Rachel!" Mikey Ray's usual smile was gone; he waved his arms high in the air to catch her attention. "We found an injured man up on the south pasture," he shouted from the wagon.

Rachel's heart pounded seeing a man's body lying across her buckboard covered in a woolen blanket. Her mind flashed to her husband, Josh, coming home to her this way more than a year ago. Only Josh's injuries had been fatal. He'd come home to her, dead.

She squeezed those haunting memories away with a quick blink of the eye and focused on the wagon. She couldn't make out who the man was; his face was covered in a shabby beard and felt hat. Jess reined the two mares in and brought the wagon to a halt just steps from her front porch. "He's in a bad way, missy," Jess said. "Looks like he's been shot and robbed. He was on foot, his horse probably stolen, too. Figured he'd freeze to death out there."

Rachel gazed into the wagon. "Who is he?"

"Don't know."

"Okay, let's see to him. Bring him into the house."

"The house, missy?" Jess asked, his bushy brows gathering like a storm. "You don't rightly know him."

"I know one thing, Jess. He'll freeze to death out in the bunkhouse. He's likely frostbitten. He needs warming up real fast."

"But you alone with little Johnny, and this stranger?"

"I'm not alone, Jess. I've got Josh's Peacemaker and his Winchester and you've seen me use 'em. Now, bring the man inside. I'll build up the fire in the hearth. We'll put him into Johnny's room for now. Take off his wet clothes and wrap him in a dry blanket on the bed. Johnny fell asleep in the main room near the hearth so be as quiet as you can manage."

Rachel went inside, tiptoeing past her sleeping little boy as he lay on a bundle of quilts, and added logs to the fire. Her ranch hands moved the man inside her house and laid him on Johnny's bed, the room partitioned from the main room by a curtain. She heard the injured man groan in pain. Quickly, she began heating water on the cookstove to cleanse his wound. She made as little noise as possible, hoping Johnny wouldn't wake.

Once Mikey Ray and Jess had the stranger situated, they walked out of the bedroom. Jess had a scowl on his face—he'd been with her for years and since Josh's murder he'd been overly protective.

"I don't know about this, missy."

"Jess, do me a favor." She took his arm and walked him to the door. "Cook up something good for the boys tonight, something to warm them on such a chilly night."

"I'll do just that and I'll be bringing you a portion of supper when I'm through."

Rachel cast him a smile. "You mean you'll be checking up on Johnny and me."

He scratched his jaw. "That, too. I can ride into town to get the doctor."

"You will, but wait until dawn. The weather's real bad right now and I don't need to worry over you tramping six miles through the night to fetch the doctor. I know how to help this man," she assured him. Jess was getting up in age and was too stubborn to let anyone else go for help. Tomorrow, Rachel decided would be soon enough. Being a doctor's daughter, Rachel had learned early on how to tend an injury.

She saw the men to the door and then turned her attention to the stranger out cold on her son's bed. She sent up a silent prayer to her father and all his wisdom to give her the guidance she needed.

Rachel walked into the bedroom with a bowl of warm water and a bar of lye soap ready to cleanse and dress a wound. She looked at the man's unshaven face and longish hair and couldn't quite make out his features. His eyes were closed. She always could tell a man's intent in the quality of his eyes.

Rachel sat down on the bed, careful not to disturb him too much, and peeled back the woolen blanket to take a look at the bullet wound. The injury was on the right shoulder and the blood had congealed from the frost. A good thing or he might have bled to death. Rachel was thankful once again when she noted the exit wound in his back. The bullet had slashed straight through and she wouldn't have a need to go digging.

"You'll be on the mend soon," Rachel said quietly as she swabbed at his shoulder. She was fully aware of the man's state of undress, but she'd seen a man naked before many times and wasn't a wilting willow about it.

This man was powerful and capable, she presumed, noting the breadth of his shoulders and the length of his body. A bandit had robbed him and left him to die out in the bitter cold. She could only look upon him as a victim for now, but she'd put Johnny to bed in her room and bolt the door at night. Rachel had learned the hard way that a widow had to keep from falling victim herself, and the best way to do that was to always be on guard.

After she cleansed the wound thoroughly, she wrapped his shoulder in bandages, and then covered his frigid body with more blankets and a quilt. She rubbed his body over and over, up and down, watching for signs of improvement and hoping for some color to come to his face.

He didn't stir, but for involuntary groans and moans of pain. Rachel had grown up hearing those sounds. She left the man with no name to check on Johnny a few times. When her son woke up, she fed him from the meal Jess had delivered to her, giving him bits of carrot and potato and spicy stew.

Johnny made the sweetest, sour face when he chewed on the stew, but he ate it. He had a hearty appetite, just like his father in that regard.

After checking on her unconscious patient, Rachel bedded down with Johnny in her own room. She bolted the door shut, not that she'd feared the stranger at this juncture. The man was too weak to wake, much less move.

She napped in intervals and stoked the fire, keeping the house extremely warm and worked on her patient several times through the night with a technique her father had taught her, trying to circulate the blood. When her arms couldn't take the struggle any longer, she retired to her bedroom for the rest of the night.

There wasn't anything more she could do for the stranger.

Cooper Garnett slid his eyes open slowly, the lids weighted like bricks of clay. Through the narrow slits, a young boy appeared before him, and Cooper searched his addled brain, coming up with one conclusion. He'd died and gone to his maker and the Good Lord saw fit to reunite him with his son, Donny.

A female voice, soft as a summer breeze, cautioned the boy, and Cooper lifted his lids to find a woman standing over him, her arm on her toddler son. "He needs rest," she said to the boy.

A measure of happiness entered his heart as the blurry visions filled him with relief. He *had* to be in Heaven, joining his family and putting him out of his misery. Jocelyn was here and so was his little son. It was too much to hope they hadn't died in the fire that claimed their lives. It was too much to hope they hadn't been robbed and left for dead in a burning house.

Cooper groaned, not from the pain shooting through his shoulder, but from memories that haunted him each day. He'd been too late to save them. He'd missed the murdering bastard by only minutes. He'd ridden in and witnessed hot flames sear through beams that fortified his house. Panicked and spurred on with dreaded fear, he'd bounded from his horse and ran inside, soot and smoke scorching his eyes. A falling post knocked him out and branded his back. A sole ranch hand coming back early from the range had rushed in and pulled him free before the fire claimed him. How often he wished it had.

But now he was with Jocelyn and Donny again. Somehow, someway, they were here with him and tranquility surrounded them. Since that fateful day he'd never known more peace.

"Come on, Johnny," the woman said, taking the boy's hand. "Let the man sleep."

Johnny? Not Donny? Had he heard right?

Cooper's eyes widened. His mind cleared from wishful sentiments. He focused hard and noted the boy's blond locks, the woman's hair of the same hue. As she moved to brush by him, he grabbed her arm, the sudden movement making him wince. He strained to make out her features. "Who are you?"

"I'm Rachel."

Her voice was soft, but wary, and he recognized it now. She'd nursed him from his wound. She'd been the one taking care of him. Not Jocelyn.

Heartbreaking pain welled up inside, the disappointment hollowing out his gut and shredding it to pieces. His body sagged and he released her arm. "You took me in."

"My ranch hands found you shot and left for dead on my land. Yes, I took you in. I've been tending to your wound."

"The boy?" he asked, glancing now at a youngster that only resembled his Donny by size.

She set a proprietary hand on his shoulder and her eyes glowed with pride. "This is my son, Johnny Bodine."

Cooper glanced away then closed his eyes. He couldn't bear to look at the woman with her child, not when his immediate wishful hopes had been dashed. How fresh the heartache was still. The rawness of it burned clear through him.

"What's your name?" she asked softly.

"Cooper Garnett," he whispered.

"Do you know who shot you, Mr. Garnett?"

He focused on her concerned eyes. Pretty eyes, he noted grudgingly. Why didn't she let him die? "Someone who wanted my horse and belongings, I suppose."

She lifted her boy into her arms, and he immediately clung to her neck, laying his head under her chin. The loving image was reminiscent of Donny and Jocelyn, and Cooper remembered what he aimed to do and why he should be grateful this woman saved him. He couldn't die, not until he claimed justice for his wife's and boy's deaths. "Where's Mr. Bodine?" he asked.

"I'm a widow," she whispered, as if the pain of that truth still hurt. "How's your shoulder feeling?"

"Like it saw the front end of a stampede."

"It's healing up nicely. You're strong."

Cooper touched the spot where the bullet went through, bandaged now. He recalled the sharp shot slicing through him, catching him by surprise and jerking him from his horse. "You know doctoring?"

"My father was a doctor. I know enough. Doctor Reynolds was out here yesterday and checked on you. He said you'd make a full recovery."

"You likely saved my life."

"I probably did," she said in earnest. "Good thing the boys found you when they did or you might have frozen to death. You've been unconscious for two days."

"Son of a bit—" Cooper held up his oath and squeezed his eyes shut briefly. He was damn tired of losing time.

"You need more rest," she said, ignoring his outburst. "You had fever during the night. I'll bring you some broth shortly."

His nod was slight and pained him some. "Appreciate it."

He watched Rachel leave with her boy and then closed his eyes. He'd been tracking the man called Brett Hollings all the way from Nevada. He'd lost time right after the fire to heal up from injuries to his scorched back. It had taken a full month to recover and get his mind in the right place. No man should have to witness his family's demise. No man.

The only clue he'd had was that the ranch hand that'd saved him saw the robber fleeing the fiery scene, hanging on to the strongbox that held the Garnett payroll. He'd caught fire to the left side of his body and by all accounts, his face suffered burns that would be recognizable. He couldn't figure out if the man deliberately torched the house, or if it'd been an accident during the commission of the crime, but the fact remained that Jocelyn and little Donny had died in that fire.

It had taken Cooper three months to find out the man's name and another two to track him to the Cedar Flat area. His instincts told him it hadn't been Hollings who'd shot him. Cooper had been careful not to arouse suspicion. Brett Hollings didn't know he was being tracked, and Cooper would make damn sure it stayed that way. Which meant that Hollings would still be in the environs.

Cooper meant to kill him.

Or die trying.

Rachel ladled broth with bits of beef and potato into a bowl and set it on a tray along with a biscuit. She pulled the curtain back and entered Johnny's room. Cooper Garnett took one look at her and tried to sit up higher in the bed. His rugged face twisted in pain and he let go a vivid curse.

His impatience reminded her of Josh. Her husband was forever moving faster than his feet could take him. "Hold on, Mr. Garnett. I'll help you sit up."

She set the tray on a side table and reached around Cooper's body, under his arms. "Hold on to me," she said, "and let me do the work. Whatever you do, don't struggle with your bad shoulder."

He pierced her with a look, his eyes dark, his brows elevated. Heat crept up her neck. It'd been a long time since she'd been this close to a man. Even though his beard covered most of his face, she could tell Cooper Garnett was a handsome devil.

He took hold of her around the waist, his fingers splayed over her hips. She couldn't think about how good it felt having him touch her. She'd seen him naked from the waist up and knew he was sturdy and powerful. Her blouse brushed his skin and the tips of her breasts skimmed over his chest. "Now wiggle up slowly as I lift you."

Cooper did as he was told, his gaze never leaving hers as he scooted up with her aid. Her heart fluttered, and she turned away from him before he could see her blushing cheeks.

"There, that does it," she said, reaching for the tray. She set it on his lap and continued to avert her gaze. "I imagine you can feed yourself, but if you need me—"

"Rachel."

"What?" She met his eyes.

"I can feed myself."

She cast him half a smile and nodded.

"I'll need my pants."

"Why?" She hadn't expected that. Why would he need his pants in order to eat? He wouldn't be able to put them on unassisted and she wasn't ready to help him. Not yet anyway. It was all she could do to stop from turning red as a tomato from lifting him up. For all her blustering about being a doctor's daughter, she realized she'd never tended a man like Cooper Garnett before. Not without her father's presence and assistance.

A grin slowly spread across his face. "Why do I need my pants? Can't very well get up when nature calls without them now, can I?"

Rachel pictured him in his undergarments and nothing else, the image so profound, she couldn't meet his eyes. Instantly, she admonished herself for being such a foolish ninny. "I'll get them for you once they've dried. I washed them out this morning along with your shirt. They were covered in blood."

"I see."

"Besides, I doubt you can put them on without reinjuring your shoulder. You'll need help."

One brow arched up as he assessed her. With a hard gleam, his eyes roamed from her blond hair to her shoulders and lower to her breasts, his gaze lingering just enough to bring more heat to her face before he met her eyes again. "I'd best be putting my own trousers on."

She swallowed.

With his right hand, he lifted the spoon and dug into the broth. She watched him take a few spoonfuls without much fuss. "'Course, if I run into a problem with the clothes, I'll give you a holler, you knowing about doctoring and all."

Rachel's eyes went wide and a protest was hot on her lips until she noted a quick smile emerge from under Cooper's beard.

She whipped around and her gown brushed the edge of the bed as she made her way out, closing the curtains with a swipe of her hand.

She marched into the main room and put a hand to her chest. "Heavens," she whispered as an unexpected tremble coursed the length of her. Why was the sight of Cooper Garnett and the deep timbre of his voice so, so…appealing? With only youngsters like

Mikey Ray and her dear old friend Jess around the ranch, had Rachel forgotten the heat of a real man's gaze? Had she forgotten what it felt like to be touched intimately? Josh had been gone a year and a half now and how she missed him, but she was still young and her mourning time was over. She couldn't abide the loneliness much longer. The winters were fiercely cold and lonely without a husband beside her.

"Maybe I should take Robert Livingston up on his offer for a buggy ride after church," she murmured as she set Cooper's clothes closer to the fire. Robert didn't spark any longing in her, but he was steady and gentlemanly and held a good job at the bank. He was forever asking her to picnic with him. Maybe it was time she thought about it.

"Here he is, Miss Rachel," Mikey Ray said, appearing in the doorway with Johnny. "We had us a good time in the bunkhouse with the boys, didn't we, Johnny?"

Johnny bobbed his head up and down and ran to Rachel, clinging to her skirts. She patted his head and smiled into her son's big loving eyes. "Did you mind Jess and Mikey Ray?"

"I minded, Mama," her boy said. At a little over eighteen months old, Johnny was especially bright and talkative for his age. On cold nights, Rachel would sit down with him before the fire and read to him. He loved to listen, to mimic words and before she knew it, he was making short sentences on his own. As smart as he was, he was also adventurous for a little one, and Rachel was forever trying to keep up with his antics.

She often asked Jess or Mikey Ray to watch him for an hour or two whenever they could spare the time to give her son some male companionship. As a result, both the men had come to love Johnny as much as Johnny loved them.

"How's the stranger doing?" Mikey Ray asked, standing in the doorway, taking a quick glance at the curtain.

"Come in outta the cold and have a warm biscuit and I'll tell you so you can go back to report to Jess." Rachel grinned, catching him, but Mikey Ray just shrugged it off. He never minded doing Jess's biding. The two fought like cats and dogs at times, but they also cared about each other like father and son.

Aside from one recent incident with a hired hand, Rachel

considered herself fortunate in having a small but dedicated bunch of ranch hands.

She buttered a biscuit and handed it to him. "The stranger's name is Cooper Garnett and he doesn't know who shot him. They robbed him of all his possessions and stole his horse. He came to, just a while ago. That's all I know right now."

Mikey Ray dug into the biscuit and with a nod, he spoke with a full mouth. "I'll tell Jess." He swallowed then took another bite and waited this time to speak once he'd finished the biscuit. "Mighty good, Miss Rachel."

"I'll send a batch to the bunkhouse." Rachel set a dozen more biscuits into a basket and covered it with a checkered cloth. She had three other boys, the same age as Mikey Ray working for her that made up the whole of the Double J outfit. She was shorthanded and couldn't afford to keep up with the bigger, more prosperous ranches in the area who paid their men better.

"Here you go." She handed the basket to him. "And be sure to share those biscuits."

"I will. Thank you." Mikey Ray strode to the front door, then stopped and turned. "Do you feel safe in here, now that the stranger's awake?"

Rachel took a deep breath, remembering another time when she'd had to fend off the lurid advances of her foreman. Seemed that some men thought that *widow* meant *willing*. She'd never put herself in that position again. "I'm not in any danger. I sleep with my Winchester under the bed."

"I'll tell Jess that, too."

Rachel watched Mikey Ray close the door and leave.

"I won't be giving you cause to use that Winchester."

Rachel spun around to find Cooper Garnett leaning against the curtained wall, his chest bare but for the bandage on his right shoulder, and filling out his long johns with a capacity that made her blink, then blink again.

Heavens, the man gave her pause and palpitations at the same time.

"Unless you refuse to give me my clothes, Miss Rachel."

Chapter Two

Rachel stepped back, caught unaware by the stranger and bumped into Johnny. She bent to pick him up and held him close as they both looked at the man. "They're not dry yet." She pointed toward the hearth. "There's such a chill in the air, it takes—"

"I'll take them anyway," he said, his body bent as he moved with slow, measured steps toward the fireplace.

"Wait! You can't wear those. You'll catch your death in them. I have some clothes that might fit."

He stopped and arched one brow.

"They're..." she muttered, and bit her lower lip. "They were my husband's work clothes. I, uh, you can wear them."

Oh, God. The words just slipped from her mouth and now she had to follow through with her offer. She had a drawer full of her husband's clothes just taking up space, but until now she hadn't been able to part with Josh's things. It was selfish of her—she should have given them to Mikey Ray and her other ranch hands. But she kept them as if...as if having them meant she still had a part of Josh with her. That she hadn't lost him entirely. Some nights, she'd take out his shirt and lie down on the bed clinging to it, breathing in the scent and remembering until she was lulled to sleep.

Cooper Garnett's eyes narrowed and he stared at her. "You sure?"

"Yes, I'll get them right now, but you have to promise to get back into bed. You're still weak."

His breath came with a heavy sigh. "I won't be arguing that point."

He turned and walked back into Johnny's room, and Rachel let out the breath she'd been holding when she saw him lie down on the small bed. He didn't frighten her so much as made her jumpy and she couldn't figure the why of it.

She set Johnny down and took his hand. "Come with Mama."

A few minutes later, with an armful of clothes and Johnny playing with a toy in the other room, she strode across the house to face a resting Cooper Garnett. "These should make do." She set them next to him on the bed.

He gave her a slow nod. "Tell me, was there any sign of the man who shot me and left me for dead? My horse? My belongings?"

"No, I'm sorry. One of my men alerted Sheriff O'Reilly of what happened, but maybe when you're up to it, you can give him a better recollection."

Cooper leaned his head back. "I wish I *had* a better recollection. Fact is, I don't remember much, other than being shot and thrown from my horse."

"So, you don't know who might have done this?"

He shook his head, his eyes darkened by frustration and anger. "Guess I was in the wrong place at the wrong time, is all. Someone wanted my horse and my gear."

"You're not from around here," she said, curious about the stranger.

"I'm from Nevada. Have a ranch there."

Rachel waited for him to tell her more, but he remained silent. She needed more answers than that. "What brought you out here? You're a long way from home."

Cooper took a deep breath and stared into her eyes. His hesitation made her think he wouldn't answer her question. Finally, and after much thought, he responded in a hard cold voice, barely above a whisper. "I could lie to you. I could tell you I came on business, trying to expand my herd or buy some land here. But you saved my life and I owe you. Fact is, I'm tracking someone who stole from me. Been tracking him for months now and the search led me to these parts."

Rachel blinked. The vehemence in his voice made her nerves

stand on edge. Whatever was stolen must have been valuable. "So maybe he was the one who shot you?"

"There's a slim to none chance of that. He doesn't know I'm after him. I've been very careful. But if he was the one who shot me, he'd think I'm dead now, which would make my search easier. His guard would be down. I don't believe that's the case, though."

"Will you go to the sheriff?"

"I plan to."

Rachel took a big swallow, and fear must have shown on her face because the minute he noticed, the hardness in his eyes softened. "You don't have to fear me, Rachel. I'm just a man seeking justice. I meant it when I said I'd never give you cause to use that Winchester."

She'd never turn away an innocent victim, but she had Johnny to worry over and she needed assurances that this man wouldn't bring harm to her family. She was glad to hear he wasn't taking the law into his own hands, but seeking out the sheriff. Rachel's mood lightened some and she smiled. "Unless I don't give you back your clothes."

His lips lifted slightly. "You've been more than kind to me. I'll find a way to repay you."

"There's no need to repay me."

Cooper's lips twisted and then he glanced at the clothes. "I'll be needing to put those on now. Nature's calling."

Heat crawled up her throat as she tried not to appear embarrassed. "I'll leave it to you, then. There's an outhouse in the back," she managed, wanting to squirm right out of her skin at such an intimate conversation. "Do you need any—"

"I'll manage, Rachel." He lifted up from the bed and took the clothes in his hands. "Appreciate this."

Rachel scurried out of the room, pulling the curtain closed but not before noting color draining from Cooper's face as he lifted his arm to put on the shirt. She could almost feel his pain, but pride and a sense of decorum that she appreciated had him refusing her help.

A short time later, Cooper emerged from the room, dressed in Josh's clothes. The shirt fit him tight across the chest and the trousers belted at the right point on his waist. All in all, the fit was almost perfect and for a moment Rachel couldn't breathe. Cooper didn't look a lick like Josh, but seeing him in those clothes brought back memories that pained her heart.

She said nothing as he made his way through the kitchen and out the door. She had no idea how on earth he managed to pull his boots on, but he had dressed himself and she was thankful for it. She didn't have the gumption to dress a stranger in Josh's clothes.

But ten minutes later, when Cooper hadn't returned, Rachel glanced out the kitchen window to find the sun lowering on the horizon creating dark shadows across the entire yard. She saw Cooper then, slowly making his way back to the house. He lost his footing at one point and stumbled, catching himself with his right arm against the branches of a tree to stay upright. Pain slashed across his face.

"Lord above!" Rachel understood a man's pride, but as the woman doctoring him back to health, she couldn't abide him hurting himself further.

She walked through the back door and strode over to him. His face was pale, his eyes bleak. Instantly, she put his arm around her shoulder and took some of his weight. "Lean on me, Mr. Garnett. We'll walk slow."

He wasn't in any shape to argue. Clearly, he'd taxed his strength by dressing himself and making the trip to the outhouse. "You're a stubborn one," he muttered quietly.

"Only half as stubborn as you. And with a mite more sense."

She walked him up the steps and into the house. Their bodies brushed in intimate ways that would have made her blush fully, but for the weakness of the man beside her. He leaned more and more of his weight on her and she picked up her pace, fearful he might collapse before she got him into bed. He clung to her tight, and once they got to the bedroom, he gave up the fight entirely and landed on the bed, taking her with him.

She found herself tangled in his arms, strewn across his body. "Oh!"

He was hard as steel, but warm, too. His heat encompassed

her and his labored breaths blew tendrils of her hair off her forehead.

He groaned from deep in his throat.

"Are you all right?" she whispered, twisting carefully off him so as not to injure his bad side. She felt a true measure of guilt that she'd actually enjoyed being in his arms for those brief seconds. It wasn't Cooper Garnett that warranted those feelings in her, she surmised. It was that she'd been alone so long and that one moment of being held had reminded her of the woman she'd once been—a woman who'd had warmth and love in her life.

"Depends," he said quietly.

"How so?" Rachel moved off the bed and stood above him.

"On the one hand, my shoulder aches like the devil and I'm weak as a newborn pup, but on the other hand, I've got me the prettiest doctor in California tending my wounds and looking out for me."

Rachel didn't miss the compliment nor did she acknowledge it. But it warmed her through and through. She straightened her dress and when she looked into his eyes, she found him staring at her. She felt a sizzle of awareness, having him look at her that way. But just seconds later, he closed his eyes and before she stepped out of the room, she heard snores that meant deep and much-needed sleep for her patient.

The weather was cool after such a hard rain and light snow, but Rachel turned her cheeks up to the sun and let the penetrating rays fill her with warmth. It was a glorious, blue-sky day with clouds forming cotton puff patterns above. She swept the front porch as sunshine seeped into her bones. Johnny sat in the big oak chair watching.

"Mama," he said, his tiny voice a constant source of joy, especially when he spoke her name. He pointed to the corral. "Look, horses, horses."

"Yes, horses," she said, for the umpteenth time this season. He loved to point at objects and say their name. It was a game she'd begun playing with him months ago…now she almost wished he wasn't so astute. When he was awake, he'd barely let her have a quiet moment of thought to herself.

"Barn." He pointed. "Mik-key."

"Yes, that's the barn. And that's Mikey Ray."

Rachel waved to her ranch hand and he smiled, giving her a wave back.

"Coooo-per," her son said, pointing to the door at her back.

She whirled around and found Cooper Garnett watching her. He leaned on the doorjamb, looking better than she'd seen him look since she'd taken him in. His eyes shone bright, the dark hue in them more vivid and clear. His stance was stronger and even though he favored his right shoulder, the favoring wasn't as pronounced now. He'd lain low since she'd helped him inside from the outhouse, two days ago. He ate what she brought to him and slept most of the day, regaining his energy.

"Mornin'," he said, gazing at her intently.

"Good morning." Why would the sight of him looking healthy and on his way to a full mend make her tingle?

"You're looking well. I've got biscuits and eggs heating on the stove if you're hungry." She put up the broom and shook out her apron. "I can—"

"Don't, Rachel." He stopped her abruptly, his voice harsh. He took a look at Johnny, who seemed mesmerized by him, and turned away instantly, his eyes cold. "You don't need to serve me."

Rachel slumped her shoulders. "You sure are grouchy this morning."

He blinked and rubbed his beard several times, eyeing her. "I've got to—

But a commotion in the corral interrupted him. Horses whinnied wildly and backed up against the fence, herding together in a fit of panic. Mikey Ray had just entered the pen to pick his mount today and he yowled as he got caught in the frenzy. Rachel saw him get sandwiched in between two mares. He was in danger of getting crushed. She cried out when she saw a frightened mare buck and knock the boy down.

"Get me your rifle, Rachel. Now!" Cooper took off toward the corral.

Rachel didn't hesitate. The command in Cooper's voice had her running into the house and grabbing the Winchester she kept under her bed. She raced back outside and found him pulling Mikey Ray out of the corral to safety. "He's hurt!"

He grabbed the Winchester from her hand. "Looks like a mountain lion," he said, leaving her with her ranch hand and striding around the corral with a steady sure-footed gate. He spotted the stalking animal and it took off running.

Rachel, bent over Mikey Ray, jumped when a shot rang out. She jumped a second time when another shot fired. "It's okay, Mikey," she said, smoothing his hair from his face. She touched the spot cautiously where she'd seen the horse kick him.

"Ow!"

"Sorry. I have to open up your shirt and see your injury." Working with care, she unbuttoned his vest and then his red shirt. There was no blood on his undershirt, which was a good sign. But as she pushed it up gently, she saw bruising already appearing on his skin, angry red splotches on his youthful chest. She touched him gingerly and he flinched each time. "I'm sorry, Mikey Ray," she said, her heart aching to see him in so much pain and obviously trying hard not to show it.

"What's…it…look like?" he muttered? "Am…I…gonna… live?"

Rachel hid her smile. The boy was scared. "Of course. I think you've got broken ribs. Does it hurt to breathe?"

"Everything…hurts," he managed quietly, "when…I breathe."

Cooper appeared, holding the Winchester. She was thankful for him being there. All the others, Jess included, had ridden out on the range already. He didn't make mention of it, but she knew he'd killed the mountain lion. "How's the boy?"

"I think he's got a few broken ribs."

"He's lucky then. Could have been worse."

Mikey Ray peered up at Cooper, his blue eyes fading into oblivion. "Would have been…" he huffed out, not finishing his thought. His eyes closed.

"Mama…Mikey."

Rachel turned to find her son by her side, gazing with big frightened eyes at Mikey Ray. "He's going to be okay, Johnny." She hugged him around his little waist. "Mikey needs to rest."

"Where do you want him?" Cooper asked.

"In the bunkhouse. I'll wrap his chest and then ride into town to get the doctor, but do you think you should—"

Before she got the words out, Cooper Garnett had picked up Mikey Ray and carried him through the bunkhouse door. Rachel lifted up her son and followed, hurrying her steps to keep up with Cooper. To her amazement, he showed no signs of weakness now, though he had to be taxed after chasing down the mountain lion and then carrying Mikey indoors.

"Thank you," she said, once he'd settled the boy down on one of the four beds. "Mikey, I'll be back. I've got to gather a few things to take care of you."

The boy nodded, his eyes still closed, his face twisted in pain.

"Johnny, you stay in here with Cooper." She set her boy down and glanced at Cooper. He took a look at Johnny, his eyes unreadable, before nodding. She'd never left Johnny alone with Cooper, not for a second, but she wouldn't be gone long and Cooper had just risked his own well-being to save a stranger and her horses. He was a decent man. "I'll be right back."

Rachel raced into the house and got the things she needed to wrap Mikey Ray's chest. When she returned, she found Johnny in the corner of the bunkhouse, exploring with ever-inquisitive eyes. Cooper stood right where she'd left him, his gaze trained on her son, watching him.

She spent the next twenty minutes with Mikey Ray, wrapping him with yards of white gauzy fabric she'd planned on using to make a new petticoat. The boy tried hard to be brave, but his pain was evident. When she was finished, she whispered quietly, "Try to sleep. We'll have the doc out here as soon as we can fetch him."

She rose and stretched out her back and the kinks from her neck. Johnny had latched on to her skirts and she touched his little shoulder. She found Cooper watching her with dark, hooded eyes. There was a hardness to them that didn't soften the way most people's eyes did when they looked at her with Johnny.

She didn't have time to dwell on Cooper, though he was beginning to fascinate her. "Will you stay with Mikey Ray while I ride into town to get the doctor?"

Cooper took a deep breath and stared into her eyes. "I have a better idea. I'll go. I can get there much faster than you. Besides, I wouldn't know what to do, if the boy…the boy needed anything."

Rachel took a pitying glance at Mikey. She knew Cooper was right. But he had already done so much and he had injuries, as well. "Can you make it? You've only just begun to recover."

He nodded, a look of confidence written on his face. "I can make it just fine. I'll need a horse and directions into town. How far?"

"About six miles."

He nodded and strode to the door. "Show me your fastest horse and I'll mount up straightaway."

Rachel walked outside with him, holding Johnny in her arms. "I'm grateful, Cooper. For all you've done today and—"

"You saved my life, Rachel," he said briskly. "Fetching the doctor is hardly repayment."

"You saved Mikey Ray. He might have been crushed to death if not for you."

"I did what anyone would do."

Rachel wouldn't argue with him, yet she wondered why Cooper found it so hard to accept her thanks.

They headed to the corral. The horses seemed to have calmed down some, as if they'd forgotten the imminent danger they'd been in just minutes before. They stayed somewhat huddled still, but they looked at peace.

"Have you had predators threaten the ranch before?"

"Only a hungry wolf or two, trying to get at the chickens. Never a mountain lion. They usually don't come this far into the valley. The ranches closer to the Sierras have more of a problem."

"They're starving," he said. "The one I shot was skin and bones. Makes them desperate. You'd be smart to keep that Winchester close at hand from now on."

Rachel shivered and hugged Johnny closer to her chest. Cooper's gaze flickered just a moment when he looked at Johnny and then he turned away to peer into the corral. "I bet that gray is fast."

Rachel smiled at his astute observation. "You know your horses. That's the one I was going to choose. You'll find what you need in the barn."

She raced to the house and came out with Josh's fur-lined suede jacket and Cooper's hat and handed them to him, then gave him directions to town. She watched him saddle and mount the horse. "Doc Reynolds's office is on the edge of town. You won't miss the sign above his door. He'll recognize you."

She waved to him from the barn door and Johnny mimicked her actions. Her son loved to wave hello and goodbye to people, smiling and expecting a similar reaction in return.

Cooper glanced at them both, then nodded curtly and was gone.

Cooper managed to push his mount and get to Cedar Flat in less than an hour. As he approached the outer buildings of town, his heart strummed hard against his chest with expectation. He'd come this far to find the man responsible for murdering his family. Finally in Cedar Flat, he couldn't waste a second to get the doctor for Mikey Ray. Yet he scanned every alleyway and the sidewalks leading to the livery, saloon, bathhouse and other establishments, cautiously looking for the scarred man as he made his way down the main street.

The onetime gold-mining town still showed remnants of the Rush with an assay office and an emporium selling mining equipment, but from what he'd learned, most people who'd survived the played-out claims nowadays earned their living by ranching. Cooper had a lead that a man with a terribly scarred face worked one of the ranches up here.

He pressed his hat farther down on his head and continued on to the far edge of town, feeling a measure of disappointment. It couldn't be that easy, could it? That he'd find Brett Hollings, or whatever name he was using now, on his first ride into town. The unbearably cold weather didn't help matters. Most men on the street wore woolen scarves that covered half their faces. It wouldn't be hard for Hollings to disguise himself while out in public.

He reached the house with a sign overhead that read Doctor's Office and reined in his mount. Without pause, he knocked on the front door and was greeted by a kind-faced woman with graying hair. "I'm here from the Double J Ranch, ma'am. My name is Cooper. Is the doctor in?"

The woman shook her head and said with apology, "Not at the moment. He's checking on a patient but he'll be back soon. Would you care to come in and wait?"

"No, ma'am, but thank you for the offer. Will you give him a message for me?"

She smiled as if she was used to this request. "Certainly."

"One of the ranch hands at the Double J nearly got crushed by a corral full of horses this morning. Mrs. Bodine wrapped his ribs, but he's in great pain."

"Oh, dear. Yes, my William will want to see him. What's his name?"

"Mikey Ray. I don't know his last name."

She pulled in her lower lip. "Yes, I know the boy. I'll be sure to give my husband the message. He'll want to ride out to check on him. I expect him back very shortly, Mr. Cooper."

Cooper didn't correct her. He'd deliberately given her only his first name. He'd been careful not to alert anyone through his travels of his surname. He didn't want to tip off Hollings that he was after him. To all, he was simply Cooper. Which reminded him that he'd given Rachel his full name while he was nearly unconscious. He'd have to do something about that when he got back. "Thank you, ma'am. Oh, and by the way, I'm searching for my half brother. He'd been burned in a fire not long ago. Wonder if the doc ever mentioned a man he'd treated with a burned face and neck?"

The woman thought for a second then shook her head. "No, I haven't heard of such a man. Maybe you could ask my husband directly when you see him."

"I will. Thanks again, ma'am."

He tipped his hat, left the doctor's house and headed straight for the sheriff's office. Luckily, the sheriff was in and he spent the better part of the hour explaining who he was, what crimes had been committed against him in Nevada and his search for Brett

Hollings. He'd explained how he'd come to be at the Double J Ranch. Sheriff O'Reilly asked him a passel of questions about his being shot and left for dead and took down a written report. The sheriff's arched brow and tone of voice told him he was skeptical that Cooper's shooting had nothing to do with his wife's killer, but Cooper knew in his gut that the two incidents weren't linked.

Like every other sheriff in every other town, O'Reilly first gave Cooper an admonishment not to take the law in his own hands. Cooper hid his true intent by nodding. Fact was, Cooper wanted to avenge his wife's and son's senseless deaths himself.

And then came the sheriff's vow to keep an eye out for the scarred man. Again to Cooper's disappointment, the sheriff hadn't seen or heard of a scar-faced man working in the territory. Cooper had accomplished what he could for now. He shook hands with the sheriff and mounted his horse.

On the ride back to the Double J, Cooper's mind whirled and a plan formed in his head. He didn't have a dime to his name at the moment, Hollings having robbed him of most of his ready cash. The fire that killed his family also destroyed all his belongings, but he did still have the ranch and about eight hundred head of cattle. While he'd recuperated from his burns, he'd sold off half his herd to meet his payroll for the year and fund his search. He'd instructed his trusted foreman to keep the ranch going, but Cooper wouldn't ever live there again. He couldn't go back to stay. He wouldn't rebuild.

Memories of Jocelyn waving farewell to him, holding little Donny in her arms in front of their home that last day haunted him. He'd been bent on building his herd and had taken off that morning to make a deal with a neighboring rancher. It had taken nearly the entire day of negotiating and by the time he'd returned home, all was lost.

He'd let his family down. He hadn't protected them and almost equally as bad, he was starting to forget them. Each day, the memory of what his life was like ebbed just that much further in his mind.

He couldn't remember the exact color of Jocelyn's caramel eyes now. He could barely recall Donny's toothless smile or the dimple on his right cheek. He'd forced those memories away in order to survive the torment, but the guilt stayed with him, always with him. And now…now all that was left was bitter hatred of the man who'd claimed their lives and the revenge that Cooper would someday claim.

Hollings was in the vicinity. He had to stay on here and find him. This was as close as he'd come to catching him. As he approached the Double J, he saw Rachel in front of her house waiting with watchful eyes. Her son stood clinging to her skirts again.

They reminded him of what he'd once had and of all he'd lost. She'd saved his life yet he could hardly abide seeing the two of them together. When he looked at them, all of his own failures slashed through him, worse than the stinging ache burning in his abused shoulder. Worse than the weakness in his body now. He'd taxed himself today and felt the drain of fatigue claiming him.

He pulled up and noted stiffness in Rachel's stance. "The doctor was here already," she said, trying to keep accusation from her tone. "He gave Mikey Ray laudanum. The boys are hitching up the wagon. They're gonna take him to his folks to rest up."

Cooper didn't want to notice the clear blue in Rachel's eyes. Or the way the bodice of her dress clung tight to her curves. He didn't want to note how pretty she was or the kindness in her heart, but he did and that alarmed him. "That's good."

He dismounted and came face-to-face with her. Blond waves, like golden wheat, framed her face as the cool breeze blew by. She pulled those strands back behind her ear. "The doc says he'll be okay, but it'll take weeks for him to heal. What, uh, what took you so long?"

Did she think he wouldn't return? Did she think he'd take her horse and leave town? Was that why she stood rigid, her eyes sharp with curiosity. "After I delivered the message to the doctor's wife, I went to see Sheriff O'Reilly."

"Oh."

"I explained about the shooting. He took a report from me."

"I see," she said, nibbling on her lower lip. "I, uh—"

"I came back, Rachel."

She closed her eyes. "I'm sorry. After all you've done today, I should have known."

Cooper took her arm, a simple gesture that he'd done a thousand times with Jocelyn, yet the heat of the contact struck him like lightning. He ignored the sensation and the way Rachel gazed up at him. "I need to speak with you. Inside."

She nodded, and he kept his hand under her elbow, helping her up the steps of the house. "Come on, Johnny," she said and her son obeyed, following them into the house. She pulled her arm free the second they were inside.

"Have something to eat," she said immediately, a rosy blush coloring her face. She made herself busy pulling muffins from the oven. The room smelled of warm cinnamon and sugar. "They're from yesterday, I didn't have time to bake this morning with all that's happened. I'll make eggs for you. You must be famished."

"I am," he said honestly.

"Thank you for going after the doctor. And for…everything else."

Cooper was dog-tired and took a seat at the table. Johnny crawled up on the chair next to him and watched him with wide eyes. Cooper's heart lurched in agony; the boy was so beautiful and it was hard to look at him and not feel miserable. But Cooper had no choice now. He had to put his plan in action.

"Looks like you'll be shorthanded, with Mikey Ray gone."

Rachel tossed her head back, a derisive laugh escaping her throat. "We were shorthanded *with* Mikey Ray here. Now, it'll only be harder."

She set a mug of coffee in front of him. He warmed his hands around the cup. "Doesn't have to be."

Rachel looked at him.

He stared back.

She was a smart woman. She knew his intent.

"You?"

"I need work, Rachel. I have only the clothes on my back." He glanced at the shirt he wore, one of her husband's. "Well, not even that."

She blinked and became thoughtful.

"It would only be temporary. Until you didn't need me anymore."

Rachel put her head down, staring at the tips of her boots. "I suppose that makes sense. You know ranching." Then she gazed into his eyes, almost talking herself out of it. "I can't pay you much. That's why I employ boys. They don't expect—"

"Whatever it is, will be fine." Cooper paid his ranch hands thirty dollars a month, the going rate. He figured Rachel paid her men half that amount, but he didn't care. What he needed and wanted was a legitimate reason to stay in Cedar Flat.

Rachel hesitated a moment and he imagined she wasn't easily fooled—his exhaustion must have shown on his face. "You were shot four days ago. You're still recuperating. Are you up to it?"

He could only answer with the truth. "I will be. I'm getting stronger every day."

"I see you as my patient first. I won't expect you to do too much."

"I'll do my share," he told her with a healthy dose of pride.

She smiled and set the eggs and muffins in front of him. "I forgot how stubborn you are."

"Do we have a deal?"

Rachel sat down with a mug of coffee of her own. "Yes. We have a deal. Tomorrow, you'll move into the bunkhouse, Mr. Garnett."

Cooper set down his coffee cup. "About that. From now on, I'm just Cooper. It's safer for all concerned that nobody knows my real name."

"But Jess and Mikey Ray know—"

"I'll have a talk with Jess later."

"But why?" Rachel blinked and took hold of Johnny, who was trying to climb up onto the table. She set him back into the chair and turned to gaze into Cooper's eyes.

"I told you, it's safer that no one knows I'm here. Do you want to back out of our deal now?"

She shook her head quickly. "No. We need the help."

He nodded. He wouldn't put anyone at the Double J in danger. If Hollings got wind of it, he might try something and Cooper would die before allowing that to happen. "Then I'll be your patient one more day. Tomorrow, you'll be my boss."

Chapter Three

Rachel had jumbled feelings about giving Cooper a job at the ranch. She needed ranch hands desperately. With Josh gone and now Mikey Ray laid up, the Double J would suffer. The boys were working twice as hard for half the pay. It wasn't fair to them, she knew, but there was little she could do about it. So in that regard, hiring Cooper had been a blessing. He was capable and intelligent and he did know ranching.

On the other hand, he was a mystery to her and kept to himself. She wouldn't pry into his life, but she wanted to know more about him. The incident this morning confirmed to her that he could be trusted. He'd saved Mikey Ray and come back to the ranch, when for more than a few moments this morning she'd wondered if he would.

With Johnny in her arms, she marched out to the henhouse to gather the day's eggs. Even with all that had happened today, ranch life was constant. The chores didn't go away just because there was strife. She'd already laundered clothes and baked two loaves of bread.

As she approached the henhouse her thoughts turned to Mikey Ray and she prayed he would recover quickly without a great deal of pain. She'd kissed his forehead as a way of farewell and bundled up her day-old muffins to send home with him. His family had a homestead on the other side of the valley, so he would be cared for, which gave her a measure of comfort. It was times like these that she missed Josh the most. He was her stability and her center. His love had always made ranch life bearable.

She was alone now, and with the Christmas holiday approaching, sadness she wouldn't display to her ranch family surrounded her. She'd do her best to make the holiday cheerful. With that resolve in mind she helped herself to today's offering in the henhouse. "Be careful, Johnny," she said, allowing her son to pick up the last egg and put it into the basket. It was a ritual she'd started a few weeks ago with her boy.

"Careful, Mama." With infinite care, her son set the egg on top of all the others.

She squeezed him tight. "That's good, baby. You did that just right."

Johnny looked at her with pride. "I…good."

She chuckled. "Yes, you are."

With a smile on her lips, she exited the henhouse and walked around the corner of the barn. What she saw then stopped her short. Cooper Garnett, with his bare back to her, held a long blade to his soapy face. Scars that had healed well spread across his back, but they didn't blur the perfect image he made, broad of shoulders and rippling with bronzed muscles that led down to a waistline hugged by his well-fitting trousers.

Rachel reminded herself to breathe.

Lord above.

After Cooper returned from town, he'd been so exhausted he'd gone into Johnny's room to rest. Rachel figured he'd be sleeping the entire day and night.

She'd never thought he'd be up already, looking so…fit. She watched him shave, taking long smooth strokes to his uplifted face. The sight of him sent tingles down to her belly. She was instantly reminded of his touch on her arm this morning. The way she ignited like a prairie fire when he held her and led her into the house.

She couldn't tear her gaze away and a deep sense of longing besieged her.

"Afternoon, Rachel," he said, his back still to her.

Heavens, she hadn't noticed the glint of the mirror hanging from a nail on the barn wall. He'd seen her watching him through the reflection. Rachel wanted to die right on the spot. Slowly, she set down Johnny, who had become fidgety in her arms.

"Cooper," she managed.

He rinsed out his blade in the blue porcelain bowl that sat atop a barrel. "Jess lent me shaving supplies. I figured I needed to clean up before starting work tomorrow."

She swallowed. Maybe he hadn't noticed her gawking.

Then he turned around and the full force of his appearance immediately struck her. Her mouth gaped open. My God, he was more handsome than any man she'd ever seen. Even with his face dotted with soap, and his dark hair so long it touched his shoulders. The bullet wound, open to the air now and healing, added to his rugged, earthy appeal. With the shabby beard gone the sharp, strong lines of his face appeared as though they'd been sculpted by a master.

"Rachel," he said, his tone deep and filled with warning. "Don't be looking at me like that."

How could she help it? Burning heat climbed her up face. "I, um, sorry." She averted her gaze to glance at Johnny. He was sitting down in the dirt, mesmerized by a trail of black ants crossing the yard. "Don't touch," she cautioned.

"I won't," Cooper said, and as her head snapped up, her face flamed again.

"I was talking to my son."

"I know, but I'm talking to you…assuring you." He wiped the remaining soap from his face then laid the full force of his dark gaze on her. So, he had seen her ogling him and thought to tell her she wasn't appealing to him. He wouldn't touch her. That was fine with her.

Or was it?

He rinsed his face and put his shirt on as he studied her. "I was burned in a fire some time ago."

"I'm sorry," she said, gathering her wits now. "When I tended your bullet wound, I noticed them. I've helped treat burn victims before so I recognized them as such." She'd wondered about the reason behind those scars, but afterward she'd forgotten about them, more intent on saving her patient's life. "Was it terribly painful?"

Cooper blinked and a frown stretched across his features. "Nothing I couldn't endure."

She was more than curious about the burns now, but his face

had closed off. She had enough painful memories of her own to know how speaking aloud your innermost agony could ruin a perfectly fine day.

"I'd best be going now." He buttoned his shirt and turned away from her. "Jess wants to speak with me."

Rachel watched him head toward the blacksmith shed, swallowing her chagrin in one huge gulp. She took Johnny's hand and walked to the house. She'd made a complete fool of herself in front of Cooper Garnett. She should feel tawdry and wanton, but at the moment, all she felt was hopelessly lonely.

Cooper cursed under his breath, walking away from Rachel and her boy. He wouldn't get involved with her. He couldn't. He was no good for anyone, much less her. He wouldn't take advantage of a widow with a kid—no matter how pretty she was or how sweet and generous.

No matter how she looked at him just seconds ago, with want and need so damn obvious in her eyes. She was lonely. He knew that. He'd witnessed her at odd moments during the days and nights she'd tended him when a glimmer of sadness gave her away. Or something she'd say would ring of heartbreaking pain.

Cooper understood that all too well. In many ways, he and Rachel were alike. They'd both lost someone they'd loved. They both were scarred that way, but Rachel was ready to move on with her life. She was young enough to forge ahead with a good man and build a future. Cooper didn't think past catching Hollings and making him pay. He had no other future. He lived solely to kill a man.

He met up with Jess by the blacksmith shed as he was putting away tools. "You a smithy, too?" Cooper asked, curious about the man who treated Rachel like a daughter.

"You can say that, I suppose. I prefer being the cook, but we all pitch in with whatever needs doing. I worked for a smithy when I was a boy and I get by with hooping a barrel or repairing equipment. You got any experience?"

"As a smithy? Some. Like you, I worked every part of a ranch before I got my own."

Jess nodded, then eyed him carefully. "You saved Mikey Ray

this morning, so I'm indebted to you, but I just gotta say one thing before we move on. It's about Rachel."

Cooper pursed his lips. It'd been a long time since anyone gave him a lecture. "Go on."

"That gal is a good woman. I been with her since the start of this ranch. When Josh was alive. She loved him something fierce and the poor man got shot needlessly. Never got to know his boy. He never got to live his life with the woman he loved. Rachel had it rough, Garnett. And I'm here to tell you, don't do anything to make her life harder." He sighed deeply. "You get what I'm saying?"

"I already figured as much. I got it, Jess."

Jess eyed him up and down, scrutinizing his appearance. "You're the right age. You're not bad-looking and Rachel's got a pure heart. Someone's already tried to take advantage of her and—"

Something in Cooper's gut pulled tight. "Who?"

"That's not my business to say. Someone she trusted betrayed her and she took it hard."

"I won't do that," Cooper said. "I owe her my life."

"You can't stay in that house once you're healed up."

"I'm moving into the bunkhouse tomorrow morning. I'm here to work, that's all, Jess."

"All right, Garnett," he said, studying his face carefully. "I'm taking you at your word."

Cooper nodded and figured this was as good a time as any to explain to Jess about his name. It wouldn't make the old man feel any better about him, but Cooper had to tell him just enough to keep everyone at the ranch safe. "About my name…"

Cooper sat at the table with Rachel as they ate a meal of roasted chicken, boiled carrots and fresh bread. She held Johnny on her lap, feeding him first as the boy shot food clear across the table, squirming in her arms and making a mess of his meal. "Johnny, I do declare you're ornery today!"

She set him down and let him wander the room. She sighed sharply and the sweet patient look that always found her face had disappeared. "I'm sorry for the mess."

"Don't be," he said as he filled his belly. "The food's good. You're a fine cook, Rachel."

She glanced at him and he noted lines of fatigue around her pretty blue eyes. Guilt assailed him quickly. She'd been taking care of the ranch, her boy, cooking and cleaning and then he'd shown up wounded nearly on her doorstep. He'd been an added burden to her. He winced at the thought.

"Thanks, Cooper."

"What do you like to do at night?" he asked.

Her head lifted and she shook it, as if deeply puzzled. "Do?"

Jocelyn used to sketch. She had a penchant for it and after Donny was born, she'd spend any spare time she had creating pictures of the three of them as a family. He'd framed the one that she'd done of them in front of their house. All those sketches had gone to ashes in the fire. "For yourself? Do you have any enjoyments?"

"It's a joy just to get Johnny down at night so I can catch a few winks." She spoke lightly with a grin, but Cooper only nodded, seeing through her attempt at a joke.

After he finished the meal, he rose from the table and took up the dishes before Rachel had a chance to gather them.

"What are you doing?"

"Helping," he said gruffly. "I'll take care of these. You go on. Get Johnny down. Get some rest yourself."

She bounded up and faced him squarely. "That's not necessary."

"I say it is."

She narrowed her eyes until only a hint of blue shot out. "I can't have you—"

"Yes, you can, Rachel. You've tended me for days. I can see you're beat."

She glared at him and shook her head.

"What? You think I can't wash a dish? I've washed plenty in my day. I've taken care of myself for thirty-one years. Go on. Spend some time with your son."

He shot her a look of encouragement. She glanced at Johnny, sitting upright on the floor and at that very moment, the boy lifted his arms to her and wiggled his fingers, beseeching her to pick him up. Cooper turned away from them and moved through the doorway that led to the small kitchen. He listened to Rachel's soft voice as she spoke to Johnny in the patient way she had of dealing with the boy. Later, he heard sounds of her reading him a story. He couldn't make out her words, but the lulling timbre of her voice soothed him and made him glad he could give her this small amount of enjoyment.

He took his time with the cleanup, listening for the quiet, and when he was sure Rachel and Johnny had fallen asleep, he entered the main room. To his surprise, Rachel sat in a chair next to the blazing fire, knitting.

"I thought you went to bed," he said.

"Johnny's down. But it's too early for me."

He studied her for a minute, unsure what to do next.

"Sit with me," she said as she continued to transfer bright colored yarn back and forth on the needles. "It's warm by the fire."

Firelight flickered softly, setting a yellow glow of light around her head, making her hair shine golden and her face appear angelic. The rest of the room fell in shadows succumbing to the dreary cold night. Cooper hesitated.

She lifted her eyes to his and smiled a beautiful smile. "For a few minutes, Cooper."

The invitation in her eyes wasn't coy, but heartfelt, and he couldn't refuse her. Not because he felt obligated, but because he couldn't seem to turn away from her and the serene picture she made. He lowered onto a bench seat facing her, bracing his arms on his knees and leaning in.

She arched a brow but didn't comment that he hadn't taken a seat in the chair beside her. "Thank you for this time. It wasn't necessary. You don't have to repay me for tending you."

"That's exactly why I want to," he said quietly.

Her eyes softened even more, and Cooper leaned back, away from her, away from the heat of the fire.

She went on. "It's a treat to have a few hours of quiet time in the evening."

"Is that your enjoyment?" he asked, gesturing to her knitting.

"Well, yes. I suppose it serves that purpose, as well. I knit things for Mr. Woodcock at the mercantile. He sells them for me.

And now, with Christmas approaching I'm making gifts for the boys."

"Scarves?" He recognized the long pull of yarn fashioned in an intricate design.

"Yes, mittens and socks and sweaters, too. It's what they need on these cold nights."

Cooper chuckled to himself, but Rachel had caught the grin on his face.

"What's funny?" she asked.

"Oh, nothing. I was just remembering when I was their age."

"And what was that?" Rachel set her knitting on her lap and smiled warmly, eager to hear what he had to say. He'd gone and done it now. If he weren't still recuperating from a bullet meant to take his life he'd have his wits about him and wouldn't have let her trap him into answering. But the sweet glow in her eyes and the smile on her face told him that wasn't an option. Damn his tired mind, he couldn't come up with a viable lie, so he told her the truth. "Most boys that age, well, when I was that age, I'd trade a sweater for a pretty young gal to hold in my arms, to keep me warm."

He waited for her blush, something he noticed her do now and again, but she only smiled as she picked up her knitting again. "I remember. When I met Josh, it was that way. He couldn't hold me in his arms long enough. We had quite a courtship. It lasted all of one week." She stopped with a knitting needle ready to cross over the other. "I didn't even *like* him when we first met. But he told me he'd change my mind and he did."

Cooper only nodded, not willing to ask more questions. He feared Rachel would return the sentiment and he didn't want to tell her more about himself than he had to. "It's been quite a day," he said finally.

Rachel glanced at him with a hint of regret in her eyes, and Cooper's thoughts of getting to bed vanished. For whatever reason, Rachel enjoyed his company and he wouldn't disappoint her. He didn't want to see loneliness on her face, not tonight.

He sat with her for another hour, chatting about inconsequential things and learning about only what Rachel chose to tell him. He stoked the fire several times and stared into the flames as she conversed with him.

After she put up her knitting, setting the needles, balls of yarn and half-finished garments into a basket, Cooper stood when she did. Their bent bodies came up at the same time and their heads bumped.

"Oh!" Rachel chuckled, her eyes bright with laughter.

Cooper instinctively reached out to steady her. He held her arms just above the elbows. "Sorry."

"Clumsy of me," she said.

Cooper's lips lifted at one corner. "You all right?"

She swallowed and closed her eyes briefly. "I'll be fine."

The connection between them was strong—a jarring jolt, an instant in time like the flash of bright lightning, burned through his gut and he warned himself to be careful. He rubbed her arms gently without pretense or ill intent for just one second. "Sometimes, I think it'd be nice to be that young boy again." He sighed and dropped his hands away.

Rachel gazed at him, but he refused to return the warmth in her eyes. He shouldn't have said anything. He shouldn't have touched her. He took a step back. "Go on to bed, Rachel. I'll take care of the fire."

She paused, and in that moment, Cooper saw something in her eyes he didn't want to see. Hope.

His next words were harsh, ruining the moment, ruining the day, but he needed to say them for both of their sakes. "You'd best be saving those looks for your beau, Rachel. Not one of your hired hands."

Her mouth gaped open and the slap came fast and hard across his face.

"I don't have a beau, you fool. And that look was only for what I'd lost. Certainly not for you!"

She marched into her room and shut the door firmly, but not hard enough to wake her son. He heard her slide the bolt closed.

"Good," he muttered, glad she'd shut him out. He'd hurt her out of necessity and her shutting him out gave him no option—no way he could go into her room and ask for forgiveness. "It had to be done," he said, mostly to convince himself.

But he went to bed that night not convinced of anything. And hating that even more.

Cooper worked on the ranch for the rest of the week, doing minor chores that kept him close to the house. Rachel's orders, Jess had said, and Cooper wasn't in any shape to argue the point. Working full days taxed his strength and after supper, he usually slid into his bunk and slept soundly through the night.

Rachel hadn't exactly gone out of her way to avoid him these days, but when she was within eyesight, she'd made sure not to send more than a glance his way. He'd seen her every day sweeping the porch, gathering eggs, laughing with Jess or sending over her baked goods to the bunkhouse, always with a smile on her face.

"You going into town tonight?" Chick Winstead asked on Saturday morning as he mounted his mare. "It's payday." The young ranch hand grinned, exhibiting an eagerness to spend his hard-earned cash drinking whiskey and playing faro in the saloon. "All the boys go. We'll miss Mikey Ray, though. His pa said he ain't fit to come back to the ranch or do much else for weeks. Gosh, he must hate being laid up like that."

"I imagine so," Cooper said, filling a bucket of oats for the horses. "What time you boys thinking about going?"

"After supper. We still got to put in a full day's work."

Cooper had been waiting for an opportunity to get back to town. It would give him a chance to meet other ranch hands that may know Brett Hollings. "I might just meet you all there."

"Okay," Chick said. "We'll look for you."

Cooper nodded and watched the boy ride off toward the east pasture, wearing a woolen coat and a tattered scarf around his neck. Overhead, gloomy gray clouds blocked out sunlight.

He was nearly finished with his chores today—there was only so much repairing a man could do around the buildings. The real work was done out on the range, pulling free mud-stuck cows, building fences, checking on the health of the herd. This week, he'd fixed a roof over the equipment shed, repaired three stable stalls that had broken latches, helped pull a calf from its pregnant mama, and now, as Cooper glanced around looking for work, he found only one thing left to do.

But that required confronting Rachel.

Truth was, it was a damn sight easier to put her out of his mind when she wasn't talking to him. But she was paying him to work and he wasn't going to let a little thing like her anger get in the way of doing what needed doing.

He walked around to the back of her house and found her bringing in clothes from a clothesline stretched between two trees. She was humming pleasantly, her throaty little sounds causing him to slow his steps. He approached her, listening as the tunes settled on him with a sense of peace.

Dried leaves crunched under his boots and she turned, startled. Then her face pinched tight and she whipped her head back around. "Good afternoon, Cooper."

He smiled at her weak attempt at good manners. "Rachel. So, you're talking to me now?"

"I never *wasn't* talking to you." She pulled a few of Johnny's small trousers from the line and folded them into a basket.

"You pack a mean punch," he said. "My face stung for an hour."

She didn't respond.

"I'm apologizing for what I said."

"No need."

Her feathers were still ruffled. She wouldn't look at him. "There's a need," he said quietly.

This time when she turned to face him, she searched his eyes for sincerity. "Because I saved your life?"

"Not only that. You deserve better treatment. I spoke harsh that day. I could have tempered my words and not hurt you. Fact is, Rachel, I'm only here a short time. Wouldn't do for us to—"

"To what, Cooper?" she asked pointedly, her pretty face in a scowl. "To have a decent conversation? To share a few moments together?" She rushed the words out, shaking her head in frustration.

He arched his brow. "That's not what I'm talking about."

She set the basket down and stared at him, her hands set firmly on her hips. "Besides, you didn't hurt me. You…you infuriated me."

"Look, Jess told me about a man who didn't treat you kindly. Someone who betrayed your trust. I'm not about to—"

"Jess shouldn't have said anything. He's overprotective of me, but the fact is, I handled Hank on my own. He didn't hurt me, not in that way."

"Who was he?"

Her shoulders slumped. She looked away for a few moments and then finally turned back to him. "My ranch foreman. I hired him shortly after Josh died. He seemed to take over so easily and I was indebted to him for helping keep the ranch from falling apart. I liked him, but not in that way. It was too soon and I was still grieving. The baby was all I could handle. But he took my gratitude as a sign of something more. Something I wasn't offering. And then one night, he decided he'd take it anyway, coming to me uninvited." Rachel stared at the ground for a moment. Her face twisted, as she seemed to struggle with the recollection. "That's when I pulled my Winchester from my bedside and threatened to shoot off the parts of his body he couldn't control."

Cooper stifled a chuckle, this not being a funny subject and all, but the image in his head wouldn't go away. "Did you now?"

She nodded with a look of satisfaction and pride. "I did. I ordered him off my land. Told him to pack up and leave that night. And he did."

Cooper was about to tell her she wouldn't have to worry about that happening with him, but he held his tongue. She had more to say, her eyes fixed on him. "I'm through grieving, Cooper. And I think I can decide on my own what's good for me. Not Jess and not you. If I want something, and I'm not saying I do, but if I want something then it's my decision. Seems to me, that's only fair."

"It is." He couldn't argue the point.

"Are you in some sort of trouble, Cooper?"

Puzzled, he barely shook his head. "No."

"Married or betrothed to someone?"

Again, another short shake of his head.

She stared at him, her eyes clear and brilliant blue. "Then you don't find me at least a little bit—"

He looked at her, her face a ray of sunshine against a stark black sky. She wore a heavy coat, but he knew what lay underneath. Not only the youthful, curvy body of a new widow, but he knew her heart—a heart that had been damaged by anguish. Cooper didn't want to add to her pain, but she was earnest and brave to speak so plainly to him. "You're beautiful, Rachel. There's no doubt."

She sighed and a small smile lifted her lips.

He searched her face, ready to reach out to her, to touch her cheek and bring her close into the folds of his arms. She looked at him, as if seeing the debate going on in his head. Her eyes drew him in like the pull of a river's current. It was hard to stay on the bank and not dive in. But he didn't move a muscle. He stood his ground, watching her breaths come in rapid bursts. "Another man might be able to give you what you ne—"

"I accept your apology, Cooper," she said, with false bravado. She turned away briskly, but not before he saw disappointment fill her eyes. "Did you come back here for another reason?"

"To chop wood. I noticed your woodpile was low," he said to her back.

"You'd b-best...g-get on with it then."

And Cooper would have done just that if he hadn't seen her hands tremble as she lifted a white petticoat from the clothesline. If he hadn't heard the deep desolation in her voice. He moved behind her and put his hands on her rigid shoulders. "Don't think I will now."

She stood quiet.

"Rachel?"

She put her head down.

"Turn around."

She moved slowly and faced him, the wind picking up enough to blow blond strands of hair onto her cheeks. Then she began speaking, and the words rushed out in a nervous stream that didn't sound anything like the woman who'd saved his life. "You don't owe me anything. It's just that I thought that we, that is, you and I, well, I was begin—"

"Be quiet now, Rachel."

She stopped suddenly, surprised by his command. "Did you just tell me to—"

"I did. I want your mouth open to me, but for a different reason."

"Oh," she said with a little gasp.

Then Cooper stepped closer, bent his head and kissed her.

Chapter Four

Rachel's heart pounded in her chest. She couldn't breathe all too well, either, because Cooper Garnett was kissing her and time seemed to stop in that very moment. His lips were cold when they came down on hers, but it was only a brief second before warmth radiated all around them. He pulled her closer by the collar of her coat and she rose on tiptoe to garner the full impact of his kiss.

It was wonderful. *He* was wonderful. She wouldn't think about how little she knew about him, or what his true circumstances were. She wouldn't think how foolish this was, because at the moment, nothing seemed better in her life. This wasn't a tentative kiss born of obligation. No, Cooper kissed her hard, crushing his lips to hers as if he meant it. As if she mattered to him. As if he couldn't get enough.

He slanted his lips over hers again, nipping at her, whispering soft words and holding her around her waist, drawing her up closer with one hand while the other weaved into the wind-tangled tresses of her hair.

She knew by the impact of his kiss, that Cooper Garnett did nothing halfway. He was a man who exacted the full extent of his power and intelligence in everything he attempted. She'd only seen him in a weakened state and now that he was recuperating, he'd allowed her to see the man he truly was—a man who claimed what he wanted without hesitancy or intimidation.

Rachel smiled at the thought. He wanted her.

And while she kept waiting for guilt to override her desire, it didn't come. She wasn't swamped with a need to uphold her loyalty to her deceased husband. She wasn't feeling terrible remorse, that another man, a *new* man, held her in his arms.

Her love for Josh would never diminish, but Rachel was ready to forge ahead with her life.

And that revelation brought an intense sense of relief.

She wrapped her arms around Cooper's neck, teasing her fingers though the hair resting on his shoulders. She found the strands amazingly soft for such a strong man. The move intensified Cooper's kiss, his lips pressing harder against hers with more demand. Small whimpers of delight escaped her throat. Her once-empty body now flooded with heat and desire that whipped through her so powerfully she gasped in surprise. Her breaths came up short. Her heart rate accelerated.

It pained her to move away from his mouth for even a second. He made her feel alive and vital and finally…like a woman again. The hollowed-out shell had been filled with life. She gazed into his eyes, fluttering hers, hardly believing she could be so brazen. "Johnny's napping."

He took half a second to allow her intent to seep in. Then he touched his forehead with hers, looking down at their boots standing toe-to-toe, and the shake of his head was enough to crush her. "No, Rachel."

She stepped back. The blow of rejection was instantly replaced with unguarded anger. "No? No? You kissed me like you—"

"I won't take advantage of you."

"I thought we had this discussion already," she said through lips ready to tremble. If she let her anger go, mortification would set in, and she couldn't face that now.

He wouldn't look at her. He heaved a heavy sigh. "It's not right, you and me. It could never be right."

"Why?" she asked, truly confused.

"I came here for a reason, Rachel," he said quietly but with the full force of his will. "I won't stay after I find what I'm looking for. I'm no good for you."

Rachel swallowed the lump in her throat and her pride. She had nothing left of it anyway. "Maybe that's fine with me."

His eyes turned black as the night. "You deserve more than that."

Her eyes filled with moisture. "Noble of you," she scoffed, shame rising with each moment she stood within his grasp.

Cooper rubbed the back of his neck, eyeing her now with such tenderness that she could barely stand it. Did he pity her—the wanton widow with no morals? Whatever he was thinking, he wouldn't share his thoughts. They met each other in a long stare, then Cooper confessed. "You're not easy to walk away from, Rachel."

The words meant little to her. "But you will."

He squinted as if in great pain. "Got to."

But he stood there, waiting. And Rachel was the one to walk away. She picked up her basket of laundry and with her head held high, she walked through the yard and into the house.

It was a small victory, but at least she had that.

If nothing else.

Cooper rode into town, meeting up with the boys from the Double J Ranch at the one saloon in town. It was cowboy payday and that meant wranglers and ranchers from all over the county overflowing out the doors of the crowded establishment. Cooper had money in his pocket now, enough to lay down some bribes if need be to get the information he wanted.

Might not be necessary, he thought. He had all night to see the comings and goings at the White Stallion Saloon, and so he took up a seat in the corner giving him the best advantage and drank whiskey, waiting and watching. Chick stopped by with his friends and they sat down for a spell, but soon the impatient boys itched to lose their money gambling and left him alone.

After two hours, Cooper's patience ebbed, as well. He'd refused three dance-hall girls their illicit advances, thinking instead of Rachel and her pretty blue eyes beseeching him today in her yard. His willpower strained to the limit, he'd had to refuse her. But all the way into town, his thoughts kept coming back to her and the powerful need inside him.

He'd not thought of a woman in that regard since Jocelyn's death just six months ago. But every time he thought of his wife now, Rachel's image came into view, casting a ray of light over the shadow in his mind. He couldn't figure it.

He put Rachel out of his thoughts and got up from his seat, angry now that he'd wasted time waiting and watching for a man who clearly wasn't here. He strode to the bar and ordered another whiskey, lying through his teeth, asking about his long-lost half brother who'd been burned on the face and neck to everyone who'd stand to listen.

The barkeep was his best bet, so he palmed him some cash, asking him to keep his eyes and ears out for such a man and report his findings back to Cooper.

After another hour of speaking with strangers and drinking whiskey, he waved farewell to Chick and the boys. Stinking drunk now, Chick told him they were staying in town overnight with tomorrow being Sunday and all. They'd repent in church for their sins tonight, Cooper figured.

He rode back to the ranch alone with his thoughts. While he should be thinking of his next strategy for finding Hollings, he kept drifting back to Rachel and the soft sweetness of her mouth. She tasted like warm honey and everything good. He had enough whiskey in him to let his willpower wane with impure thoughts of her. His body ached with need and tightened just thinking about what she'd offered him.

While he could have, and maybe should have eased his lust with the saloon girls in town, Cooper found no such desire for them. He'd go straight to hell for wanting Rachel like he did and not even the frigid cold night could hamper his need for her.

When he got to the ranch all was quiet, but he cursed when he saw Rachel's lamp lit in her room. She was awake and probably knitting up those Christmas gifts. No one was around. The temptation to go to her was strong even as the effects of whiskey wore off.

He dismounted his mare and took a few minutes to unsaddle and groom the horse, putting it into a stall in the barn. By the time he walked outside again he hoped to see Rachel's lamp extinguished. But instead, he saw the shadow of her silhouette framed by the window as she moved across the room with haunting beauty.

"Ah, hell," Cooper muttered as he gave up the fight.

He knocked softly on Rachel's door.

When she finally opened it, she faced him with a question in her eyes.

He scanned her, seeing the beautiful outline of her body from under the cotton nightdress she wore. "Maybe I'm not so noble after all."

Rachel opened the door wider, glad to see Cooper standing there. His comment and the intense look in his eyes gave her hope. She gestured for him to come inside, and he entered quietly, removing his coat then let go a deep sigh as if he'd somehow lost the battle he'd been waging. She found herself being lifted up in his strong arms and carried into her bedroom. "Tell me no, Rachel," he whispered with deep conviction.

"I won't." She stroked his jaw tenderly and laid her head against his chest. She wanted him here, more than even she imagined. Denying him wasn't possible.

He accepted her decision with a slight nod she felt rather than witnessed. He set her down near her bed carefully, her feet touching the floor light as a feather. "You're back early."

He touched her cheek, the back of his fingertips ever so gentle, as if they were memorizing her skin. "Were you waiting for me?"

Dread had settled in her belly thinking he might be with a saloon girl in town. "I didn't know if you'd come home at all tonight," she whispered.

She saw him flinch when she'd said *home,* but his next words comforted her. "I couldn't stay away from you."

He nuzzled her throat, placing tiny kisses there, breathing in her scent and rubbing his nose in her hair. "This is a wagonload of wrong, Rachel." The warmth of his breath tickled her throat. "But when I'm with you, I forget everything bad in my life."

She arched her neck, relishing every sensation, and closed her eyes, his kisses making mush of her brain. "I feel…the same."

"Do you?" He drizzled kisses up her throat now, his lips moving to her chin, her cheek and then finally, he set his mouth on hers and she inhaled deeply, her heart pounding. Little pools of heat curled down past her belly and she moaned lightly. Cooper parted her lips then and stroked her with his demanding tongue. Sensations ripped through her rapidly as he tasted the hollows of her mouth. With a groan, his tenderness gave way like a match to dry prairie grass. Flames erupted and his breathing quickened.

In one swift move, he pulled her nightdress up and over her head, baring her to him. His hands were on her instantly, tender but urgent as he caressed her skin and stroked over her back. His palms warmed her and brought chills at the same time. She leaned closer to him, murmuring his name.

Then he stopped and stepped away. Her heart stilled.

He gazed at her, naked to him but for a modest covering below her waist. "Rachel," he said, shaking his head and whispering in awe as he lifted her face to his, "You can't be real."

She smiled deep in her heart. "I'm real, Cooper."

His eyes shone bright with lust and craving. The look alone ignited fiery heat inside her that melted her bones. He dropped his hands and unfastened the buttons on his shirt. She helped him then carefully spread the material wide across his shoulders, noting his injury, healing well now. He pulled off his shirt and Rachel put her hands on his chest.

He closed his eyes as she stroked him, her fingers sifting through fine hairs and nipping at the twin disks that grew pebble hard. He was rippling with glorious muscle, and she touched him over and over, until his restraint vanished. He growled deep in his throat and once again lifted her, the look in his eyes one of an animal ready to devour his prey.

He came down on the bed kissing her with enough fire to burn clear through the mighty Sierras. Her body curved into his, his manhood pressing her belly, yearning for release. He held her head steady in his hands and moved his mouth to her throat once again, this time with sweeping long strokes of his tongue. She arched up, anticipating his next assault, and when his mouth found her awaiting erect nipple she cried out. Every stroke made her whimper with delight and whatever he couldn't accomplish with his mouth he managed with nimble fingers.

Her body moved in rhythm with his. Wild undulations made her pant out her breaths. Cooper shed the rest of his clothes with smooth movements and then, he rose above her, both of their bodies aching for the release that would join and then claim them.

He touched the most sensitive place between her legs and found moisture there. His fingers brushed over the spot again and again. An aura of bliss surrounded her like an unseen halo as she surrendered to him and simply enjoyed every caress.

The fire barely flickered, the burning logs falling victim to the cold but all Rachel knew now was heavenly heat. Cooper looked deep into her eyes and she nodded, anticipation growing. Carefully, he joined them, his manhood filling her and stretching the boundaries of her body. He waited with fierce eyes for her to accept him.

There was a little ache as she accommodated his size, her muscles remembering how to give way. Then he moved slightly and she moaned with pleasure and arched her hips, telling him without words that she was ready. He moved slowly, deliberately, and she came alive with each one of his thrusts that brought her desperately closer and closer to ultimate pleasure.

Cooper kept his eyes locked with hers, watching her, protecting her. She saw his restraint and the care he took to bring her fulfillment even as he drove deeper inside her. He was beautiful in body and mind, but he held secrets that always kept his expression tight and his thoughts well bound. Except for now. Now she saw him without the mask. She saw him clearly for the first time. And she gave herself up to him.

"Rachel," he ground out, his breaths coming short and quick.

She reached up and wrapped her arms around his neck. "Cooper."

The fury inside him unleashed and he moved faster and faster. Rachel's pleasure escalated, her body bending to his will, arching and moving with him, then against him until they'd risen as far as they could go. The dam burst and a flood of sensations ripped through her, making her sweat and moan and cry out. Every sliver of her being was shed in that moment. She waited for the pain, the guilt and the remorse for what she'd done to assault her, yet nothing but joy rippled through her.

Cooper lowered onto her and kissed her lips, her cheek and then her forehead. He held her tight and rolled over, bringing her into the circle of his embrace. She laid her head on his shoulder. Both were breathing hard, deep in thought.

"I didn't hurt you?" he asked in a quiet whisper.

"Do I look hurt?" Her voice was soft.

He chuckled and tightened his hold on her, brushing his lips through her hair. "No, you look beautiful."

She snuggled deeper into his chest, breathing in the scent of lust and man, earth and power. How much she'd missed that. How much she'd missed feeling vital and alive. She sighed and couldn't hide her contentment or the satisfaction she experienced in Cooper's arms.

He squeezed her gently and kissed the top of her head. "I can't stay all night," he said, and she understood he meant to protect her reputation.

Oh, but she wished it so. Nothing would be better than to wake up in Cooper's embrace. She murmured softly, "I know."

"I can't chance it for you, in case the boys decide to come back early tomorrow."

"But you can stay a few more hours."

At least she didn't have to worry about Jess coming home and finding out about this. On paydays, he visited his elderly sister two towns away and came back in time for the next workday which would be the day after tomorrow.

"That I can do. I'm not ready to leave you just yet."

Rachel smiled. "And I'm not ready for you to leave."

The lay together for a long time in the darkened room, dozing for short spans of time. But the thirst they felt for each other wasn't sated and Cooper made love to her again, this time with much less restraint. She was taken up in a storm of passion that shortened her breaths and sped up her heart, the sound of its beating pounding in her ears.

Her heartbeats had barely gotten under control when Cooper rose from the bed. "It's almost dawn," he said, pulling on his pants and turning to her. The sight of him, standing over her, his dark eyes gleaming with regret, stilled her heart. She didn't think she'd ever get accustomed to having Cooper Garnett, half-dressed and handsome as a devil, looking at her in such a way.

You can't be real.

Those softly uttered words would stay with her forever.

"I have to go, Rachel."

She sat up on the bed, covering herself with the blanket. "Come for breakfast?"

Cooper thought on that for half a second and was about to shake his head, when she added, "Please, Cooper. It's not unusual for me to cook meals for the boys this time of year when the weather turns bad. No one will think it curious to find you here for the morning meal. And well, I'll be going into town for the church service afterward. Reverend Alton is expecting me to lead the choir today. We'll be singing our Christmas hymns."

"You're going to church today?"

She nodded and immediate shame washed over her. How could she rationalize what she'd done? Even as Cooper put on his boots and buttoned his shirt, evidence of their transgression assaulted her with full force. Yet, she had a difficult time thinking that what they'd shared was anything but wonderful. "Do you think I shouldn't go now?"

Cooper's face tightened. He set this jaw firm and spoke with conviction. "No, Rachel. That's not why I questioned you. I'm not a churchgoing man, but if anyone deserves the Lord's blessing, it's you." He became real quiet and his face twisted in pain before he looked away. "I wanted to spend more time with you. I…" he began, and let out a heavy sigh as he gazed at the dying embers in the hearth. "I have something to tell you. Something that might change what you think of me."

Fear entered her heart, but she concealed it with a smile. "Cooper, you're a good man. I couldn't think anything else."

He shot her a sharp, warning look. "Rachel, you don't know me."

"I think I do," she said, but her own conviction started to ebb when she saw the dire look in his eyes.

"I gotta go. Sun's ready to come up." He bent his head and kissed her lightly on the lips then stroked her cheek.

She relished that slight touch and gazed into his eyes. "Will you come for breakfast? You can tell me what you need to say then."

He nodded. "I'll come."

She watched him walk out of the bedroom and listened for the front door to shut behind him. The minute he was gone, undeniable loneliness overtook her.

She lowered onto the bed and stared up at the ceiling. "Dear Lord," she whispered ever so quietly. "I've fallen in love with Cooper Garnett."

Chapter Five

Cooper was going to hurt Rachel. There was no doubt in his mind of that truth. If he had a half a brain, he'd tell her about the real reason he was in Cedar Flat then ride off her land without a look back. He was bound and determined to accomplish the first, but couldn't quite manage the latter.

He needed to stick around these parts to find Hollings.

He called himself ten times a fool for seducing Rachel. He should have been stronger. He should have resisted her sweet smiles, honey-blond hair and sky-blue eyes. He should have stayed in town overnight. No use thinking backward, he reasoned as he closed the bunkhouse door and met with gray clouds overhead that moved in quickly, threatening a fierce winter storm.

He wasn't looking forward to facing Rachel this morning. Not after the night they'd spent satisfying each other's needs. He wasn't a man who could do right by her. And today he had to tell her.

He knocked on her door, just past eight. It'd been only a few hours since he'd seen her, yet when she opened the door and he looked at her face, all his rightful reasoning faded into the beautiful hue of her eyes. He tipped his hat. "Morning."

She welcomed him with a sunny smile. "Morning."

They stared at each other.

Yearning deep in his gut nearly knocked him to his knees. He thought better than to act on it. He strode past her, removing his hat, attempting to ignore how striking she looked in her Sunday dress. It was a frilly little beige thing that rode up high on her neck and hugged her curves with lace everywhere. Her hair was tied up in loose curls that touched her neck soft-like. "Pretty," he said.

A pleased expression stole over her face. "Thank you."

The boy was there, too, and the second he noticed Cooper, he scrambled up from the floor and stood by his mother. "Cooper."

"Yes, Cooper is here for breakfast." Rachel told her son.

Johnny moved to Cooper's legs and touched the hat he held in his hand. "Like it."

Cooper released the hat, and the boy was all too eager to plop down on the floor right there to examine it.

"Don't get dirty now, Johnny, and take care with the hat," Rachel said to her son. "He likes big hats," she explained, and Cooper nodded. His mouth dry, he couldn't quite get the words out that would explain his situation. The boy, clad in a clean white shirt and trousers, ready for church, was a constant reminder of the child he'd lost. His own son would have been nearly the same age, had he lived. He'd be dressed up in his Sunday best, playing with his father's hat, getting ready to go to church with his family.

"I have breakfast all ready. Come," Rachel said softly, aware of his discomfort somehow, "sit down." She led him to the table that was already set, the food in covered bowls on the table.

"Smells good."

She dished up his plate and set it in front of him. "You worked up an appetite last night."

He snapped his eyes to hers, and her grin would have made him smile if what he was about to do wasn't so damn serious. "Rachel, about that."

She spared a glance at Johnny, making sure he was occupied and then turned to Cooper, staring deep into his eyes. "It wasn't a mistake, so don't try to convince me of it. If believing that makes me a bad person, then I'll do my best to repent in church today. I'll try to—"

Cooper stood, grabbed her wrist and pulled her close enough to mingle their breaths. He looked down into her eyes. "I told you last night, you're not the one who needs repenting."

She set her hands on his arms and stroked him gently. Her touch warmed everything cold inside him. "Do you need repenting?" she asked softly, her lips trembling.

"I do. I'm not fit to be here with you. Maybe you shouldn't have saved my sorry life."

Rachel blinked and tried not to show him how much his grim assessment unsettled her. "I'll never be sorry I saved your life."

"Not even if I mean to take another?"

Rachel stared at him, searching his eyes for a long moment. Cooper didn't back down; he didn't soften his glare. She needed to know his full intentions. "You can't mean—"

"I'm searching for the man who murdered my family, Rachel. The coward who set my ranch house on fire, killing my wife and boy."

The news that he'd had a family and the harsh way he spoke to her startled her speechless. She slumped in the chair, shaking her head. Finally, when she seemed to have absorbed all that he'd said, she gazed up at him and whispered so softly he barely heard her, "Tell me."

Cooper eased himself down beside her, feeling defeated in one respect, seeing the light in Rachel's eyes go dark. But at the same time, it was right that he shed the burden he held buried inside. Sharing the facts with Rachel would insure that she stay away from him now. She'd realize, once and for all, that he wasn't a man worthy of her. He was on a single-minded mission and had no room in his bleak heart for anyone, much less a widow with a child of her own.

He held nothing back when he began his explanation. "My wife, Jocelyn, and my boy, Donny, they meant everything to me…."

Rachel listened to it all, asking a few quiet questions as he told her the events leading up to his being shot on her land. He held nothing back, baring his soul and anguish with a venomous accounting of his hatred of Hollings. He looked away from her as he spoke, staring straight ahead, too cowardly to witness the pain and regret in her eyes.

When he was through, he glanced at her and the moisture pooling in her eyes told him everything he needed to know. She knew the truth now. She wouldn't harbor soft feelings for him. He'd accomplished his goal.

"You don't have to do this." Her sorrowful plea tore at his gu

"I do. I will." He left no room for doubt.

She rose abruptly, wiping away the tears that had leaked onto her cheeks. "Hitch up the wagon," she said, her body stiff and her tone formal. She was his boss, and this wasn't a request, but an order. "I'm expected at church."

Cooper hesitated a moment, watching Rachel gather her things, dress Johnny in his heavy burlap coat then put hers on. She held the boy tight to her chest and waited, refusing to look at Cooper. It's what he wanted, he told himself. Her disgust. But somehow, he hadn't really expected it.

He strode outside, noting angry clouds gathering overhead as he made his way to the barn. He hitched up the buckboard wagon and brought it to the front of the house. Rachel and Johnny waited on the porch. She handed him a covered basket and he put that in the back of the wagon. Then she set Johnny onto the seat herself, and she climbed on too quickly for him to lend his aid.

He took the loose reins in his hands, reluctant to give them over. "Rachel, there's a storm coming. Maybe you shouldn't go."

She grabbed the reins from him gently, careful not to touch him. Her smile was a little too sweet. "I know this land better than you, Cooper. The weather will hold. We'll get to town before it breaks."

He glanced at the threatening clouds once again and shook his head. "Doubtful, Rachel. Don't go."

"I'm going," she said stubbornly.

"Then I'll take you into town myself."

"No." Her lips barely moved when she added, "I'm no concern of yours."

Cooper winced at her clipped tone. Even if the storm held off until she got into town, how would she manage to get home? But she wouldn't hear another word on the subject. He already knew that. He watched her ride off, keeping Johnny close with one hand on him and the reins in the other.

Ten minutes later the sky above made a liar out of her.

Rachel couldn't get away from the Double J fast enough. She'd held her tears at bay, restraining them until she was off her land. Now they flowed freely past her cheeks and mingled with the light drizzle raining down her face. She hurried the horses along the path. Johnny would never notice her tears, the rain being the best disguise. He'd never know his mother's heart was breaking.

For Cooper.

And for his loss.

He'd had a wife. A child. Rachel had been stunned to hear it. He'd had a family, much like the family she and Josh and Johnny had been. Cooper's wife and boy died in a tragic way. But as Cooper had spoken the words, grimly distant and detached from reality, she knew of his anguish and she'd been jealous, God forgive her, of the woman who held his heart. The woman Cooper would sell his soul to avenge.

"Dear Lord," she muttered quietly, trying to still her anger. But the rage kept building as she thought of the danger Cooper might be inviting. Rachel had already mourned the loss of one man she'd loved. It had been an accident. Josh had the misfortune of being the identical twin brother of a bounty hunter after the lawbreaking scoundrel, Rusty Metcalf. Bodine had been relentless in his pursuit, so when Metcalf saw Josh in town, he'd mistakenly thought him the bounty hunter out to bring him in. Metcalf took aim and shot her unsuspecting husband in cold blood.

Now Cooper was bent on pursuing a heartless killer, mindless of the danger he might be in. Recklessly, Rachel had thrown caution to the wind and fallen in love again. She'd given herself to Cooper and now she regretted it. She couldn't go through that torment again. Of loving and losing another good man.

"Mama…I'm cold," little Johnny said, snuggling under the blanket she'd draped over him.

"I know, Johnny. Pretend we're sitting in the warm church. Afterward we'll have hot apple cider and cookies at Pastor Alton's. I promise."

Johnny shivered beside her and a crack of thunder made him jump up. "It's okay," she said, trying to comfort, but then the sky opened up and rain poured down in buckets. The road, already sodden from a hard winter had quickly turned to thick black paste. The wagon slowed, even as the horses tried pulling them free of the soaked earth. Rachel was half the distance to town. She could forge on, or turn back and go home. But going home meant dealing with Cooper, and she didn't have the courage to do that right now. She called to the duo of horses, the strongest in her string, to get going. She clucked her tongue, but no amount of encouraging could get the wagon moving faster.

Hard rain hit her cheeks. Thunder boomed and a flash of lightning lit the sky. Johnny cried out and she did her best to comfort him, snuggling him deeper into the blanket that was two dry threads away from being drenched. She *had* to turn back. She had no choice now.

"Stay here, Johnny. Mama's going to turn the horses." Rachel climbed down from the wagon, her booted feet sinking into three inches of mud. She trudged to the front of the horses and grabbed hold of Blaze's bridle. Another clap of thunder boomed overhead, and the mare jolted nervously, shoving against Rachel's shoulder. She felt herself flying backward, knocked off her feet into thick layers of sludge. Her head met with something hard on the ground. Sharp pain exploded and she cried out. Her mind spun as the cold ooze of the earth sucked her farther down. She fought to keep her eyes open, but she lost that battle all too soon, and they closed against the blinding rain. Her fading thoughts were of Johnny, alone in the wagon.

"Rachel, Rachel, wake up, darlin'."

Rachel's eyes opened slowly to the sound of Cooper's gentle voice. He held her carefully in his arms. A sense of peace washed over her. Was she dreaming or was he really here, holding her close, looking at her with softness in his eyes. Her mind muddled and her thoughts scattered like fallen leaves swept up by the wind. "Cooper," she uttered, barely able to catch her breath.

He lowered her to the bed, the chill in her bones warming now as she felt the familiar sag of her mattress underneath her. "W-what happened?"

"You got caught in the storm," he said, his eyes roving over her slowly, intent on his examination. He sat on the bed beside her. "Do you remember?"

The minute she did, her eyes went wide and she tried to lift up. "Johnny!"

Cooper wouldn't let her rise. With care, he grabbed her shoulders and eased her back down. "He's fine. Stay down and rest. I'll get him."

Cooper left her side for a moment. When he returned, her beautiful boy was clinging to Cooper's neck. He was wrapped in a blanket, soaked to the bone. "I'm going to get the fire going and dry him up. Just rest, Rachel."

"Don't go," she said, focusing on her son. "Please."

"Mama's hurt," Johnny said, shivering and pointing his finger at her.

Cooper set Johnny down and built a fire in the hearth, explaining, "Your ma hit her head on a rock. But your mama's head is harder than the rock." Cooper sent her a sideways glance. "She's going to be just fine."

Johnny seemed to absorb every word. He nodded, watching Cooper toss a match into kindling. The fire blazed to life, fascinating her son.

"We've got to get you dry, Johnny," Cooper said, hunkering down next to Johnny. He faced her son on his knees and removed the blanket wrapped snugly around him, then began peeling off his wet clothes. When he was through, Cooper dried him with a towel, rubbing his skin gently up and down then tousling his mussed hair, making Johnny giggle.

Rachel's head ached liked the dickens and a quick flash of memory reminded her why. She recalled the storm, and all that occurred before it. But seeing Cooper with Johnny eased the pain in her head some, witnessing for the first time Cooper's gentle way with her boy. Up until now, Cooper barely regarded Johnny and she'd wondered if he didn't like children. But now she knew the truth and her heart ached, seeing the father Cooper had once been. Seeing the care he gave Johnny, despite his reluctance, made her love him even more.

Johnny rubbed his eyes, a telltale sign of his fatigue. Though it couldn't be more than ten in the morning, her baby had already been through a grueling day.

"Kiss Mama," Cooper said, lifting Johnny in his arms, then lowering him at an angle enough for Johnny to plant two moist lips to her cheek. She smiled and thanked God for Cooper's rescue today, berating herself for her silly foolish pride that put her son in danger.

She didn't want to think about Cooper's would-be act of vengeance. Not now. It hurt her head too much. All she wanted...was right here in front of her. Her son and the man she loved.

"Thank you, Johnny. I love you so very much." *And you too, Cooper.*

When he reached for her, Cooper pulled him away. "You'll see your mama later. She needs to rest." Cooper caught her eye then, and she nodded. "I'll be back to deal with your injury," he said.

Rachel watched him leave the room holding Johnny in his arms. The scene was almost too hard to witness because she wanted it so. She wanted Cooper to stay, to make her whole again. To make the three of them a family.

Rachel closed her eyes tight and made a wish.

The only one she had for Christmas.

Chapter Six

An hour later, Rachel sat up in her bed, sipping coffee that Cooper had laced with a bit of whiskey. For her nerves, he'd said, and to warm her up. She winced at the taste, the liquor burning her throat as it went down. The storm raged outside. No telling when it would let up. She'd been careless and rash and let her stubborn pride win out over rational thinking. Now she saw the error of her ways.

"Thank you," she offered to Cooper, who sat in a chair across from her. "For coming for us."

This was the first chance she'd had to truly thank him, and she didn't have words enough to show her appreciation. After he'd gotten Johnny to sleep, Cooper had returned to her room. He'd washed the slight blood from her head and undressed her. She'd protested, but then realized she didn't have the strength to argue. He'd taken her muddy clothes off her down to her chemise and left her to clean herself up while he brewed a pot of coffee in the kitchen.

Now, she was relatively clean, dabbed with rose water and didn't smell as much like cow dung.

Cooper looked down into his mug of coffee, shaking his head. "It was a fool move, Rachel."

"I know," she admitted.

"You put your life in danger," he said, his voice stern and angry.

She couldn't disagree. She'd put Johnny's life at risk, and she'd never forget it or forgive herself yet she couldn't help but defend her actions. "Not deliberately."

"I warned you and you should have listened."

When she thought he'd continue lecturing her, he said instead, "I'm to blame. It was my fault."

Her head snapped up. "No, it wasn't."

"I hurt you, Rachel. It wasn't my intent." He looked at her now, his gaze roving over the flow of her hair. "And you lashed out."

"I'm prideful."

"Yeah." He almost smiled in agreement and then his voice took on a fierce tone. "I couldn't stand it if you or the boy got hurt on my account."

"We won't," she lied. She already knew that the day Cooper left for good, both she and Johnny would miss him terribly for the longest time. "I mean, I won't do anything so incredibly... thoughtless, again."

A log fell in the hearth and the fire blazed, outlining the angles of Cooper's handsome face.

"But won't you reconsider, Cooper? Won't you let the authorities handle the situation with Hollings?"

"I won't rest until that man is dead."

A chill ran along her spine at the cold way he uttered that statement.

"I can't expect them to find Hollings," he went on. "He's been drifting from place to place. Spending my money." He shook his head and his expression grew even fiercer. "He took *everything* from me."

Rachel hurt for him. She understood the kind of pain that burned a hole in your stomach day in and day out from grieving. She set her cup down and rose to kneel in front of him. Her hand went to his face, her fingers brushing over his skin lightly. "I'm sorry for your loss."

He held her hand to his face, crushing her palm to his cheek, and he closed his eyes briefly. "You matter to me, Rachel."

She lifted her lips to his and kissed him.

He pulled away from her, his voice strained with regret. "I should go. Leave the ranch before—"

"Is that what you want?" she breathed.

He sighed, the heavy sound coming from deep inside. "Don't,

Rachel. You tempt me and I'm not strong enough to resist you like this. But mark my words, I will have to leave you one day."

In that moment, Rachel knew what she wanted. And that was Cooper—on his terms if it had to be that way. The longer he stayed, the longer she'd have to change his mind. He wasn't a killer. She'd never think of him that way.

"But you're here now. That's all I'm asking."

He touched the strands of hair just below the bruised knot at the back of her head. "You're injured."

The greatest injury was to her heart, not her head. "It doesn't hurt anymore."

Cooper took her arms gently and lifted them both up so they stood by the fire. He kissed her soundly on the lips, brushing their bodies close. She trembled from his touch, from being so near him. Was she wrong to want this time with him? To feel his strength and power, his warmth and comfort for just a little while?

He wrapped both arms around her waist and pulled her even closer, his mouth claiming hers in heated, hungry kisses. She fell into him, yearning for more. Had it been just last night that they'd been together like this, when he'd made her feel womanly and alive again?

He scooped her up easily and carried her back to bed. She watched him shed his clothes as the rain continued to fall with far less rage. It was eerily dark and noiseless now, but for the pings hitting the window and rooftop.

She marveled at how beautiful a man Cooper was. Firelight danced shadows across his body but couldn't hide his pure manly form, the breadth of his shoulders that led to a narrowed waist. The bed took his weight with a creak and groan, and Rachel slid aside to make room for him. He took her back into his arms immediately, his gaze watchful, taking care that he wasn't hurting her.

The only way he could truly hurt me is to leave, she thought.

And then, Cooper banished all thoughts from her head. He made love to her with slow and deliberate moves that made her breaths quicken and her body arch and ache for more. He nuzzled her neck and moistened her skin with his tongue, causing unabashed cries of pleasure to surge from her throat.

She swallowed hard and tried to catch her breath every time his hands caressed her breasts, every time his mouth wreaked havoc with her lips.

She witnessed a fiery gleam in his eyes, his expression taut and filled with lust. And when he rolled over and beckoned her with a gaze so hot it would surely melt snow, she rose over him and made love to him in much the same fashion as he had her. She relished his body with her mouth and moistened his skin with her tongue.

"Rachel," he groaned, his kisses intense and his arms about her possessively. She loved the feel of him, the way she could bring him pleasure. He held her firm now, his hands splayed over her waist. And in his next breath, Cooper lifted her atop him, bringing her down onto his shaft, filling her body with him.

She ached for him in every way and she took him inside her with shameless joy. He guided her with sure eyes, his body responding to her every move. The pleasure heightened and she closed her eyes to him, absorbing every bone-melting sensation, riding Cooper as she was, fully aware that she'd never forget this moment, not if she lived one hundred years.

"Now, sweetheart," he urged. And they rode the storm out together until lightning struck one last time and the last drops of their passion were shed.

Rachel sank down on Cooper, exhausted and happy, her body still humming. He held her tight and planted kisses on her forehead. They lay there for several minutes until their breaths calmed. Then he whispered, "Will you do something for me?"

Anything. "What is that?"

"Stay in bed and try to rest. The storm's over. I've got to see to the fire and check on the livestock."

Rachel snuggled against him. She wanted to ask him to stay in bed with her, but she knew he was right. She needed to rest, to gain her strength back from the ordeal out on the road. "I'll rest."

He kissed her one last time then got out of bed. "I'll check on you later. Get some sleep."

Rachel nodded, watching him dress by the fire. When he left the room, her eyes drifted closed. Her heart heavy now, she realized that with the storm passing and the boys coming back to the ranch soon, her time alone with Cooper was almost over.

* * *

Cooper left the comfort of Rachel's bed. He wasn't thinking clearly. He had to get a grip and shake the cobwebs from his addled brain. He stared out the window in the main room, watching light drizzle ebb and clouds overhead disperse. The skies would lighten soon as the sun forced its way through the gloom. The earth would dry and life would continue on as usual.

His respite with Rachel was a mistake, though the mistake felt too damn good. He'd been a fool to weaken to temptation. There was no way around hurting Rachel when he did what he came here to do. His recovery and this storm had interrupted his plans, but now he had no excuses, no reason not to fully engage in finding Hollings and setting that part of his life to rights.

Cooper left the window and strode quietly to pull the curtain back and check on the boy. Johnny slept peacefully, his little body curled up and snuggled under a heavy quilt. The boy had been frightened and near hysterical when Cooper had found him on the wagon, ready to try to climb down to help his mother. He'd been freezing cold and shivering. Cooper was only glad he'd gotten there in time before the boy was injured.

He'd rescued Rachel and Johnny from the elements and he was grateful to have saved them, but it didn't make up for his leaving his wife and child unprotected on the ranch. He hadn't *saved* them. How many times had Jocelyn asked him to teach her how to shoot a gun? How many times had she wanted to learn how to protect herself? Cooper argued that he'd never leave her in danger so he'd denied her time and again, asking for her trust. Perhaps his pride had been at stake and it had bolstered him when she'd dropped the request. She had trusted him. And in the end, he had betrayed her.

Cooper watched the boy sleep, mesmerized by Johnny's sweet breaths sliding up and down his little chest. He was an innocent child who'd deserved a family, a mother and a father to love and raise him. Cooper shook his head at the thought.

It wouldn't be him.

He couldn't fail another family.

Cooper put on his heavy coat, lifting the collar to the cold and strode outside. He had cows to milk, horses to tend, stalls to muck and eggs to gather. He wouldn't let Rachel down, at least not in that respect.

He did his work in intervals, checking on Rachel and Johnny before moving on to the next chore. He needed to keep his mind on other matters, but every so often he'd lose the struggle and fist his hands tight, thinking about the day when he would leave the Double J Ranch and Rachel behind.

She was alone before you came and she'll be alone when you go.

But she wasn't entirely alone, he thought. She had Jess and the boys. She had friends in town and neighbors nearby. That thought brought him a measure of solace.

He filled a bucket with oats and carried it around to the horse stalls. "There you go," he said to Blaze, giving her an extra helping. "You had yourself quite a day." It wasn't the horse's fault that Rachel had been shoved down and hurt. In truth, he'd hitched up the most docile horses for her ride into town. A more spirited horse might have reared up and trampled her.

Cooper made his way into the house to check on Johnny. The boy had been napping for almost three hours. When he peered behind the curtain of his room, he found Johnny sitting up on his knees, looking a bit bewildered, his blond hair tousled from sleep. "Where's Mama?" he said, clutching his blanket.

Cooper removed his coat and strode over to him. "She's napping, just like you."

Johnny crawled the length of the bed and once he reached the foot he lifted his arms to Cooper. "Up."

Cooper's gut twisted tight and he hesitated a moment. The hopeful look on the boy's face melted the cold in his heart. He lifted Johnny in his arms and held him to his chest. The boy set his head on his shoulder, and Cooper closed his eyes, breathing in Johnny's little boy scent and the sweetness of his skin.

Just minutes later, Cooper sat with Johnny on his lap as the main room's fire snapped and crackled. He held a picture book in his hands and Johnny pointed out and recited each object. The boy was amazingly bright for his age and adept at learning. His mother would have no trouble with his schooling in that regard.

Cooper felt another presence in the room as the scent of roses wafted in. He turned his head to find Rachel in the bedroom doorway, watching.

Her eyes gleamed and her face filled with quiet joy as she looked at the two of them and the scene they must have presented. Her expression appeared full of hope and expectation. He wanted to shout out, no. Don't look at us this way. Her soft wishful smile ripped him to shreds.

He rose immediately, putting Johnny down on the chair with the book and stared at her. "You look rested."

She moved across the room. "I slept well." She lifted her son and settled him against her hip. Gently, she fingered a few stray strands of hair off his forehead and kissed him there.

"Mama, Cooper learned me."

Cooper stiffened when she cast a knowing look his way before responding to her son. "I saw that, sweetness."

"How's your head?" he asked her.

"Better. It doesn't hurt anymore. I'm feeling fine."

"Okay then." He glanced out the window to find sunshine breaking through the clouds. "I've got more chores to do."

"O-okay," she said, her eyes dimming. Disappointment filled her expression when she realized his withdrawal and Cooper knew it was for the best. Tomorrow, he'd continue his manhunt. "I'll see you at supper."

He nodded, then put his coat and hat on and walked out the door. The sooner she got used to not having him around, the better.

Chapter Seven

Two days after the storm, Cooper received a message from Chick, who'd just gotten back from a trip into town. "The sheriff has news he says you'd want to know. He wants you to come into town soon as you can."

Cooper lowered the brim of his hat, hiding the expectant expression on his face. Finally, maybe he had a lead. "Did he say anything else?"

"Nope, just for me to get the message to you."

"Okay, thanks."

A hundred notions muddled his mind, but the one that stuck, the one that gave him both peace and a sense of dread, was that the sheriff knew something about Hollings.

It was late in the afternoon and he was done repairing fences along the northern edge of the pasture. He'd put in a full day's work and wouldn't sleep a wink all night if he waited for tomorrow to see the sheriff.

Chick was halfway to the bunkhouse when Cooper called out, "I'm going into town. Tell Jess not to wait on supper."

Chick acknowledged him and when Cooper turned his head, he saw Rachel on the porch, her gaze locked with his. With determined steps, she marched down the stairs, coming straight toward him. "Why are you going into town, Cooper?"

He winced, seeing the concern in her eyes. "That's my business."

"I see," she said, her blue eyes sparking fire. His rude response didn't stop her. "What business?"

Cooper sighed. "Rachel, the sheriff wants to see me."

She blinked and her words escaped with a gasp. "He's found Hollings."

Cooper rubbed the back of his neck. "I don't know that for sure."

"But you're hoping." She rushed the words out like an accusation.

He couldn't look into her eyes. He peered down at the tips of her boots, nearly touching his. She was beautiful and kind and spirited, but he couldn't let that persuade him. Not after he'd come so far. "Yeah, I'm hoping."

"Cooper, let the sheriff handle it," she pleaded.

"Rachel, we've been over this."

"What are you going to do?" she asked, her voice a mere whisper. Her eyes went soft on him and tugged his heart in ten different directions.

He took his hat off and ran a hand through his hair. "I'm going to see the sheriff, is all."

"But you're coming back tonight. Promise me you won't run off to hunt that man down by yourself."

Cooper slammed his eyes shut briefly, realizing he shouldn't have gotten close to Rachel. He left her with the truth before riding into town, "I can't make you that promise."

Now Cooper stood inside Sheriff O'Reilly's office hearing news he hadn't exactly expected to hear. "Mr. Garnett, we've found the man responsible for shooting and robbing you."

Cooper's brows rose in astonishment. He'd been so bent on getting Hollings, he'd hardly given the other crime a thought.

"He's locked up in there."

Cooper glanced at the door that separated the office from the cells and nodded. The sheriff shoved a gun, holster, some cash and a daguerreotype toward him. He pointed to the image of Jocelyn, Donny and him on that picture frame. Cooper's body went rigid. Of all the things stolen, that likeness was what he'd missed the most. "That's how we knew these were your belongings. We believe the horse he was riding is yours."

"How did you find him?" Cooper asked. "And who is he?"

"He's a drifter. He doesn't come from these parts. Name's Clyde Berkins. He'd tried shooting Guy Wimbley, a local hired hand, as he was leaving town after dark. He took his shot and missed. Guy ran chase and downed him with a bullet to his shoulder. He's gonna live to stand trial. Not too bright a fella. You'd think he'd have left the county after what he did to you. You want to see him?"

"Yeah," Cooper said, and he was led to the other room where the man stood behind bars. Cooper didn't say a word. He looked into the eyes of a killer, seeing no remorse, no regret on his face. The man was cold as a block of ice, brazen in his returned stare. After a few seconds, Cooper turned to the sheriff. "I've seen enough."

The sheriff had him sign for his possessions and took him out back. Cooper took one look at his bay, Bell, and let out a curse. He stroked her gently, careful not to touch the welts on her body.

"Some men got no respect for anything," the sheriff said with disgust. "Leave her at the livery with Mattie Sanders and he'll fix her right up. Might take a few days of healing, but she'll be fine."

"I'll see to it." Cooper slid his hand down her snout with care. "You haven't heard anything about the other matter?" Cooper asked. "Nothing about Hollings?"

"No, sorry to say. He might have moved on."

"Maybe," Cooper said. And maybe it was time he did the same.

On Saturday morning, four days before Christmas, Rachel packed a basket of pecan pies and sweet muffins she'd baked the night before then tied the woolen socks she'd knitted for Mikey Ray with ribbon and strode out of the house with Johnny in hand. "We're going to visit Mikey Ray and his family," she told her son. "He'll be glad to see you, sweetness."

She closed up the house and stepped down from the porch, walking toward the buckboard wagon. Cooper stood by the hitched team, waiting.

She narrowed her eyes. "Where's Jess?"

"He's not taking you. I am."

Johnny released her hand and ran to Cooper, looking up at him. "Why? Is something wrong with Jess? He wanted to see Mikey Ray."

"Nope, nothing's wrong with Jess." Cooper cast her a guilty look, one that he might've been able to disguise from someone else, but not from her.

Cooper had ridden off the ranch every chance he'd had this past week, going into town for supplies, finding excuses to visit other ranches, and she knew the reason why. He was deep in pursuit of a killer. Rachel's heart plummeted thinking about it. After he'd come back from the sheriff's office with news that they'd found his shooter, Rachel had been relieved. She'd thought that would have been enough to appease him for a time. But ever since then, he'd used every spare moment he'd had to continue his search.

"I know why you're going, Cooper. Mikey Ray's homestead is clear across the county. I doubt you've gotten that far as yet."

Cooper lowered the brim of his hat and took the basket from her hands. "Couldn't be that I want to see the boy."

Rachel's mouth curled down. "It would be the Christian thing to think, wouldn't it?"

"Then you should be thinking it."

He set the basket in the back then helped her up, his arms wrapping around her waist. Their eyes met and she found no comfort in their deep depths except for the slightest flicker in his eyes. But oh, having his hands on her again brought back such yearning.

She adjusted her position on the seat and Cooper hoisted Johnny up, giving him a bit of a twirl, enough to make her boy giggle. They set off for the Hanson homestead, Johnny's questions and excitement over the trip keeping them both from speaking their minds. The ride was long and Johnny began fidgeting. Rachel had trouble keeping him still in her lap. She'd tried calming him, playing games and singing songs, but Johnny's attention lapsed, and she struggled with her hold on him.

"Settle down, boy," Cooper said in a stern voice, reaching out to put his hand on Johnny's shoulder. "Mind your ma."

That was all it took. A stern reprimand from Cooper and Johnny immediately settled on her lap. He stared at Cooper and the next time Cooper glanced at him, Johnny grinned.

The little devil.

They reached the homestead by midmorning and were greeted by Mikey Ray's entire family. Rachel introduced Cooper to the boy's parents and brothers and they all thanked him for saving Mikey from a herd of frightened horses.

Mikey looked well rested and announced he would be returning to work on the ranch after the holiday. When he bent down to give Johnny a big bear hug, Rachel saw firsthand his recovery. He lifted Johnny in his arms and carried him into the house without flinching.

Not a minute after his mother set out the basket, Mikey Ray dug into one of the cinnamon-and-raisin muffins she'd brought along. He jammed half of it into his mouth. "This is delicious as ever, Miss Rachel."

"Mikey, I'm so glad to see you're feeling fit. And with a hearty appetite again."

"He's eating more than a grizzly," his mother, Marie Hanson said. "I can't seem to stop him. Pretty soon you'll see what I mean with your boy. Now, isn't your Johnny just the sweetest thing."

They all looked at Johnny, who at the moment had become curious about a crocheted handkerchief covering a small round table. His little hands grabbed for it, and before Rachel could stop him, he yanked and a thin, beautifully etched crystal flower vase fell onto its side and began to roll off the table. Cooper was there instantly, catching the flower vase with one hand, while scooping up Johnny with the other.

"You saved the day again, Cooper," Mikey Ray said with a grin. "That was my ma's favorite vase."

Cooper righted the handkerchief and the vase.

"Not to worry," Mrs. Hanson said in a rush. "No harm's been done."

Rachel strode over to Cooper and faced him with gratitude. Johnny hung sideways against Cooper's hip, like a sack of potatoes. Apparently, her son loved it. She reached for Johnny, taking him out of Cooper's arm. "Thank you," she whispered, nearly mortified. For the rest of the day, she kept Johnny within her reach.

"I'll be sure to wear my new wool socks, Miss Rachel," Mikey Ray said as he bid them farewell once their visit was over. "Thank you kindly."

"You're welcome, Mikey Ray. We'll be seeing you at the ranch soon. Merry Christmas."

"Merry Christmas to you, too," Mikey Ray said with a wave. The entire family, all five of them, came outside to see them off.

Rachel waved to them until they were no longer in sight. Then she turned back around and adjusted Johnny on her lap, tossing a light blanket over him. He rested his head on her chest and she knew he'd be napping in just a matter of minutes.

"Well? What did you find out?" she said to Cooper, sounding like a chirpy little bird.

"About what?" Cooper held the reins and stared straight ahead.

"You went outside with Mr. Hanson and Mikey's older brothers for a smoke. I saw you through the window. You were questioning them."

"And you want to know what I found out?"

"Yes, I do."

He glanced at her and shook his head. To his credit, genuine concern formed in his expression. "You really *don't* want to know."

"I do," she said firmly with a nod, but when he remained silent she touched his arm. "Cooper, this affects me, too."

His lips pulled down. "I know. I didn't mean for that to happen."

"But it did."

He was quiet for a few more seconds. When he finally spoke, his voice held no emotion. "You know Mikey's father and brothers hire themselves out to local ranches for work. Jed is a smithy at the Bar K and Mikey's other brothers work for the Circle Six Ranch."

She knew that. She could only afford to hire one Hanson, the youngest, since she paid lower wages than most other ranches. She waited patiently to hear more.

"Well, both Mr. Hanson and Jed know of a drifter who keeps to himself. They've seen him in town a few times. He never says much and he's always wearing a scarf around his neck, even if the weather is clear. His hair touches his shoulders and he's got a beard. They say he looks sort of strange."

Rachel's heart stilled. "You think it's him?"

Cooper shook his head. "Don't know. Jed said he might be working one of the smaller spreads up by the foothills."

Rachel swallowed the news with dread spreading through her body. She was certain of one thing. Cooper would go in search of his family's killer and there wasn't anything she could do about it.

Christmas was fast approaching, and Rachel continued with traditions she'd started when Josh was alive. During the nights leading up to the holiday, she invited all her hands to the house after their meal to help her with stringing popcorn for the little pine tree she'd asked Cooper to chop down for the holiday. She served hot cider and baked pumpkin muffins then led them all in cheerful Christmas songs. The younger boys helped her tie colorful ribbons and lace onto the tree.

The house filled with neighbors stopping by with Christmas cakes and good wishes. Except for Cooper, who was always deep in thought, everyone's mood was light and cheerful.

Rachel didn't press him on those nights, but she didn't allow him to escape from the festivities, either, which seemed his inclination. She'd conjure up little chores for him to do, making sure he was always part of the group. Johnny loved the commotion and was always in the middle of everything. Too often, she'd see Johnny reach for Cooper's hand. It broke her heart to witness Cooper bond with him and know that maybe one day, he'd be gone.

Two nights before Christmas, as the celebration continued in the evening, Chick handed her two gifts, one tied with a pretty pink ribbon and a bigger one tied with blue. "This is from all of the boys," he said. "The pink one is for you, of course. Johnny gets the other."

"Thank you," she said, her heart truly touched with warmth. She opened her gift and marveled at the pretty pendant, etched with a rose design that they'd given her. "It's lovely. I'll wear it on Christmas Day," she said. Then she cast a look at her boy, who had quieted some, sitting on Jess's lap concentrating on the story Jess was telling him. "I'll save Johnny's for Christmas morning."

A short while later, Rachel said good-night to everyone, handing them their gifts as they returned to the bunkhouse. She'd knitted a wool blanket for Jess, and scarves and socks for everyone else. As Cooper was leaving, she stopped him with a gentle hand on his arm. "Can you stay an extra minute?"

He nodded and waited by the door. He didn't speak much these days, his expression always pensive with a distant look in his eyes. Rachel went to her bedroom and brought out a package she had tied with simple string. "This is for you. Merry Christmas, Cooper."

"You didn't have to do this," he said, humbled.

She put the package in his hands. "Open it."

Cooper stared at her a moment. She nodded her encouragement. As he pulled the strings loose, the surrounding brown paper unfolded and the plaid shirt she'd sewn appeared. He lifted it up and took a second to admire it. "Did you make this?"

She tilted her head and smiled. "I thought you might be tired of wearing Josh's clothes."

"It's thoughtful," he said, fingering the fabric before folding it up again. "Thank you. I don't have a mind for Christmas, Rachel. I can't celebrate—"

"I…know."

"I wish things were different. I wish I had a special gift for you."

She met his eyes and spoke softly, from deep in her heart. "I only want one thing from you, Cooper."

He looked at her with such pain on his face she could barely stand it. "I can't give you what you want."

She touched his cheek and lifted up to brush a tender kiss on his lips. "I wish things were different, as well."

She turned away from Cooper then, and as soon as she heard him close the door, tears she'd held back bravely streamed freely down her cheeks.

Chapter Eight

The next morning, the day of Christmas Eve, Rachel walked toward the barn and wasn't surprised to see Cooper standing by her buckboard wagon. He would accompany her to town and it wasn't because she was such engaging company, but because Cooper was bent on his search. He'd managed to convince Jess that he needed to see as much of the county as possible in the shortest amount of time.

And Jess, she suspected, was only too happy to give up this trip to town. Somehow, over the past weeks, Jess had taken a shine to Cooper and thinking himself a matchmaker of sorts, had seen to it that she and Cooper spent a good deal of time together.

When she reached the wagon with Johnny in hand, a frown pulled her lips down when she met with Cooper's stare. His eyes, filled with determination, and his stance told her he was ready for her argument. After last night, with her tears spent and her heart aching, Rachel didn't have any fight left in her. Cooper's will had won out.

He helped her climb into the wagon as he'd done many times before, his hands always gentle yet firm on her waist. She tried not to long for his touch or for the simplest of gestures that set her heart and mind spinning. She tried not to think about him at all. But that was proving darn hard to do with him wearing the new shirt she'd given him, looking perfect in red-and-gray plaid and handsome as the devil. She tried to focus solely on Johnny and making him comfortable for the ride.

They rode in silence for a spell and on occasion she caught Cooper glancing at her with a questioning look on his face. She ignored him until finally, after several more minutes of silence, he turned to her. "Have a bee in your bonnet, Rachel?"

She shrugged and glanced around. "I'm not wearing a bonnet and last I looked, there are no bees around here."

"Uh-huh. You want me to believe that you're not sore with me about something?"

"No, I'm not sore at you."

"I'm not believing that."

"Well, I don't…I don't rightly care what you believe, Cooper Garnett."

"Okay, but it's too dang pretty a day to be mad. The sun's out bright and clear and you should be happy."

"I'm happy," she lied.

"I'd sure like to hear you sing one of them Christmas songs."

"You would?" Rachel turned to him fully, confused by his sudden interest in the Christmas spirit. "Why?"

"'Cause the only thing prettier than the way you sing is your sweet smile. Figure I'd get both if you sang a song."

Cooper was, in his own charming way, trying to make up for hurting her last night. In her heart, Rachel believed she'd never really have him until he put the past behind him. She also believed he truly didn't mean to cause her harm. But knowing it and trying to justify that truth wasn't easy. She'd never met a more stubborn, determined man in her life. "Which song do you like?"

"'Joy to the World,' is real nice."

Johnny tugged on her skirt. "Sing, Mama."

Rachel had no choice now, and though she narrowed her eyes at Cooper, he was wise enough not to smirk when she sat up straighter in the seat and began to sing. After a few verses, her mood lightened and the smile that Cooper thought so pretty, returned to her face.

Once they reached town, Cooper asked, "Where do you want to stop first?"

"Oh, I'd like to say hello to Pastor Alton and his wife and then I should stop by the bank, before I go to the mercantile."

Cooper drove the wagon to the church. He waited while she and Johnny had a short visit with the Altons. Rachel brought them fresh oatmeal cookies and a mince pie and wished them a Merry Christmas before returning to the wagon.

Then Cooper drove the wagon farther into town toward the Bank of California. Robert Livingston, who'd just stepped out of the bank, caught sight of her and waved. Rachel almost wished Cooper would drive on, but Robert had already taken measures to greet the wagon. He had a smile from ear to ear and Rachel cringed inside. He'd been a persistent would-be suitor and Rachel tried time and again to discourage him. "Hello, Miss Rachel. I'm so happy to see you this morning. Might I escort you into the bank?"

"Well, uh, yes. That would be fine." Rachel turned toward Cooper. "Would you stay with Johnny while I take care of some business?"

Cooper gave a cursory glance to the younger man and nodded an acknowledgment. "Livingston."

Robert inclined his head. "Mr. Cooper."

"Do you two know each other?" Rachel asked, looking from one man to the other.

"Well, uh, yes. I met Mr. Cooper a short time ago. He, uh, had some questions for me…about his half brother. Poor man had been burned in a fire."

Rachel needed no further explanation. Cooper probed everyone he met about the scarred man.

"Go on, Rachel," Cooper said. "Get your business done."

Robert helped her down from the wagon. He held her a little too close and too long for her liking. She pulled away as soon as her boots touched the ground, straightening her gown. Out of the corner of her eye she saw Cooper shoot Robert a cool glare, and Rachel's mood immediately lifted.

Once her bank business had concluded, Robert insisted on escorting her back outside. He didn't try to conceal his frown when he found Cooper standing beside the wagon with Johnny in his arms, waiting.

"I'll take it from here." Cooper smiled at Robert. "We have one more stop before we head home."

An awkward moment passed, and then Robert bade her farewell, wishing her a Merry Christmas.

Rachel's heart lurched. If only Cooper meant it. If only the Double J was truly his home. Yet, she couldn't help but be encouraged by his bout of jealousy.

As they rode farther into town, Rachel noted Cooper's eyes darting from one establishment to another, his gaze honing in on every rider, every male walking along the sidewalk. He was a hawk, searching for his prey.

"This shouldn't take long," she said, once they crossed town to the Cedar Creek Mercantile. "I'll drop off these extra scarves and socks to Mr. Woodcock. And while I'm there I'll get us some candies for Christmas."

"Mmm, candy," Johnny said. "Candy, Mama."

Rachel chuckled. "I know, sweetness. You be good for Cooper and I'll bring you a licorice stick."

"I be good," her eager boy said with a big grin.

Rachel bounded down from the wagon without Cooper's aid this time and grabbed a basket of her knitted ware. She walked inside the shop and Mr. Woodcock greeted her kindly. "Nice to see you, Miss Rachel. I dare say you have perfect timing."

She sent the shop owner a smile. "How's that, Mr. Woodcock?"

"Well, Mr. Brown, just right now, stopped in looking for a new scarf."

"Oh, that is good timing." Rachel set down her basket on the counter, giving Mr. Brown a cursory look. He was a contradiction, she thought, wearing fine clothes, but his hair was overly long and his beard scruffy. The black scarf around his neck was shabby and ready to be replaced. "Would you like to try one of color?" she asked. "I have light brown or how about this gray one?" She lifted both for him to see.

"Thanks, ma'am." He took the darker one and removed his old scarf in a hurry to try the gray one she handed him.

That's when she noticed his neck. His scarred neck!

Rachel's heart raced, pounding against her chest so hard she very nearly swayed right there by the counter. She disguised her panic and concealed her inspection of his face. From this close, she noticed red slashes on the left side, under his beard. As he wrapped her scarf around his neck, his hair shoved aside and that was when she knew for sure she was looking into the eyes of Brett Hollings, the man who'd killed Cooper's family.

"I'll take two," he said quietly to Mr. Woodcock.

She froze. Time seemed to stop. Somewhere in her mind she realized Hollings had cast her a strange look before moving to the back of the store in need of other items.

"Rachel?" Mr. Woodcock called out. "Rachel, dear. Are you ill?"

Rachel blinked, then looked at him, her body trembling. "N-no." Her mind muddled for another second, then barely able to say the words, she breathed out, "I have to go."

She exited the shop in a stupor and stood woodenly on the sidewalk. Seconds ticked by. She knew she couldn't hide this from Cooper, but everything inside her screamed with dread.

Slowly, she walked to the wagon. Cooper was playing a tickling game with Johnny. Her boy's giggles broke her spell. She climbed up on the wagon and sat down beside Cooper.

"Ready to leave?" he asked, his smile broad.

Yes. She could tell him to leave. She could go home with him and keep him safe. But his search would never end. He'd move on eventually. He'd go from town to town, drifting, seeking justice and a way to redeem himself from the guilt that plagued him. Rachel couldn't deceive him. But oh, how she wanted to.

"Rachel?" he asked, finally noticing her state. "You're white as a sheet."

She turned to him, her mind made up and her heart breaking. "Cooper, listen to me. You're a good man. A decent man. I know it in my heart. I love you. Truly and wholly, I love you. We can be a family. Together. The three of us. If you do the right thing. If you just let the law—"

"Rachel, honey, what are you talking about?" He appeared puzzled, but there was softness in his eyes. For her. Could it be that he loved her?

"Hollings." She squeezed her eyes shut.

"What about Hollings?" His tone immediately changed and she snapped her eyes open.

"I think he's inside the mercantile. I saw a man with burns on the left side of his face and neck. He's...*scarred.*"

Cooper's expression shifted. His eyes grew cold. The angles of his face tightened. Everything she knew of Cooper Garnett had instantly changed. He reached in the back of the buckboard and withdrew a shotgun.

"Take the boy and go home, Rachel."

"Cooper, no. I'm not leaving."

Cooper jumped down from the wagon and handed her the reins. "You don't want to be here. You don't want to see what I'm about to do."

Tears sprang from her eyes. "Cooper, *please*."

He shook his head. "Once it's done, I'll head back to Nevada. Pick up the pieces of my sorry life. I won't be worthy of you. You won't want to know me."

"That's not true!"

His stern voice lent no room for argument. "I swear I don't want you in the middle of this. Take Johnny and leave." He glanced at Johnny and then shot her a long look with regret darkening his eyes. "This is goodbye, Rachel. Now go."

Rachel's hands trembled, but she managed to hold on to the reins and click them once. The wagon lurched forward. Cooper stood there and watched her drive away.

The last thing she heard was the cocking of his Winchester rifle.

Rachel couldn't hold her despair inside too much longer. It was all she could do to drive her team to the Double J without breaking down completely. She'd shushed Johnny so many times on the ride that he'd finally just lain across her lap and quieted. The minute she reached home, she handed a befuddled Johnny over to Chick then ran straight into Jess's arms. The poor man had just come out of the barn when she'd thrown herself at him, sobbing.

Between broken cries, she explained what had happened in town. Jess held her tight and consoled her. "It'll be all right, missy," he whispered in her ear. "It'll be all right."

"I can't stomach it, Jess. I just can't. Not again." She rested her head on his chest, dampening his shirt with her tears.

"I know. I know. But think on it this way. Cooper's a capable man. He's smart. He won't put himself in harm's way."

"You didn't see the look on his face. Or in his eyes." An uncontrollable shiver shook her. "I'll never see him again."

"You don't know that, missy. Have faith that he'll get through it."

She'd shed a river of tears already, but they still kept coming. "Oh, how I pray he does. But he's leaving anyway. He's going back to Nevada. He says…" She gulped a breath of air. "He says he won't be worthy of me. I won't want to know him."

"C'mon, let's get you inside. I'll stay with you until you calm down." She clung to Jess and together they walked to the house. Then a ray of hope entered her heart. "I hope Sheriff O'Reilly got there in time."

"Now, how'd the sheriff know anything?"

"I went straight there after leaving Cooper. I couldn't think of any other way to help."

"Well, then, maybe he did get there in time."

Rachel nodded, feeling slightly better. "Maybe he did."

Half an hour later, Jess left her after she'd assured him that she would be all right. No amount of consoling could diminish the fear she held inside. No amount of cheering up would fill the void in her heart. She felt empty and hollowed out, the pain reminiscent of losing Josh. But the difference was, Cooper had had a choice in the path he chose.

He could have walked away.

He could have alerted the sheriff and allowed the law to decide Hollings's fate.

Instead, Cooper chose to take matters into his own hands.

She'd confessed her love for him and it hadn't mattered. Nothing she could have said would've stopped him. It hurt her terribly that his vengeance meant more to him than her love.

She glanced at Johnny sitting on the rug by the fireplace, playing with a spool of yarn. She sat down next to him, stroking his fine silky hair. "You've got yourself all tangled," she said quietly. She saw the glow of innocence in his eyes, the wonder and joy. She had Johnny to love and she was grateful to have him. She adored her son, but she wondered if it would always just be the two of them? Was she meant to live the rest of her life alone?

She couldn't fathom loving any other man. She loved Cooper.

She would continue to love him, even as her life moved on. Even if a dozen Robert Livingstons came calling, she would turn them all away.

"Sad, Mama?" Johnny looked up at her quizzically.

"No, Mama's not sad. It's almost Christmas, Johnny," she said as cheerily as she could muster. "We'll have our celebration tomorrow. Want to help Mama make pie?"

Johnny nodded, and she untangled the wool strands wrapped around his chubby hands. "C'mon," she said, lifting him.

She had no life left in her, but she went about the motions of her daily chores pretending to Johnny, Jess and herself that she could survive another tragic loss.

Jess had checked on her during the day and later in the evening he brought her supper, a rich soup he'd prepared for the boys. He'd stayed and eaten the meal with her, sending her worried glances. It was all she could do to keep from breaking down again in front of him. The elderly man had become like a father to her. She didn't want to cause him further alarm. Her pain would be met in the late hours of the night and in the hours before dawn when she didn't have to disguise her anguish from peering eyes.

"I'll be back later," Jess said as he rose to leave.

"You don't have to," Rachel insisted.

Jess smiled a sweet smile. "Indulge your elders, missy."

"You'll tell me if you…if you hear anything?"

His eyes wrinkled with uncertainty. "I doubt that's gonna happen tonight. We won't be getting word from town."

"Just promise you'll tell me."

"You know I will," he said before walking out the door.

Drained of energy, Rachel put Johnny down to sleep early and sat by the fire in the main room staring at the licking flames until only embers burned. She got up to douse the fire completely, when Jess knocked on her door.

The dear man was concerned about her.

She tried pasting on a smile, but she knew she couldn't fool him. She opened the door and gasped.

Cooper stood on her threshold.

She was so relieved to see him, she wanted to rush into his arms, but the hard look on his face stopped her cold.

"Hollings is dead."

Rachel squeezed her eyes shut for a second, absorbing the truth. Any sliver of hope she had vanished in that instant. Dreadful emotions landed in her belly like a deadweight. She inhaled deeply and held her tears back. Thoughts raced through her head, but she couldn't find the words.

"I'm sorry, Rachel. For putting you through this."

She nodded slowly. Her limbs shaky, she leaned against the edge of the door for support.

"I didn't kill him."

Her eyes lifted to his, puzzled.

"I couldn't do it, Rachel. I went into that mercantile with every intention of murdering him. When I saw him, my blood ran cold. He didn't recognize me right away and I could have shot him dead right there by the penny candies. But then something flashed in my head. I recalled the cold, ruthless look in Clyde Berkins's eyes. The man who shot me and will probably hang for the offense, pretended no remorse when I saw him in that jail cell. He was a hard, unfeeling man. A man with no soul. And I knew if I shot Hollings in cold blood, I wouldn't be much better than him. I didn't want to be like him. Because of you. And what you mean to me."

Rachel's mind swirled and another fraction of hope entered her heart. "But you said Hollings is dead. How did that—"

"I took him in. I had the rifle pointed at his back as we walked toward the sheriff's office. Two young boys got into a fistfight in the street. There was a lot of shouting and I got distracted for an instant. Just one second passed and Hollings wrestled the Winchester from my hands. He was ready to shoot me when Sheriff O'Reilly sent a round into his gut. Hollings died before he could get off a shot at me."

"Oh, Cooper." Tears spilled from her eyes. "You could have died."

"But I didn't, Rachel. And it's because of you that I'm standing here. The sheriff told me what you did. How you went to him for help. You saved my life again."

Rachel trembled so much she thought she'd collapse. But Cooper was there instantly, bracing her shoulders, his strength seeping into her as he held her firm. "I rode out of town headed for Nevada, Rachel. But I didn't have the strength to leave you like that. I doubled back and, well, here I am."

"Yes," she said with a smile, her body beginning to recover from the shock. "Here you are."

Cooper's dark eyes pierced hers with sincerity. "When Jocelyn died I didn't think I could let anyone else into my heart. But then I met you, and it took me all this while to realize that I've been given a second chance. I love you, Rachel. I love you and Johnny so much, it tears me up inside to think of a life without you. You've healed my injuries, sweetheart, but you've also healed my heavy heart. You've saved my life twice now, but I'm greedy. I need you to save me once more."

"H-how?"

"Marry me, Rachel. Let me love you until the day I die."

Rachel stared at him in wonder. Was it true? Cooper loved her and wanted to marry her. She swallowed hard and blinked several times. Sudden joy, the kind she thought she'd never experience again, the kind that makes you whole and fills you with happiness, washed over her. Her prayers answered, she moved closer to him, meeting his beautiful dark eyes. "Yes, yes. I'll marry you, Cooper."

He brought her into a tight embrace. "I love you, Rachel."

"I'll never tire of hearing it."

"You won't have to," he said. Tipping her head up to him, he brushed an exquisite lingering kiss to her lips, a kiss that spoke of long nights and bright futures. "I'll tell you every day."

"Thank you, Cooper."

"You have nothing to thank me for, sweetheart."

"But I do. You said the other day that you wished you had a special gift for me. Giving us both this chance, a second chance at love, is the most precious Christmas gift I will ever receive."

Cooper grinned. "It's going to be a special Christmas."

"Because we have each other."

"And Johnny," Cooper said. "I want to help raise that boy."

Rachel's heart swelled with happiness. "Josh would want that."

"And you?"

"I couldn't think of a better father for Johnny."

Cooper wrapped his arms around her shoulders and together they entered her house. "Welcome home, Cooper."

"Merry Christmas, sweetheart."

"It is. It's the merriest day of my life."

* * * * *

COMING NEXT MONTH FROM

HARLEQUIN®
HISTORICAL

Available October 26, 2010

- **REGENCY CHRISTMAS PROPOSALS**
  by **Gayle Wilson, Amanda McCabe, Carole Mortimer**
  (Regency)

- **UNLACING THE INNOCENT MISS**
  by **Margaret McPhee**
  (Regency)
  Book 6 in the *Silk & Scandal* miniseries

- **LADY RENEGADE**
  by **Carol Finch**
  (Western)

- **THE EARL'S MISTLETOE BRIDE**
  by **Joanna Maitland**
  (Regency)

REQUEST YOUR FREE BOOKS!

 HARLEQUIN® HISTORICAL:
Where love is timeless

2 FREE NOVELS PLUS 2 FREE GIFTS!

YES! Please send me 2 FREE Harlequin® Historical novels and my 2 FREE gifts (gifts are worth about $10). After receiving them, if I don't wish to receive any more books, I can return the shipping statement marked "cancel." If I don't cancel, I will receive 6 brand-new novels every month and be billed just $4.94 per book in the U.S. or $5.49 per book in Canada. That's a saving of 20% off the cover price! It's quite a bargain! Shipping and handling is just 50¢ per book.* I understand that accepting the 2 free books and gifts places me under no obligation to buy anything. I can always return a shipment and cancel at any time. Even if I never buy another book from Harlequin, the two free books and gifts are mine to keep forever.

246/349 HDN E5L4

Name	(PLEASE PRINT)	

Address		Apt. #

City	State/Prov.	Zip/Postal Code

Signature (if under 18, a parent or guardian must sign)

Mail to the **Harlequin Reader Service:**
IN U.S.A.: P.O. Box 1867, Buffalo, NY 14240-1867
IN CANADA: P.O. Box 609, Fort Erie, Ontario L2A 5X3

Not valid for current subscribers to Harlequin Historical books.

Want to try two free books from another line?
Call 1-800-873-8635 or visit www.morefreebooks.com.

* Terms and prices subject to change without notice. Prices do not include applicable taxes. N.Y. residents add applicable sales tax. Canadian residents will be charged applicable provincial taxes and GST. Offer not valid in Quebec. This offer is limited to one order per household. All orders subject to approval. Credit or debit balances in a customer's account(s) may be offset by any other outstanding balance owed by or to the customer. Please allow 4 to 6 weeks for delivery. Offer available while quantities last.

Your Privacy: Harlequin Books is committed to protecting your privacy. Our Privacy Policy is available online at www.eHarlequin.com or upon request from the Reader Service. From time to time we make our lists of customers available to reputable third parties who may have a product or service of interest to you. If you would prefer we not share your name and address, please check here. ☐

Help us get it right—We strive for accurate, respectful and relevant communications. To clarify or modify your communication preferences, visit us at www.ReaderService.com/consumerschoice.

HH10R

*See below for a sneak peek from
our inspirational line, Love Inspired® Suspense*

*Enjoy this heart-stopping excerpt from
RUNNING BLIND
by top author Shirlee McCoy,
available November 2010!*

*The mission trip to Mexico was supposed to be an
adventure. But the thrill turns sour when Jenna Dougherty
and her roommate Magdalena are kidnapped.*

"It's okay. I'm here to help." The voice was as deep as the darkness, but Jenna Dougherty didn't believe the lie. She could do nothing but lie still as hands slid down her arms, felt the rope around her wrists.

"I'm going to use a knife to cut you free, Jenna. Hold still."

The cold blade of a knife pressed close to her head before her gag fell away.

"I—" she started, but her mouth was dry, and she could do nothing but suck in air.

"Shhh. Whatever needs to be said can be said when we're out of here." Nick spoke quietly, his hand gentle on her cheek. There and gone as he sliced through the ropes on her wrists and ankles.

He pulled her upright. "Come on. We may be on borrowed time."

"I can't leave my friend," Jenna rasped out.

"There's no one here. Just us."

"She has to be here." Jenna took a step away.

"There's no one here. Let's go before that changes."

"It's dark. Maybe if we find a light…"

"What did you say?"

"We need to turn on the light. I can't leave until I know that—"

"What can you see, Jenna?"

"Nothing."

"No shadows? No light?"

"No."

"It's broad daylight. There's light spilling in from the window I climbed in through. You can't see it?"

She went cold at his words.

"I can't see anything."

"You've got a nasty bruise on your forehead. Maybe that has something to do with it." His fingers traced the tender flesh on her forehead.

"It doesn't matter *how* it happened. I'm blind!"

Can Nick help Jenna find her friend or will chasing this trail have Jenna running blindly again into danger?

Find out in RUNNING BLIND, available in November 2010 only from Love Inspired Suspense.

SHLISEXP1110